SPHERIA

by

Cody Leet

COPYRIGHTED MATERIAL

Editing by Michele Jacklin (www.linkedin.com/in/mjacklin).
Cover Design by Isabel Robalo (www.isadesign.net).

Stuff You Should Know transcript used with permission.
Gizmodo is a trademark of Gawker Media, used with permission.

First Edition, 2016, Version 1.0.10

ISBN: 978-0-9977513-0-7 (Trade Paperback)
        978-0-9977513-2-1 (Hardcover)
        978-0-9977513-1-4 (eBook)

No Trees Harmed, LLC.
56 Brewster Rd,
South Windsor, CT 06074

www.notreesharmed.org

Dedicated to my descendants,
that they might remember me when
I no longer walk this Earth.

ACKNOWLEDGMENTS

Special thanks to Jan DiRuzzo, who believed I could write this since I was 12. I would honestly never have attempted it without her encouragement. It took a while, but I did it!

Thanks to my loving wife and kids who allowed me the time and freedom to get this project done.

Thanks to my parents who always encouraged me to try anything, and when doing so give it my best.

Thanks to the indie authors who inspired me by example including Hugh Howey, Andy Weir, and E.L. James. And the hosts of the Self-Publishing Podcast (sterlingandstone.net) and the Authority Self-Publishing podcast (authority.pub) for their wisdom.

Thanks to Josh Clark and Charles W. "Chuck" Bryant from the Stuff You Should Know (www.stuffyoushouldknow.com) podcast for permission to reprint some of their dialog. Thanks to Gizmodo (www.gizmodo.com) for permission to use their name in a fictitious article.

Thanks to my creative team: Michele Jacklin for fixing my typos and grammar, Isabel Robalo (www.isadesign.net) for designing an awesome cover and being a pleasure to work with, and my beta readers, Rick Baumgartner, Therese Arkenberg, and Mohammad Hamad, for their invaluable feedback.

Most of all, *thank you,* my readers! I really hope you enjoy this as much as I enjoyed dreaming it up.

CONTENTS

PROLOGUE

Photons flickered like frantic fireflies, blinking out of existence. Then they appeared elsewhere as if by magic. In a desperate attempt to hold onto life, they acted. Some died, and some lived; their destiny was not of their choosing.

The doorbell rang. It was Aunt Mayra from Victoria coming for the annual Australia Day cookout. Graham lingered in his bedroom, trying to prolong his peace before encountering her. It wasn't that he didn't like her, because he actually did, especially when she brought him gifts. There were just two things that nagged at him about Aunt Mayra: her persistence and her kisses. He promised himself he'd be respectful this time.

His parents greeted her at the door. After the usual pleasantries, their voices trailed off to the kitchen. The TV in his room began playing a new video, "Beds are Burning," from the local Sydney band Midnight Oil. He muted it so he could hear the conversation down the hall. But the voices were too distant to make out anything.

He shrugged to himself and resumed his work, which he took very seriously. It wasn't real work – more like research – and wasn't even research since it wasn't related to any school-work. It was his hobby: exploring what makes computers tick. More so, trying to make them, for lack of a better word, think.

Graham heard Aunt Mayra's footsteps heading toward

the bathroom, which was right next to his room. After a bit, the toilet flushed, and the sound of running water seemed unsettling. A moment later, Graham's door was pushed open, and Mayra poked her head into his bedroom.

"My little Graham! Wow have you grown! Aren't you gonna come give your Auntie a big old hug? After all this time?"

"Yes Auntie, how are you?" He rose and gave her a brief hug. Oblivious to his dodge attempt, she responded with her typical kiss on his mouth. He knew this was going to happen, so had prepared by pressing his lips together. He smiled at her, proud that he'd avoided any direct saliva contact.

She looked around, and not finding another chair, sat on his bed. He gave her a "you want to talk more?" look and returned to his desk. Amber squares blinked on and off on the screen of his Apple II computer. His father had bought it "to calculate taxes," but that coincidently aligned with Graham entering high school. He soon monopolized it to teach himself programming, which secretly his father endorsed.

"Here, I brought you something," Aunt Mayra said, handing him a wrapped package.

He tore the paper, revealing a calculator with a solar panel.

Mayra looked proud, and added, "I saw this in an electronics store in Canberra. It never needs batteries. Cool huh? I knew it'd be right up your alley."

"Yes, it's great. Thank you. This will help with my math homework."

"Okay, but no cheating."

"Of course not. We're allowed to use calculators now."

Mayra cocked her head and squinted at him. Then she gazed at his computer screen for a rather long moment, perhaps mesmerized by the changing patterns. She finally asked, "What game are you playing?"

"It's not a game," Graham responded. "It's a simulation." Indeed, even though it was called the Game of Life, the word 'game' was a misnomer. In truth, it was a simulation of, well, life, albeit very primitive life. The simulation was developed as a mathematical way to express how life can function under a simple set of rules. It consisted of a grid of squares, any of which could be either on or off, with on representing being alive.

He was about to explain the whole concept and the rules to Aunt Mayra but thought better of it. Instead, he just said, "These dots represent bacteria fighting for survival. If they get too crowded, they kill each other. If they get isolated, they die of loneliness. And if they've got some friends, they multiply. It's a program that simulates artificial intelligence."

"Artificial intelligence!" Mayra echoed. "That's silly. How can a machine have intelligence?"

Graham resisted the urge to roll his eyes. "Well, it doesn't really. It just behaves like it does, thus the artificial part. There are a bunch of experiments like this one that simulate aspects of human thought." He stood and pulled a book off his shelf. "This book explains all the ways that people have made machines think. They've been able to form symbolic relationships, solve puzzles, classify animals, and even have a conversation with you. But they don't get the computer to think for real, like where it's self-aware. That's going to take a while. But I'm planning on specializing in A.I. in college, and I will figure out how to do it for real! That's my goal, at least."

Mayra was speechless, which was unusual. She stared at the blinking screen again, then back at Graham. "Whatever silly pursuit makes you happy. Hopefully, you'll change to a real career before you graduate. Something that can make some real money!"

Her words proved prophetic. Graham went on to major in economics – but he never forgot his dream.

/ PART ONE /

ORIGIN

CHAPTER 1 - SHARD OF LIFE

"Problem solving is hunting. It is savage pleasure and we are born to it." -
Thomas Harris

The vegetation rustled around the great beast, but not enough for it to notice. The creature was focused on finding buried crystals, green ones, containing seed energy. The bright light above shown white, compelling it to forage.

Nine Polyans surrounded it, taking care to stay hidden. Like the beast, they were compelled to hunt. The shining orb above, which they called "The Source," governed their behavior.

Unlike this beast, their best source of food wasn't from the ground. Instead, it came from the heart of ones such as this. There, in the center of its two rows of three massive legs and shelf of five scooping tusks sat an enormous violet crystal, pulsing with light. That single crystal was the one that gave this creature, known as a Zalisk, and all the beings of the world for that matter, their life. Without it, they'd be mere inanimate structures consisting of connected tetrahedrons.

Each member of the Polyan hunting party was about equal in size to a single leg of the gigantic Zalisk. Being of the Soldier caste, each of them had five limbs, connected to a violet core. But rather than being lined up on the sides, their legs were evenly spaced about their roundish body. They looked like how a five-legged spider might look, were there such a thing. As they got into position surrounding the beast, it stopped and listened. Zalisks were known for severe aggression, and many Polyans had died blundering into their territory. That was how they learned to work as a team.

Hearing nothing unusual, the beast returned to sensing the ground. It paused over a patch of barren surface, then rose up, plunging its five frontal tusks into the ground. It leaned back, leveraging them into a scoop, overturning a chunk of inert brown rock. Amongst the debris was a small green crystal, and the creature eyed its prize. It moved its hulking form over the shard and aligned the point of its own violet core to its dinner. The energy from the previously buried crystal flowed into the belly of the beast. Once the new crystal was depleted and now clear, the Zalisk moved on. Its own core was a little bit brighter, almost full in fact.

The group of Soldiers had been following the Zalisk for some time. They watched and waited, letting it do the work, before taking their own meal. Now was the time.

Ga·zo, Za·zo, and Be·zo had been staying a slight bit ahead of the beast. They swerved in unison as it went, remaining in the same relative position while staying hidden. The first two each dragged the end of a long strand of chords, resembling rope. Be·zo carried a small shard of green crystal on his back. The remaining Polyans, three on each side of the Zalisk, trailed the rest of the rope. These two flanking groups kept visual sensors toward Ga·zo, waiting for the signal.

The beast paused again. Its enormous tusks swayed to the left, then the right. It attempted to sense another green crystal buried in the ground.

With the beast distracted, Ga·zo bowed, and the others stopped as signaled. He made a circular motion with one of his legs and Be·zo began to dig a shallow hole in the path of the Zalisk. Ga·zo and Za·zo each made a loop in their ropes, which they then hung from a branch in the way of the beast. These were suspended at the exact level of its outermost tusks. The others grabbed the loose ends of the ropes and stretched them around trees. They braced for them to go taut. Be·zo placed a small green crystal into his hole and covered it.

The Zalisk didn't detect anything in the current spot. Still unaware of the stealthy trackers, it shifted forward to try again. It took three more steps, paused, and sensed the crystal that Be·zo had buried. The Zalisk moved toward it, and in doing so, unknowingly slid its two outer tusks through the dangling loops. Another step and the loops caught, pulling taut. The Soldiers reacted quickly, and in unison. They pulled the trailing ends of the loops toward the back legs of the creature, seeking to bind them to the tusks.

Seeing sudden quick movement, the creature panicked. It made a loud bellowing sound and flailed its tusks to one side. Za·zo went flying through the air, along with two other Soldiers. They landed in front of the beast's deadly tusks. It immediately charged at them. But just before smashing them with a crushing blow, the Zalisk jerked back and fell sideways. The second strand had caught on a tree as the other three held it. They tied it to the creature's three exposed left legs, render-ing them useless.

The Zalisk struggled to get back up, thrashing its right three legs. The Soldiers heaved on the left rope, and the beast was rolled onto its back. Ga·zo and Za·zo scrambled up the creature's forward appendages and onto its exposed belly. Two others retrieved the strand dangling from the Zalisk's right tusk and tossed it up to them. Along with Be·zo, the three on the ground each grabbed onto one of the flailing legs and, holding tight, pulled with all their strength. Ga·zo and Za·zo went to work, binding each leg with the rope.

The creature struggled, pushing with its middle legs on each side. It was working to remove the strands connecting its tusks to its legs. They'd soon come off, but the Soldiers were ready. They snared each leg with additional strands and pulled them tight around more vegetation. This stretched the body of the creature, its legs spread wide. It lay immobile, vulnerable to the sky.

Be·zo, who was on his first hunt, was given the honor of the kill. He retrieved a bundle of clear crystals that the group had been dragging with them. He removed one and hefted it onto the belly of the beast. The Zalisk struggled against its restraints, knocking Be·zo off balance. But he recovered and climbed up. He reached the spot between its six outstretched legs and looked into its belly. There, pulsing from a day of foraging, was the life crystal: large, violet, and glowing.

Holding the clear fragment high above his head, Be·zo proclaimed the words he was taught. "This Zalisk gives us its energy, that we might move, that we might live, that we might multiply." He then pressed the pointed tip of the shard against a flat edge of the beast's core. The color began to flow into the crystal, turning it a vibrant violet, and the Zalisk's life dimmed. Be·zo passed down the saturated shard, and the others handed up another clear one, which he also filled. In this way, they removed all the energy contained in the beast, and it went limp, the struggle over. The core of the magnificent creature, still impressive in size, twinkled clear like a diamond.

Be·zo once again raised a shard over his back and this time, with the final one filled, proclaimed, "For the Colony!" The pile of crystals contained enough energy to replenish them all.

"For the Colony," the others repeated in unison.

#

Ti·ni squealed "All fall down!" as the stack of brown rocks collapsed onto its side. They tumbled into a ragged column along the ground. She laughed and began pushing them back together with her three legs, but paused when something caught her eye. A moving glow became visible in the forest just outside the Colony.

The proud Soldiers emerged from the growth. They each carried a radiant shard above their backs, displaying them like trophies. The other Polyans rushed out to greet them, and everyone danced around in a wild commotion. This was the third great haul, possibly enough to refill everyone. These shards contained more energy than a week's worth of foraging for green crystals. They formed a line and marched between the hives to the center of the Colony.

Po·ni, another three-legged Drone like Ti·ni, approached her. She asked, "Can you make a square, Ti·ni?"

Ti·ni bounced and laughed. She returned to the fallen blocks and formed them into a square platform on the ground. It was a decent job, considering Ti·ni was their latest born Polyan and had a lot to learn. Po·ni tidied up the structure a bit more.

The Soldiers approached the platform and placed their shards upon it. Everyone gathered to admire the magnificence of the combined glow. The crystals illuminated the gathering now that the Source above had begun to dim, signaling the end of the day. Whispers spread through the congregation until everyone was asking the same thing: "Where's Sa·ma?"

A mysterious voice spoke from within the crowd. "I'm here," it said. Those near the voice spread apart, and a gap emerged through the crowd clearing a path to the center. The old Polyan then hobbled to the platform that Ti·ni had built. "Today is wondrous," he said, his front illuminated by the purplish glow. "Our hunting party must be commended for another fantastic capture. Bringing down a Zalisk is no easy feat. It takes the coordination of many skilled Soldiers, and at significant risk. Today we're all blessed with their success and the Colony is stronger as a result. Come, it's time to celebrate. Let the feast begin!"

Then, as if on cue, Po·ni declared, "Let us Drones make sound!" All the three-legged Polyans started to bang their legs together in unison. Synchronized primal rhythms emanated from their motions. This was one of the few things Drones were able to do, besides menial tasks such as pushing things around. Ti·ni bounced in cheerful glee, this being her first-ever celebration. She fumbled a bit but, after a dull clank or two, was able to mimic the cadence of the others. "Aren't you a quick learner," praised Po·ni. Ti·ni seemed to swoon and stumbled but recovered. This caste, being the most numerous, withdrew from the crowd and formed a musical circle around the others.

Pu·ma then bellowed at the crowd, to be heard above the noise. "Let us Workers make sway." Upon hearing this, all the four-legged Polyans raised one of their legs into the air and tapped the ground with the beat. They raised another and did the same, and so on. As they performed their tapping dance, they spread out and formed a concentric circle just inside the one formed by the Drones. Their motion now synchronized and developed the appearance of a wave.

Next, the crowd mingling inside turned to Be·zo, of the five-legged caste. She declared to the anticipatory eyes, "Let us Soldiers dance!" The five-legged Polyans began to spin. They rotated around the central shards. Thus, they also formed a circle inside the ones shaped by the Workers and the Drones.

All that remained inside were eight six-legged Polyans. Yo·sa spoke to them, just loud enough for them to hear. "Let us Leaders eat first." This caste, being just one leg short of a god, were the wisest and most elite. They thus had the honor and privilege of eating first. Each of them, in turn, climbed upon the platform in the center of the celebration. They placed the lower point of their core upon one of the shards and drained out a bit of the violet life force inside. Once at capacity, they climbed down and made their way through all the moving circles to find a place to rest.

Now the five-legged Soldiers moved in, each performing the same act of feeding. This was followed by the four-legged Workers, then finally the three-legged Drones. The violet shards were eventually depleted, reduced to mere transparent shells again. A few of the Drones failed to get any, but nobody seemed to notice. Everyone spread out in a grid-like pattern and sat upon the ground, basking in the afterglow of having been replenished.

Near the remains of the shards, two of the four-legged Polyans were in deep discussion. Sa·ma was illustrating something to Le·ma, making outlines in the air with one of his legs. Le·ma seemed to be taking it all in. She'd learned to observe more since becoming his apprentice. Ga·zo, considered to be the chief of the Soldiers, noticed this and spoke to them loud enough so the whole crowd could hear. "Show us some learning," he teased. "Build us something, Le·ma. Build us a statue."

The Colony in unison echoed his request. "Le·ma, build us a statue. Le·ma, build us a statue." This chant was repeated until Sa·ma stood and raised a leg. The crowd became silent, and Le·ma took this as permission to appease them. She pushed the shards off, then separated the blocks making the platform. She stuck the largest six shards into the ground. Then she rested several brown blocks on top of them. To the front of the brown blocks, she attached five more small shards.

She stepped back to view her masterpiece. The crowd couldn't help but admire the beauty and symbolism of her creation. A perfect Zalisk replica stood tall before them.

CHAPTER 2 - 1% INSPIRATION, 99% FUNDING

"Genius is one percent inspiration and ninety-nine percent perspiration." -
Thomas Edison

Max walked out into the raw Belgian night. A horn blasted from below, and he walked over to the balcony railing to peer down. Two cars were attempting to take the same parking spot. The drivers began shouting profanities in French. Max knew he had that same passion in his blood. *If we realized we are all pieces of the same machine, conflicts like this wouldn't happen.*

It calmed his nerves to know he was in the tower of the Hôtel de Ville de Bruxelles. Here he could be an observer of society for a moment instead of interacting with it... instead of being the center of it. He pulled out an electronic cigarette and took a drag of vapor. The nicotine calmed his nerves.

Light footsteps approached him from behind. Turning, he saw his friend David heading toward the balcony. He stopped next to Max and looked out upon the city.

"Nice job today," David said. "It's not easy for a rookie to impress a roomful of leading particle physicists." He looked up at Max, whose dark hair blended into the night sky, making him look even thinner than he was.

Max took another drag of vapors, exhaled, and pretended to squint as if smoke blew into his eyes.

David's youthful demeanor belied his age. Max had befriended him years earlier in an online discussion forum on quantum theory. They'd formed a long distance friendship due to their shared interest in the components of the atom. This turned out fortuitous for Max, because when his friend was appointed chair of the 25th Solvay Conference on Physics, Max landed a speaker invite.

Max was thrilled to have participated in this event. The first one, in 1911, was attended by many luminaries including three of his heroes: Albert Einstein (who explained the photoelectric effect), Marie Skłodowska-Curie (the first woman to win a Nobel prize for radioactivity), and Henri Poincaré (a mathematician who created the foundations of chaos theory). It was, and still is, an invitation-only gathering and represents the best of the best.

This year the theme was "The theory of the quantum world." Max had demonstrated a radically new device. It was an honor to have shown it to the modern equivalent of those who had made it possible, people who actually cared.

"There's someone I want you to meet," David said.

"I'm kind of burnt out on meeting people, that's why I'm out here on the balcony."

Sounds from the cocktail party floated up from the conference below. The lively debates were still going on, and would go to the wee hours of the morning.

"Kid," David said, smiling at him. "It's not just anyone. It's Graham Neilson, and he loved your presentation."

Max raised a brow, Spock-style. *"The* Graham Neilson? The wealthiest man in Australia, the brilliant investor, the international playboy?"

"The same."

Max knew a lot about Graham Neilson. He had a reputation as a flamboyant spendthrift. Unlike many of his contemporaries, he used his wealth to fund eccentric hobbies, such as treasure hunting and racing fast cars. His progressive policies toward employee benefits also got him on the cover of many news magazines. Max had wondered, more than once, how he had time to run a bunch of companies and do all the cool things he did. Maybe he just had talented and trustworthy managers overseeing his companies for him.

His story wasn't atypical of other Information Age billionaires. He created something great, made a boatload of money, and used it to fund additional pursuits, all of which also made boatloads of money. His first company was started in his garage (studio apartment to be precise) where he created an automated stock trading system. This system outplayed all the other ones from competitors, and certainly anyone attempting to trade manually using just human knowledge and research. His day job was a data analyst for a large company, but he liked to offset the boredom by buying stocks. He noticed that many moves weren't tied to relevant factors like reported earnings or price ratios, but by the emotions of individual buyers. In fact, stock theory is such that the market always self-adjusts, so you can never actually make money. Unless you can predict and exploit an abnormal movement before the system has time to correct itself. This is exactly what Graham started doing, and he was good at it, *reliably* good at it.

He never revealed the exact nature of his methods, as they're a well-protected trade secret. But he hinted on more than one occasion that they used social media to exploit population trends, rather than raw statistics or the opinions of experts. Once he could turn his decision-making process into a computer program, his machine made all the trades for him. And at a much greater speed and quantity. The money started rolling in. He hired staff to handle administrative duties and formed Aboriginal Accruals as his first company. Within a year, Graham Neilson became one of the youngest billionaires ever. Aboriginal Accruals is still a privately held company and a perpetual cash cow.

Since then, Graham had formed five more companies all with the unifying "Aboriginal" moniker:

- Aboriginal Aquatics, which creates underwater exploration vehicles and tools;

- Aboriginal Augmentations, which produces prosthetics and medical devices for insertion into or attachment to the human body;

- Aboriginal Aerospace, which designs aerial and low orbit vehicles;

- Aboriginal Automotive, which builds high-end race cars;

- and Aboriginal Asteroids, which is currently researching the feasibility of mining space debris for platinum and other rare earth minerals.

Max believed that, aside from the first, that all these companies existed solely to allow Graham to create toys to use for his personal hobbies. Still, all but the last have become profitable in their own right.

"He loved my presentation?" Max repeated.

"He said it was brilliant! He specifically asked for an introduction."

"No shit?"

David responded in his typical deadpan, "I never defecate in public."

Max chuckled, then shivered. The two drivers had gotten out of their cars and were now shouting at each other, nose to nose. Their headlights blurred as Max remembered seeing Graham in the audience.

#

Max was sitting in a row of red velvet chairs on the stage, next to some of the most brilliant minds in particle physics. The conference was being held in the vast and extravagant Gothic Room. The dark wood on the walls was intricate carved and lined with eight tapestries representing the Trade Guilds of Brussels. Three offset rows of modern lights illuminated the round tables below. All of these were packed with people eager to receive the free flow of new information and ideas, fuel for the endless debates that would follow.

Loud clapping snapped Max out of silently rehearsing the speech he was about to give. Julian Farber, from the Large Hadron Collider team at CERN, had just finished presenting its plan to create Dark Matter. He walked across the stage and sat down. David rose and returned to the podium.

"Our next speaker is a young but brilliant, um, inventor."

Inventor? Max was amused at his introduction. Guess 'scientist' wasn't one of his qualifications.

"I first met this speaker on the Internet, and he had the audacity to debate with me some of the fundamental properties of the universe. Over time, however, I realized not only the need to challenge assumptions but how the only way to make progress is to change the way we think. He thought different, that's for sure. And although I don't always understand what he's talking about, he's shown me some amazing things. Things that can move our field forward, in a practical sense. I am proud to introduce Maximilian Moreau!"

The clapping resumed, although not as heavy as before, and subsided quickly. Max stood up, feeling nervous. As he made his way to the podium, he noticed one person in the audience who stood out: a tall gentleman with a bright blond mullet and a matching goatee. He seemed familiar somehow, and at the same time out of place. Max picked up the clicker and adjusted the microphone.

The slide behind him said, "Qubit or not two bit?"

Overcoming his stage fright, he leaned into the mic and said, "Thank you, David." Every eye in the room was upon him, and the silence pressed in, making it hard to breathe. He cleared his throat to buy a moment of time. "It's an honor to stand here before you. Many of you are my heroes, and I could only hope to someday be a fraction as brilliant as you. I'm not going to dazzle you all with any fantastic new theories. Or wow you with a new concept of how to explain the universe. Or even talk about new things that we don't quite understand.

"Instead, I'm going to show you how I've applied the knowledge that you all have been generating. I guess 'inventor' is appropriate, for what value are all these theories, tests, and proofs if they can't be used for something? Used to help improve mankind?"

Max advanced the presentation, and the next slide showed a large futuristic computer housing the size of a box truck. It had a control panel on one side with a screen and some indicator lights. "I'm sure you have all seen the D-Wave One quantum computer. It contains 128 quantum bits of metal niobium suspended in a super-cooled chamber. The fixture is protected from magnetic and vibrational interference by 15 layers of shielding. These qubits can perform calculations rapidly that the most powerful digital computers would spend years doing. They do this, as most of you know, by leveraging quantum superposition."

Given the audience, it was safe to assume everyone understood what quantum superposition was. Max wasn't a fan of the typical description that a subatomic particle can be in multiple states at once. Or that the particle only chooses a value when you look at it. But this was the wrong audience to have that debate with. Regardless, superposition, when connected through a series of quantum particles, allowed statistical problems to be solved. The challenge was these qubits were susceptible to the slightest disturbance. Even a train going by miles away could cause the particles to decide an outcome prematurely, producing an incorrect result. Thus, the need for extreme isolation from the outside world.

The slide advanced, showing a cup of coffee and a plate of sugar cubes.

"What if I told you all that I could improve the power of a D-Wave computer by over thirty times, make it the size of a sugar cube, make it impervious from outside interference, and have it work at room temperature, all at the same time?"

Max looked at the audience. People glanced at one another, and some even snickered. Max cracked a grin. He was hoping for this response.

He reached into his pants pocket and, making his best Steve Jobs impression, pulled out a small cubical prism-like object. It was about a centimeter wide, and he placed it on the rim of the podium. Out of his shirt pocket, he pulled a standard laser pointer. This he also set on the podium, pointing toward the cube, and turned it on. The red laser shone into the prism. It began to glow a *blue* color and started pulsing.

"What you see before you, dear scientists, is the product of your brilliance." The slide advanced, showing a close-up of a glowing blue prism, with the letters Q-U-B-E displayed above it. "I call it the Qube, which stands for Quantum Uncertainty Binary Engine. What you see before me on this podium has 3,840 quantum bits inside it. This is over thirty times more than anything ever made, and is no bigger than the tip of my thumb."

More snickers from the audience.

"You don't believe me? Believe me. I'm going to tell you how I did this. But not everything, because the process is proprietary and a trade secret."

The blond man shifted in his chair, and he was the only person who'd moved.

"The problem with quantum bits is that they're inherently unstable and subject to disturbances. So quantum computers up to now have attempted to solve this by blocking disturbances. My technique embeds the quantum bit inside a diamond lattice. This makes it stable within the system, impervious to any movements of the Qube as a whole.

"This crystal was produced by sublimating a gas of carbon and germanium particles under high pressure onto a seed plate. What formed is an artificial diamond interspersed with a lattice of defects. The germanium particles are locked inside the diamond in such a way that free electrons are held in a suspension state, thus behaving like quantum bits. These qbits are close enough together to allow interactions with each other, in a similar way to how the neurons in your brain interact. A set of lasers can then stimulate these electrons on one side, which causes a cascade of states through the entire structure, thus causing the whole system to emit a unique color spectrum. Over time, by activating them at different angles, they can be "trained" to perform complex calculations."

"The one before me has been taught to calculate any

digit of the number Pi. Let me demonstrate." Max pointed at a man in the front row. "Sir, can you please give me a number, a large one."

The man thought for a second and shouted, "78,557."

Max repeated the number into the microphone. He turned off the laser and, after a second, the Qube ceased its glow.

"Now I'm going to feed that number into the Qube using binary. When I'm done, I will leave the laser on, which will end the calculation. David, can you please tell me what 78,557 is in binary?"

David was briefed for this and ready with a special calculator. He began to recite the numbers "1-0-0-1-," and so on. With each 'one,' Max blinked the laser on, with each 'zero,' Max paused. David completed reciting the whole number 10011001011011101.

Max ended by locking the laser on. The Qube emitted a pinkish hue. Max said, "The entry speed was important, but David knew that. It's kind of like Morse Code, beep beep pause beep pause beep. The Qube read the pauses as zeros, so the number was entered as dictated by David. As you can see, the Qube is now emitting a color. The hue is its result."

The audience was silent now. Puzzled expressions dominated.

Max produced a box, similar to an alarm clock, from under the podium. He placed it next to the glowing Qube. "This is a portable spectrum analyzer. It's calibrated to convert ten different color hues into the digits 0 through 9."

Max turned it on, and it showed the number "6" on its LED display. "There, the 78,557[th] digit of pi is the number *six*. A traditional computer would take hours to calculate that, as it has to go through each digit in order, one by one. The quantum algorithm we programmed into this Qube can perform that calculation instantly, skipping to just the position we want to know about."

The audience began clapping; then they stood. Max smiled ear to ear and blushed. He glanced back at David, who gave him a thumbs-up.

Max made a downward motion with both hands and said, "please sit." The audience did so. "And that's not all. This is just a simple algorithm. The possibilities of this are... endless! I think we could make versions that could simulate the intelligence of insects, or even better."

The crowd was moved. Many had begun talking with each other, and the noise level was rising.

"Thank you," Max said, but it was drowned out by the voices.

David got up to the microphone and tapped it twice, producing loud clicks. The audience hushed. "We have a few minutes to field any questions you may have," he said.

One woman stood up and asked, "How did you get the germanium atoms to align in an evenly distributed lattice?"

Max replied, "Good question. As I said, some of this is a trade secret, and that's one of the pieces I'm not at liberty to reveal."

She sat down, frustrated.

A gentleman stood and asked, "D-Wave costs ten million dollars for one computer. How does this compare?"

"Well," Max said. "It's much more economical. However, that doesn't make it cheap. Diamond, no matter how you make it, is expensive. The exhibit before you cost in the range of forty thousand dollars to create. Much more inexpensive than previous attempts, but still economically unreachable for, say, home users. I was only able to afford this one with the research grant I was using."

Another gentleman stood up. "What is next for the Qube? What are you planning to do with it?"

"Two questions! Well, tonight I'm kicking off a tour of venture capital firms. I don't have the money to mass produce these, but I do think there could be a large market for them. With the right backing, the company we form could become the next Apple or the next Google. Heck, it could make computers obsolete as we know them today."

A woman, without standing, blurted out, "Does this present a danger if it falls into the wrong hands?"

Max stared at her, not expecting such a question from those who built careers out of furthering science despite any risks. "Well, um, I'm sure they could be used in nefarious ways just as traditional computers could."

"So what if terrorists get these? What if the military gets them?"

"Well, I haven't thought that through. I'd prefer that the Qubes are used for good rather than evil, just like anyone. But did Glenn Seaborg hesitate when he produced plutonium from uranium for the first time, knowing it'd inevitably lead to an atomic bomb? Everything can be used for good and bad. Let's just hope the good guys keep winning."

Something caught Max's eye. Among the sea of wiggling bodies, one sat firmly immovable, staring intently at him: the blond gentleman. Max tried to place where he'd seen him, but before he could figure it out, David interrupted at the microphone.

"That is all the time we have for questions. If you have more, you can talk to Max at the cocktail party on the third floor immediately following our last speaker, who I am proud to introduce now..."

#

"Those will kill you," came a deep Australian voice.

Max snapped out of his reverie and turned around. Towering over him stood an unnaturally blond man, exuding confidence and authority.

"Mr. Neilson, sir," Max stuttered. "P-Pardon me?"

"Those e-cigs, we don't know if they're safe."

"It's just vapor, harmless."

"They said the same thing about tobacco seventy years ago. We think everything is safe until we know better, but then we learn everything kills you. Have you ever heard of the Radium Girls?"

"I don't believe I have."

"It was around the beginning of the twentieth century. These sheilas worked in a factory making glow-in-the-dark analog watches by painting the numbers with radium. Some of them thought it'd be cool to paint their teeth as well so that their smiles would glow in the dark. They learned the hard way that it wasn't such a great idea when they all developed mouth cancer. We just don't know enough about how the universe works. You, of all people, should be aware of this, Mr. Moreau."

Max contemplated his e-cigarette, squinted his eyes, and drew another breath of vapors.

"Regardless," snickered Graham, "I didn't come here to

save your life, Mr. Moreau."

"Please call me Max."

"Very well, Max. As I was saying, I didn't come here to save your life, but I did come here to see your presentation. Not specifically yours, of course. I didn't even know you'd be here and even if I had, I wouldn't have heard of you. You see, I tend to go to these types of things for my own amusement: the TED conferences, the Summit Series, Learning Without Frontiers, etc. Sometimes, like now, I find attractive business opportunities. This one, however, is more than that. You said something that touched a nerve in me."

"Really? What was that?"

"Insect."

"Insect?" Max echoed, puzzled.

"Exactly. You see, I've had an idea for a long time. I realized, when you said that word, that your technology would be perfect for it. This moment is exactly why I've been building my fortune."

Max was a little confused, but he understood 'fortune.' "So you want to invest?"

"Invest? Yes and no. I want to fund the development and use of your Qubes. I want exclusive rights. I have a fantastic idea that'll make these, well, glow brighter than you can imagine. I will fund further development with $50 million and make you the technical leader of my project. You'll have a wild ride. But you have to promise me one thing."

Max was too shocked to respond right away. He looked at his e-cigarette but didn't take a drag. Instead, he shook his head and asked, "What's that?"

"That you will under no circumstances sell the technology to the military. That woman in there who asked about malicious intent was a grant developer who works for me. Her name is Dana Carter. In a way, she was speaking on my behalf. I would prefer that this technology doesn't fall into the wrong hands. And by wrong hands, I mean anyone who might turn it into a weapon."

"I think the government could do some great things with this technology," Max countered. "NASA could calculate cheaper ways to get off earth. Design materials for a space elevator, for example. Why would I want to exclude that? Why would *you* want to exclude that?"

Graham leaned back and uttered a deep booming laugh. "A space elevator happens to be another one of my projects. But I want to start with something more esoteric. Listen, I'm offering you a job, and some initial funding to expand your ideas in ways you probably have never imagined. When you get back to the States, I have a lab already set up and ready to go."

"That's a hard offer to refuse. So what's your idea?"

"C'mon. Let's go get a coldie and I'll fill you in. You're gonna love it! Oh, and you should quit the vapors, it makes you look like a drongo, and we both know you're not *that*."

Max looked at his plastic apparatus. Then, with an agreeable shrug, he flicked it over the balcony like a used butt.

CHAPTER 3 - UPLIFT PASS

"Nothing in all the world is more dangerous than sincere ignorance and conscientious stupidity." -Martin Luther King, Jr.

Le·ma struggled to keep up with Sa·ma. They were moving fast, with purpose. Through the blurred motion of the foliage, she kept her vision sensors fixed onto the straight textured lines on his body. Were he female, like her, the swirling pattern would have been less easy to track.

They'd come a long way from the Colony, much farther than Le·ma, or many for that matter, had ever ventured. Sa·ma seemed to know where he was going, so she followed without pausing to contemplate their course. It seemed to her that he was disorienting her intentionally.

They came to the base of a mountain range, comprised of blue crystal, as all the mountains were. These crystals emitted a repulsive force. The two Polyans could only get so close before the push was too great to come in contact with the smooth blue surface. This push, unique to the blue crystals, made the mountains impassable. They divided the world into maze-like sections, many of which were unreachable.

The travelers turned to the right and began moving again, following the contour of the mountains. This went on for only a brief time, and as they turned a corner, Le·ma saw something unexpected. There, on the side of the mountain, was a gaping slit, quite large, forming a passage into it.

"Here we are," said Sa·ma. "This is Uplift Pass, so named by the ancestors of my ancestors, and their ancestors in turn. Like you, I was led through this crevice as an apprentice Lumen Seeker. I was given knowledge about our world that only a select few ever receive. Today, I pass this knowledge down to you. Someday, you'll replace me as the Colony's Lumen Master and attain a special status equal to, if not higher than, that of the six-legged Leaders. Come."

Le·ma was dazzled and followed Sa·ma as he ducked into the passage. As she entered, she could feel an almost crushing force from both sides at the same time. But it couldn't repel her away because each side was pushing equally. This created a sensation that could only be described as "slippery." She began to slide forward as if floating along. Both she and Sa·ma started to pick up speed and suddenly shot out of the opposite side. They landed into a kind of bowl-shaped area of blue rock. There, Sa·ma bobbed a little above the ground. When Le·ma looked down, she discovered she was doing the same. Her legs, being repelled by the blue substance below, were suspending her above the surface.

This startled her, and she lost her balance. All four of her legs sprawled out, and she went sliding and spinning toward the opposite side of the indentation. But as it sloped up, she lost momentum and slid back from where she came. This happened a couple more times, back and forth, until she came to rest at the lowest point. Sa·ma chuckled to himself, watching as she attempted to stand. She slipped once again onto her belly. He lent a leg to prop her up, and she figured out how to remain floating upright. She practiced feeling the odd sensations below her. Eventually, she learned how to control her orientation by applying slight pressure onto her individual legs. She was walking on an imaginary, flexible floor.

"As everyone in the Colony knows, climbing blue rock is impossible," said Sa·ma. "That's not changed for us. But we're on the first step of a Lumen Walk. This cave and cup, discovered by those long forgotten, can show us things that others will never see."

Le·ma glanced up and could see that what initially appeared to be a gentle upwards slope was actually comprised of a series of steps.

Following her gaze, Sa·ma continued. "We call these the Uplift Steps. They were created in ancient times when Spheria was forming. Like the one we're on, each has a concave shape that we can rest in."

"How can we climb them?" Le·ma asked with puzzlement.

"It takes a particular skill, which I'm about to teach you. Observe me."

Sa·ma stretched two of his four legs downward on one side. This altered the balance of the repulsion and he was pushed away from his position. As he slowed, he stretched out the opposite two legs and his direction was reversed. But since he was starting higher along the curve, he went a bit farther up the opposite side this time. This he repeated, over and over, until he shot over the rim of the basin and out of Le·ma's sight.

Le·ma found this floating phenomenon intriguing, and definitely foreign to her. But in a strange way, it made sense. She imitated Sa·ma and after a few false starts, she got it. Once she found the rhythm, it became easy. She flew over the lip and landed on the higher step. Sa·ma was there waiting for her, lying on his back. He tapped his feet to his belly, showing her his approval for her achievement.

"This is fun!" she exclaimed.

"Yes, it is. One of the perks of being chosen for this path. But come, we've got many more steps to climb. We have a long journey before nightfall."

They climbed and climbed, in the same manner. There were about thirty of these steps, although Le·ma had lost count at about fifteen. Finally, they reached the top. As Le·ma slid to the opposite edge, she was startled to be looking down an almost sheer face of mountain rock. The drop was formidable and frightening. She flailed her legs, struggling to push herself backward.

"Calm, my child," said Sa·ma. "We're at the Apex of the World. This is the highest known reachable point ever discovered."

Le·ma looked up at the glowing Source. Indeed, they seemed noticeably closer to it. They were about a third of the way from the ground to the center of their spherical world where the Source floated. She stared at it in awe. It was definitely larger than she'd ever seen it. Even the lands on the other side of the Source seemed closer, although still an impossible distance away.

"Remember, it's impolite to stare at the Source. The gods dwell there, looking down upon us. When you stare at the Source, you may be staring into the eyes of any god watching us, and you may offend him. A glance is okay, but a stare not so." She averted her eyes.

"The Source looks amazing," she muttered. "I feel almost like I could touch it. What would happen if I did?"

Sa·ma glanced up at it, too long actually, caught himself, and looked away. He looked back at Le·ma and said, "It's never happened. It's said that any who touch the Source will get pulled into it. They'll dwell there forever, amongst the gods. Inside, there's endless energy and everything you could ever need or want. Nothing there can ever harm you, and you will never die. As you can see looking at the entire world, there are no mountains high enough to even come close. But enough of looking up, we're here to look down. Please, float to each edge of this basin and look upon this valley, until you get a sense of the wonder around us."

Le·ma did as she was told, having gained a good command of what she called "the push." She propelled herself, not back and forth, but in a spiral motion. This led to her sliding around the perimeter of the circular step. As she did so, she focused her attention downward and outward, looking at the ground nearby. This was different than looking upwards toward the opposite lands that formed the sphere. Details were small but closer. She could see the hives in the Colony from where she was, and even a couple Polyans moving around. She wondered if anyone would look up and see them as well. They wouldn't believe what they saw, even if they did.

The view down the other side of the mountain ridge was more spectacular still. Fingered veins of red created a web of rivers between which the foliage seemed sparser, like it was struggling for survival. It was clearly a more inhospitable place on this side, a place she dreaded visiting.

Sa·ma met her at the edge and followed her gaze. "That's the 'Proving Ground.' We'll be walking through there on the way to the Rift."

"Through there? But there is a much easier way to the Rift on our side."

Sa·ma focused on the scene below him. He saw something in the distance that he never noticed before, a violet spot on an otherwise average sea of brown, blue, red, and green. This reminded him of an old legend, and he committed the approximate location to memory.

"Sa·ma?"

"Yes?"

"I asked you why we're going through there when there is an easier way to the Rift near our Colony."

"I know, but getting to the Rift isn't the only reason we're on this walk. The journey is the reason we're here. There will be many trials along the way, as is always the case. So keep a keen watch as we cross these lands."

She looked down again. She could see a group of lumbering shapes, which resembled her statue. A group of Zalisks. She'd never heard of more than one together before. But she guessed the harsh environment forced them to band together for protection, even with their mighty tusks. Having to attempt to navigate this gave her chills.

A large spiral pattern on the ground caught her eye. It was a dreaded Troaten. Many long tentacles swirled away from its central core, awaiting unsuspecting prey to approach.

Sa·ma looked down upon the scene as well and remembered when he was an apprentice here with his master.

#

Go·ma, Sa·ma's master, pointed down toward a herd of Zalisk. A much younger Sa·ma followed the direction of his leg and saw the lumbering beasts below. He didn't see the Troaten.

"Watch," Go·ma said. "This is perfect. Our timing couldn't be better."

"Why?" asked Sa·ma.

"Shh," whispered Go·ma.

Sa·ma shrugged and watched the Zalisks wandering

through the brush looking for buried crystals. Without warning, one of the Zalisks flew into the air and was caught by three gigantic tentacles. A Troaten! Camouflaged and lying in wait, it had grabbed the closest Zalisk as it ventured nearby. It lifted it upwards toward its center. The remaining members of the herd were confused, and a large tentacle wrapped around another. Realizing what was happening, the remaining Zalisks charged the center of the Troaten. They pounded it with their tusks. This dislodged the second Zalisk, which fell to the ground, and rushed to assist the others. The Troaten then began to spin defensively, many of its tentacles forming a flailing spiral on the ground. The motion forced the Zalisks outward and held them at bay. The Zalisks attempted to poke into the whirling mass with their tusks, but each got swept aside. The herd gave up and watched as the first Zalisk, still being dangled in the air by two of the tentacles, was lowered onto the center. There, its core was pierced by the Troaten's point, and its life energy was consumed.

The lifeless carcass of inert polygons was flung over the herd and landed with a thud into one of the red rock veins. There it lay, unmoving. Gradually each piece turned red, and it sank into the river. The herd formed a line along the shore and watched their disappearing brethren. Then they turned, and moved along as if nothing had happened.

It occurred to Sa·ma that the Zalisks didn't care that they'd lost one of their group. Their lack of compassion made him sad with unexpected remorse.

Go·ma noticed his reaction and spoke. "Child, this is the natural course of things. The world is harsh. We all are competing for survival. The energy of that Zalisk has flowed into the Troaten, and will someday flow into something else. Such is the way. Remember what you saw here, for it's the basis of the story I'm about to tell you."

"This journey is to give respect to the Rift, the barrier

that separates the two halves of our world. Look around. We live inside a giant sphere, with the two halves divided by a chasm that is uncrossable, and that has no bottom. But it wasn't always this way. When the world was young, before there was even a Source in the center, our sphere was whole. Creatures could move about as desired.

"Then one day there was a greedy Troaten. He wasn't content with the energy he needed to survive; he wanted it all. So he dragged himself along the ground with his tentacles, grabbing any creatures he could reach, and consumed them. His life crystal was full and still he consumed more. This caused him to expand. Soon he'd destroyed every living thing. So he had to resort to digging for crystals in the ground, and thus he continued to get larger and larger. He became so large that his tentacles could reach clear across the entire world. He hung suspended with his body in the center, his arms embedded in the ground. There was no more food anywhere, neither creatures nor buried crystals. The Troaten began to starve. In a last desperate attempt to find energy, he spun, as Troatens do, and tore a giant chasm clear across the world. The Rift was created. But that was the end of him. There was no food, and he shrank until he was just a ball at the center of the world.

"The gods looked up at his carcass and thought it would make a satisfying home. So together they transformed his bulk into a ball of infinite energy, and thus the Source was made. Then the gods went there to dwell, where they have a view of the entire world anytime they want. They're probably watching us even at this moment."

#

Sa·ma shook off the memory and decided the story would be more appropriate to tell when they were actually at the Rift. He pushed off and disappeared over the steep edge of the mountain.

CHAPTER 4 - CELL DIVISION

"Suicide is a permanent solution to a temporary problem." - Phil Donahue

The University of Connecticut Health Center was built in 1970 on the highest point in Hartford County. It was established as the medical-dental school branch of the main university campus located about thirty miles away. In the 90's, a significant expansion added a focus on clinical research to the mix. It slowly became host to some non-clinical private research projects as well. At night, its many tall buildings, with lit windows, gave the impression of an apartment complex.

Timothy and Jill approached the academic entrance, holding hands. It was late, and a full moon ominously lit the cobblestone circle and entry. They were heading into the Lyman Maynard Stowe Library to study before exams the next day, having come from an amazing dinner at Naples Pizza down the road. Tim could still taste the pepperoni.

As they stepped onto the sidewalk from the traffic circle, Jill yanked Tim's hand and said, "You're gonna trip."

Tim looked at the curb, but Jill pointed to his left sneaker. It was untied.

Tim took two more steps and placed his backpack on the right of two pedestals. These supported a series of sculptures called "Spheres" by artist Wopo Holop. This one happened to have six round bronze objects depicting a human retina, three versions of a dividing frog's egg, the Earth, and an acorn. A few steps away, an identical pedestal presented a long jagged DNA strand, stretching between an odd faceted sphere and a smooth round one.

Tim stooped down to tie the lace on his new white sneaker. This time, he'd make a double knot. As he made the first loop, he heard a loud smack, like a steak being tenderized on a cutting board. He felt something wet on the side of his face and noticed red droplets coloring his white shoes. They looked polka dotted.

Jill released the shrillest scream Tim had ever heard. It made the hair on his neck stand up. Losing his balance, he fell onto his butt and jerked his head upwards. Staring down at him was the mangled face of a young woman draped over the spherical models, her lifeless eyes wide with astonishment.

#

Captain Brennan from campus security stood between the stone altars. A sheet was draped over the body, and Brennan's team had just set yellow police tape around the perimeter. A small group of students had gathered to one side and were gawking at the scene.

"What happened?" asked one woman.

"Sorry, we can't give any information at this time," Brennan responded. "Please move along." He waved the students away toward the building's entrance. They began to disperse.

Turning around, he walked twenty steps to the couple sitting on the bricks that circled a tree.

"My deputy said you two witnessed the accident?"

Jill sat silent, white as a ghost, and rocked forward and back.

Tim stepped in, "No sir. I mean yes sir."

"Take a deep breath," advised Brennan. Tim filled his lungs. "Okay, good. Now start over please."

Tim exhaled. "I mean yes I was there, but I was looking down when it happened. I swear the force of her knocked me on my ass. When I looked up, I thought it was my girlfriend lying there, hit by a car or something."

Jill shook her head and started sobbing.

Brennan placed his hand on her shoulder. "Honey, I know this is difficult. This is a very safe campus, and we take security seriously. From our perspective, this looks like a suicide. Apparently, she jumped from the building's roof and unfortunately, or maybe intentionally, landed on the jagged statues below. Did you see anything that might suggest otherwise?"

Jill took a few sobbing breaths. "No," she finally said, shaking her head. "I was just admiring the full moon, which looked large and almost red. Then something caught my eye, and I glanced to the right just in time to see her hurling toward me. I jumped back and she..." A sob was coming, but Jill managed to suppress it. "She landed right in front of me! It was awful. I've never seen anything so horrific in my entire life!"

"Did you see her jump?" inquired the Captain.

"No, she was already falling when I saw her."

"Well, you saw enough. You two are the only witnesses, but this is a cut and dry case of a jumper. A darn shame too. She was a pretty girl. We already identified her as an employee here, an intern actually, also a student. Must've been studying late like you two. The stress can be intense, I know, and it's a real shame what it pushes some people to do, to take their own lives rather than just try their best. A real shame."

Jill added, "There is one thing."

"Yes?"

"I didn't see her jump, but I thought I heard something, just before she fell."

"Heard something?"

"I thought I heard someone yell 'No!' But there was no one else around."

CHAPTER 5 - ARCANE PHYSICS

"There are three principal means of acquiring knowledge... observation of nature, reflection, and experimentation. Observation collects facts; reflection combines them; experimentation verifies the result of that combination." - Denis Deiderot

Le·ma was alone on the mountain. Her guide had just plummeted over the side. She rushed to the edge and watched as Sa·ma deftly navigated the slope. He slowed his descent by bounding off flat outcroppings, changing his direction. He did this about twelve times, and, after leaping from the last one, landed with a thud onto the brown rock at the foot of the mountain. He looked up at Le·ma and waved a leg. *He is insane.*

"I'll meet you at the bottom," she yelled, as she started to head back toward the steps.

"No," she heard. "You'll be on the wrong side."

She returned to the lip and yelled back at him, "What do you mean?"

"There is no passage to this region from the Colony side. You have to come down the way I did."

"If there's no passage, then how will we get back?"

"That's one of your tests. Come down. We must make the Rift before nightfall."

"It's too steep!"

"It just appears steep. Aim for the flatter parts, and you'll be all right."

"Okay."

Le·ma moved toward the edge, but just as her body crossed partly into the empty air, she changed her mind and flailed backward. But there was nothing to push against, and she tumbled over the side. She fell straight down for a few seconds then felt the repulsion as she approached the slope. There was an invisible compression, and then she was vaulted outward. She stared straight down at the brown rock below; it was approaching fast.

The slope of the mountain once again reached out to her. This time, Le·ma used two legs to ease herself into the repulsive field and instead of bouncing, began to glide down over it. She began to steer and swerved to the side toward a flatter outcropping. She quickly approached it, so fast in fact that it launched her once again into the air. Then she hit the mountain almost going sideways. She recovered and came down onto another outcropping, almost in control.

With her speed slowed, Le·ma pushed off toward another jutting mass of blue rock. She repelled off it and changed course to aim toward another, then another. A couple more and she reached the bottom with a solid thud that made her four legs vibrate. She swore they must've shattered, but they were intact.

"I could've died!" she fumed at Sa·ma.

"But you didn't," he answered matter-of-factly. "Instead, you've passed your first test."

She was shaking her legs in the air, one by one, trying to end the vibrations.

"We need to move," Sa·ma said. "Come on." He headed off across the scraggly wasteland.

From this perspective, Le·ma could see that it was different than the land on the other side of the mountain. Over there, the green plants were plentiful and thick. Over here, they were sparse and oddly shaped. They were more crooked looking, with links branching away and back again toward the center supports. Some grew toward the ground, forming arches large enough to walk under. Together Le·ma and Sa·ma passed through several of these. The arches seemed to weave across the wasteland as if Sa·ma was using them as landmarks.

"This is the Trail of Passage," he said. "Remember these arches, for they'll be your guide back."

"What do you mean? Why will *you* not be my guide back?"

"It's not the way. You must find your way back to the Colony alone."

"But you said there is no passage back."

"Indeed, there is no passage. But that doesn't mean there is no way back. You'll have all the skill necessary to get back on your own after this journey. Your final test combines everything you'll learn to make it home."

"Ugh," Le·ma said, exasperated. "What if I don't make it?"

"That is possible. This entire area is circled by sheer blue rock, leading to the edge of the Rift. There is no way through them or over them. I was the second apprentice selected by Go·ma. His first selection never returned from this quest.

It happens. Only the strong and wise become Lumen Seekers."

Le·ma remained silent. Up until now, this felt like a game. Sa·ma was her safety net. Now, the process seemed serious, and she worried that she wasn't up to it.

They trudged on for a bit until reaching one of the red rock fingers. What looked thin from the top of the mountain was actually quite vast when standing next to it. It spanned about the width of eight of their bodies.

"We need to cross this," Sa·ma said.

"But red rock is attractive," she stated quizzically.

"Yes, it is. We can't just walk across it because our feet will stick. It's possible to detach one leg at a time, but this requires leverage. Once you have all your limbs stuck, you'll be helpless. But luckily for us, the attraction isn't that strong unless you touch it." He waved a leg over the red rock. It seemed effortless. Then he let it drop, and it clanked onto the red stone.

Le·ma gasped.

"Pull me," Sa·ma commanded.

She wrapped two legs around his center and pulled back with her remaining two legs. It took all her might, and his pushing with his free legs, to detach him from the red rock. He popped back.

"Thanks!" he said. Then he asked, "How can we cross?"

"We need to make a barrier between us and the river."

"Correct. How?"

Brown Rock. She found a loose polyhedron on the ground and threw it into the river. It stuck fast in the middle, then turned red and sank as the shapes below shuffled to make room. Puzzled, but not deterred, she tore loose a hunk of green polyhedrons from the side of a plant and threw it into the river. Again they turned red and sank below.

"What's going on?"

"What do you think?"

"Well, it looks like anything that touches the river changes into red rock. But you touched it and didn't change."

"An enigma, indeed. It turns out that it'll turn almost anything red. One exception is something living, something attached to a violet life core."

"Why is that?"

"For this answer, we need to go all the way back before the world existed. This is the story of the creation."

#

A single eight-legged Polyan, named Ra·ju, floated in the darkness. He was all that existed. He made himself shine bright white, but there was nothing for the light to fall upon. He searched the void but found nothing. He was alone.

So he detached all his legs, one by one, and as he did they changed color. One became brown, one orange, one red, one blue, one green, one yellow, one violet, and one indigo. They each then sprouted seven legs of their own and became the eight gods. But unlike us, they each had a colored core. To these, he gave the suffix "ro" and named them Ta·ro, Ke·ro, Pi·ro, Ju·ro, Ca·ro, Na·ro, Wi·ro, and Su·ro, respectively.

They gathered around Ra·ju, and he was proud. But they floated in nothing, and this made him sad. So he directed his children to make a place where they could dwell and play.

To Ta·ro the brown, he said, "Go and make the lands." Ta·ro then produced a chunk of brown rock between his legs. This he shaped and smoothed and spread out until it surrounded and contained them all in a continuous sphere. This is the world in which we now dwell.

To Ca·ro the green, he said, "Go and make the plants." Ca·ro exploded in a mass of green polyhedrons that shot out in all directions. These dotted the landscape, and each of them became the plants spread about.

To Ke·ro the orange, he said, "Make life, so the land may buzz with activity." To do this, Ke·ro descended and imbued a bunch of brown rock with orange energy. Thus, the creatures that inhabit our world were born, including us.

To Su·ro the indigo, he said, "The creatures are unable to experience their world. Give them senses." So Su·ro waved at the creatures, and they sprouted sensors that allowed them to see, hear, and speak. Some plants also gained the ability to grow new sensors for future generations. But the creatures were too few, and would never find each other, so Ra·ju turned his attention to Wi·ro.

So to Wi·ro the violet, he said, "Make the creatures multiply, so that we may never run out." To do this, he shone his violet light upon them, and they found each other and increased their numbers. Soon there were too many, and they began to fight.

To Ju·ro the blue, he said, "Go and make divisions so that the creatures will not fight." Ju·ro descended to the land and rolled about, leaving a trail of blue rock in his wake. This rock was so high it became the mountains we know today. But in the valleys, the creatures were too close and still crowded.

To Pi·ro the red, Ra·ju said, "Go and make the rivers so that the beasts will multiply slower." Pi·ro descended, like

Ju·ro, and rolled around the land. As he did so, trenches formed and filled with red rock to further divide the lands. However, every time he hit a blue mountain, he was repelled and bounced off. This went on for many days, and each time Pi·ro was halted, he got angrier and angrier. He decreed that everything that touched the red rock from then on would become red as well. To do this Wi·ro, having a violet core, demanded that anything violet would be immune from this curse. But Pi·ro did not care because he just wanted to turn all the blue rock to red. But when he attempted to affect the blue stone, he was still repulsed. So he made the red rock attractive. Finally, the forces balanced and he was able to touch blue with red.

Ra·ju was angry. He said, "Enough! I will not tolerate my children fighting any longer. Your powers are from this point frozen and in balance. Blue will not be changed to red, nor will blue be repulsive to red."

The gods accepted their place and returned to the center to look upon the lands that they created. They were pleased with their work, but the terrain was dark. Ra·ju then turned to his last child.

"Na·ro the yellow, shine your brightness upon the lands so that we may see them, and the creatures may see each other." To this, he burst into a shower of shimmering brightness, and the world was filled with light.

#

"So that's why living things can touch the red and not turn red?" asked Le·ma. "But nothing else can?"

"That is why. The ancient ones, when they formed the world, created the rules by which everything behaves. Knowing how things work, and how to use their properties together, is what makes us Lumenaries. By your training, and the training I received, we know more about the world than most others, and this gives us an advantage."

"I feel privileged and grateful to you for having been selected to receive this knowledge."

"So far, it's been my privilege to be able to teach you. You're a good student, and I think your deeds will someday exceed my own."

"I doubt that, but thank you for the words of encouragement."

"Now," Sa·ma said, changing the subject. "You need to use your knowledge to get us across the river."

Le·ma was perplexed. She looked around. She thought about the story of creation. Without realizing it, she worked the problem out by speaking it.

"Okay, so the red rivers turn everything red, except the living. But living things stick to it, and it's difficult to detach oneself without help. If we put something living on it, we can walk over that!" She was proud of herself. As they walked along the bank, she found a plant leaning over and pushed it down, laying it upon the red river. Starting from the point where the plant touched the river, it turned red along its length until it reached the ground. The part over the river sank down, leaving a strip of red rock remaining on the shore.

"Why?" she asked.

Her logic was clever, so Sa·ma explained why it had failed. "Remember my story. 'The Living' applies to those with violet cores, like us, or the beasts. Plants are alive, in a sense, but they don't have a violet center so they'll turn red."

"So we need to pile up a bunch of beasts onto the river."

"Maybe, but there has got to be a better way."

Le·ma worked through the problem, replaying the scene in her mind. *I laid the plant down so we could walk across it, but then it touched the river and turned red. It would've worked if it didn't touch the river.*

A realization came to her. She strutted away from the river, found one of the arched plants, a big one, and pulled it from the ground. She dragged it and tossed it across the river so that one end landed on the opposite bank. The arch made a bridge, something she'd never seen or envisioned before.

"Perfect!" Sa·ma commended her.

Le·ma knew it would just fall over if they climbed on it. So she yanked it back over, retrieved three more, and lashed them together side by side to make a thick archway. With Sa·ma's help, she heaved this structure across the river once more. It was both broad and stable enough for them to cross, which they did.

"I solved it!" Le·ma danced with joy on the opposite side, as the Source began to dim above her.

"Come on," said Sa·ma. "I want to get to the Rift before night. It's not far now."

They marched off in the direction of the chasm that divided their world in two.

50

CHAPTER 6 - FIRST IMPRESSIONS

"There is no personal charm so great as the charm of a cheerful temperament." - Henry Van Dyke

Max tapped his foot, waiting for the elevator. He watched the numbers count down, pausing at every digit for an unusually extended period of time. He pulled out his phone and looked at the time: 10:05. He was already late for the interview. His team desperately needed this candidate to be a fit. They'd been without an intern for six weeks following the tragic suicide of their previous one.

A 'ding' was heard, then the elevator doors opened, brightening the corridor. Two kids rushed out, laughing. They dodged around Max as he stepped in.

The lift was empty. Max poked his head out the door and shouted, "Where are your parents?" But the kids were nowhere in sight. He ducked back in and the door shut. As he went to press floor seven, he noticed all the lighted squares.

"Damn kids!" he exclaimed. They'd pressed every floor before leaving the elevator.

Max pressed the numbers randomly in frustration. He pounded his fist on the panel as the elevator began moving upwards.

The door opened on the second floor. He stared out into an empty hallway. After what seemed like a full thirty seconds, the door closed.

Why the hell don't they allow you to unselect elevator buttons? he thought to himself. *It should be like check boxes on a computer form. If you press it again, it'll uncheck that option. That way if you make a mistake, you can fix it, or in the case of annoying kids, reverse their joke.*

The door opened on floor three. Carts of medical equipment were lined up along one wall. They looked like expensive devices. One resembled an oscilloscope with a bunch of dangling electrical cables. The door closed.

We've had radio buttons since the sixties. And computer interfaces with them for decades. But Otis Elevator, in all its wisdom, has never thought to allow you to unselect a floor by pressing it again.

The door opened, revealing floor four. Across from the elevator was a special fountain used to flush one's eyes out in the case of an accidental chemical burn. *I hope I never have to use one of those.* The door closed.

Max watched the floor four light go out as the elevator made its way toward floor five. The door opened.

A lab across from the elevator glowed an eerie red through its smoky white window panel. *Why'd they have red lights in there? What twisted experiments are they doing? Probably sticking sensors into monkey brains and seeing how they interpret colors. I'm glad we only experiment on fake creatures.* The door shut.

Max looked at his watch again. 10:08. "Damn." *Fucking kids.*

Floor six. A sterile cinder block wall, institutional beige, filled the view. With a sudden rattling noise, a cart of glassware sped by. It was pushed by a woman who was obviously in a hurry and had built up quite a bit of momentum. The sound startled Max from his thoughts. "One more to go," he said.

"Sorry?" asked the woman pushing the cart, as the doors closed.

Yeah, you're sorry. I'm the one who's late.

The final ding and the elevator delivered Max to floor seven. Max rushed down the hall to the lab, which was tucked away behind an unassuming wooden door. He yanked it open and it slammed into the adjacent wall. A young Asian woman looked up from the magazine she was perusing. She sat in the first of two chairs they had set up as a makeshift lobby, with a browning fern placed in between. *Reminder to self, water the plant,* he thought.

"Hello," he said. "I'm Max. Sorry I'm late. I had some issues... with the elevator." He held out his hand.

The woman put down her magazine and stood up. She had short black hair and thick black-rimmed glasses. She grasped Max's hand and shook it. "I'm Min. I hate elevators, they're always bringing me down." By the way she winced at herself, even she thought that was dorky. But Max liked that she made the joke anyway. "I haven't been waiting long," she recovered.

"Nice to meet you, Min. I can already tell you'll be perfect. Let's talk in my office and then I'll show you around."

#

Max entered Dana's office. It was larger than his. In addition to the desk, it had a separate round table for holding meetings, a mini fridge, and two small bookcases. It was also on the first floor and in Building 20, which was the name for the government grant wing of the UConn Health Center. This location allowed her to work with administrative staff directly, but didn't prevent her from collaborating with the team. Her workstation had a direct fiber link into Spheria's computer system. Max pulled one of the table's chairs over and placed Min's resume on the desk.

"This is the one," he proclaimed.

Dana picked up the resume and began to read through it.

Max glanced out Dana's window at the view of the Farmington Valley beyond the parking lot. This reminded him what an odd location a medical facility was for an A.I. project like Spheria. He'd debated it with Graham, but apparently the dean owed him a favor or two for funding some research here previously. So their space was generous and economical, and utilities were free. Also, the location in Connecticut assured they could attract talent from either Boston or New York City.

"She looks good on paper. You're sure she can take your twisted management style?" Dana asked.

"What do you mean? Everyone loves my management style. I have some of the best talent available."

"I can't argue with that." She looked at the resume again. "Her name. Min? Seems ironically appropriate. Maybe this one can handle the stress."

"Stress? There is no stress! This is pure fun. We're paid to basically play all day in a big sandbox. What more could any researcher want?"

"Tell that to Olivia."

Max frowned and slumped his shoulders. "That's still a mystery to me. Olivia was finding some intriguing trends in the data, work that she loved. She was all smiles every day. I don't get it. What would've pushed her over the edge?"

Dana glared at Max. "That's a rather poor choice of words, don't you think?"

"Right. Not my intention."

"Anyway, I agree. I don't get why she'd commit suicide. She was on a great project, a once-in-a-lifetime opportunity, working with some amazingly talented people. She even seemed to cope well with your style. As you say, you're paid to play all day."

"Yep."

Dana handed the resume back to Max and glanced at a printout on her desk.

"We have a problem, Max."

"What?"

"The paid part. The initial funding for this project is drying up. You've spent too much too fast. I know things cost more than you expected, and you increased the scope of the project somewhat. But we're going to need more, especially if you keep bringing on new people."

"Hey, we're stable with staffing now. Min is a replacement, not a new person."

"Even so, we're running out of money. We need to write some grant applications for round two funding."

"What about Graham?"

"I already asked him for more. He was standoffish and wouldn't commit to anything. He said he's going to stop by in a few weeks for a checkup, so you need to wow him. But even if he gives us more, it'll only buy us some time. To keep this project viable, we need more irons in the fire. It's not good to have only one source of funding."

"Agreed. So how do we do this?"

"I will show you. Take a few days to get Min settled. Then you and I need to focus on getting us some more money."

"Understood."

CHAPTER 7 - THE INTERVIEW

"If you're having fun being yourself and filming something that you would watch yourself, it becomes contagious for other people to watch, too." -
Zoe Sugg

Min entered her apartment. Sheila, her roommate, was sitting on the couch painting her toes. She was a knockout, from Australia even, which made her name more than appropriate.

"Hey babe," Sheila said. "How'd it go?"

"Pretty good… I think. Actually, super good if I get it. The project is amazing, one of the best things I've ever seen. This is like a computer science major's dream internship."

"Tell me more, your geekiness." Sheila was a medical student at the UConn Health Center. On the cafeteria bulletin board, she saw the ad posted for an internship and told Min about it. She didn't like computers and didn't understand Min's fascination with them. But other than that one difference, they got along smashingly.

"I'd be helping out a bunch of scientists to watch this virtual world. They've built a complete ecosystem and have created a bunch of brand new creatures, and a…"

"Hold it! 'Built creatures?' What is this, Frankenstein's family?"

"No," Min chuckled. "Not real creatures. Computer creatures. Like things living inside the computer. They call them Spherians because they exist inside a Sphere. There are a bunch of types of Spherians, but the extra intelligent ones are called Polyans."

"Huh? You lost me."

"It's like earthlings and humans. Spherians and Polyans."

"Okay, I get the names, but how's this inside a computer?" Sheila asked.

Min puckered up her lips, searching for the words to describe it. She wasn't adept at speaking 'layman.'

"Listen, why don't I just show you? I filmed the interview."

Her roommate was used to this. Min was a gadget freak, and her 'spy glasses' were her favorite. She picked them up years ago from spygear.com and had been wearing them ever since. They looked like ordinary thick-rimmed glasses, which just happened to be in style these days. But hidden in the frame on one side was a miniature camera capable of filming up to two hours of compressed video footage.

Min took off her glasses, plugged a cable into them, and hooked the other end to the TV. She put the glasses back on and sat facing the screen. It looked like her head was wired to the television, and she was about to do a brain dump, revealing her inner thoughts to the world. She picked up the remote and changed to input one. Then she pressed a concealed button on the inside of the frame of her glasses.

The screen showed a small windowless office with a plain wooden desk. Behind the desk sat a lean man with chiseled features and short curly dark hair. To one side, only half in view, stood a tall bookcase filled with imposing looking books and a shelf of blurry knickknacks. On the wall over the man hung posters of Carl Sagan, Bill Nye, and Neil deGrasse Tyson. Sheila didn't recognize any of them.

"So what attracted you to this position?" asked the man, with a slight accent. Probably French, but Sheila wasn't sure.

"That's Max," said the real Min to Sheila.

"I've always loved computers," answered Min in the video. "I especially like working with data. Not structured data like in databases, but seemingly random data like activity feeds. I love looking for patterns in the randomness, like looking for a needle in a haystack."

"That's exactly what we need. What did you think of my write-up of the project?"

"Fascinating," Min replied.

"Fascinating!" Sheila interjected. "You're such a nerd. Who are you, a chick from the planet Spock?"

"The planet Vulcan, jeez. Get your facts straight."

Max was saying. "…is going to give us insights into how cultures develop that were before now unachievable. Sure, we've visited primitive cultures, and even watched them for long periods of time. In many cases we've seen how civilization has influenced them, changed them. But real life moves too slowly, and the sample size is too small, to draw many conclusions. This simulation allows us to see firsthand how cultures can form; how social structures are created; how good must win against evil, or maybe evil *can* win. Regardless, this experiment will provide insight and knowledge about the human condition that nothing else has ever provided. It's evolutionary, er, revolutionary."

Sheila shook her head. "I have no idea what this guy is saying, but he sure sounds passionate. And he's kind of hot. I can see you two together, same color hair."

"Sheila! This isn't about how hot he is. I'm not in this to find a boyfriend. I'm interested in this work because it's the coolest thing ever and can change the world."

"Okay yeah, I got that out of what he said, right. Gotcha. He's still hot. I would date him. Even if I worked with him."

"Jeez."

"Actually, maybe not. He sounds French. They can be intense. Watch yourself with him."

"That's sooo racist. I didn't think you were like that."

"No, it's not racist. It's culturalist. Like *he* was saying. Maybe I do understand this stuff."

Max continued. "...was invented by me. It's the heart of the operation." On the video, he handed Min a small chunk of glass. She held it up to her eyes and it filled the screen. At this magnification, it sparkled like a prism made of diamond and had layers of defects inside. "We call it a Qube, which stands for Quantum Uncertainty Binary Engine. I know it's kind of a cheesy name, but I picked the acronym first and had to come up with something for it to mean. Anyway, whatever it's called, this is what gives the inhabitants of our world their brains. No, that's the wrong analogy; their brains have more data than these can hold. It's more like their soul. There's enough infor-mational state in one of these to govern their tendencies to make a choice in any given situation, to be their... personality, if you will. Their actual memories are stored in traditional hard drives. Does any of this make sense?"

"Totally!" exclaimed Min without hesitation. "This is the coolest thing I've heard in a long time. It's like science fiction, but in real life."

"That's what I was hoping you'd say. We're breaking new ground here, and everyone on my team needs passion. I was impressed by the analysis you emailed to me. You came up with some clever solutions to my exercises. Not bad for a student at CCSU. So..."

"Hey, it's a great school! They teach practical knowledge. Because I'm a numbers geek, I'm just trying to finish up all the required computer science classes to graduate. Statistics is my focus, but to get a degree in Data Analytics requires that you be able to code also, though it's not my favorite thing."

"Well, we need your skills specifically. I already have great coders on the team. Anyway, as I was about to ask, are you interested in the job?"

"Totally!"

"At least you're consistent." He cracked a smile. "I agree you're a great fit. I just have to get final approval from the project sponsor and will let you know soon. Let me show you the coolest part on the way out."

"Thanks," Min replied.

"Follow me," Max said. He got up and left the office. The camera rose and followed him out.

The real Min pressed another button on the frame of her glasses. The video skipped ahead at quadruple speed. Max was weaving between cubicles and down a hallway like The Flash.

"The most amazing thing you'll ever see is about to happen," real Min said.

"Seeing him smile is the most amazing thing I've ever seen!" Sheila quipped.

"Stop it!" Min ordered.

"Wait. Play it normal." Min pressed a button and the video returned to real time.

The camera focused on Max as he walked up to a large metal door.

"Yes, that confirms it. He's got an amazing ass. That's prime eye candy."

"I mean it!" said Min.

Max typed a code into a keypad near the door and it clicked. He turned the handle and pushed it open. The light from the room was blinding. The TV went completely white with over-saturation until the camera exposure compensated. Then walls on both sides of the room came into view. They emitted a massive amount of blue light interspersed with speckles of red. Max and Min entered what was shaped like a large walk-in closet, about fifteen feet long by eight feet wide.

"I can see from your expression you're confused," Max said. "Rightfully so. This is like nothing you've ever seen before. It's not typical, but it's our server room."

"I've seen server rooms before. They're usually darker."

"Yeah, that's what I mean. See that Qube in your hand?" Min opened her palm, not even realizing that she'd carried it from his office. "When those are powered up, they glow. These walls are covered with them. There are thousands. These are the core of the computer array."

The camera panned across the scene, and Min (and Sheila) could see that there were rectangular panels along the walls forming layers. They were like shutters, or shingles, or the flip panels at department stores displaying posters for sale. In fact, these were virtually identical to those, and Max began flipping them.

"See, this setup allows us to pack in many more of these in this tight space and still gain access to them all. Each panel is three feet tall by one foot wide, and thus holds 300 Qubes. We have eight panels, four on each side, holding a total of 2,400 active Qubes. That's how many thinking creatures we currently can have in our world at one time. But each Qube costs a lot to make, so this was all quite expensive. Luckily we were funded by an eccentric billionaire."

"Really, who's that?" Min asked.

"Graham Neilson," Max answered.

"No shit!" blurted Sheila. "He's from my hometown. A living legend in Australia."

"… that's the problem," Max continued. "We've noticed that those Polyans that act disruptively tend to have a Qube that glows red. Those that behave neutrally glow a light pink. And those that seem cooperative glow blue. We gained this insight early by watching behaviors in our first set of prototype Polyans. Now we intentionally weed out the destructive ones."

"I don't think I understand," stated the recorded Min.

"Yeah, it's deep. Remember when I said the Qube is like the Polyan's soul?"

"Yeah."

"Well, the Polyans in our virtual world aren't built to be indestructible. In fact, we've created a rather hostile environment. They die all the time. So when they die, the associated Qube stops processing and blinks. What we then do is make it available for another Polyan, so that when a new one is born, the Qube is recycled. Or, to put it another way, resurrected. That's actually more like the truth because the new Polyan inherits the previous one's core personality traits. Here, I'll show you."

Max searched the closest panel and pulled a flashing red Qube from it. "The blinking ones are connected to a deceased Polyan. They flash because they're no longer receiving data." He walked to the back of the room where a workbench supported a large computer screen and keyboard. Next to it, rising from the floor, was a round metal cylinder with a hinged lid. It was covered with thick red paint like a fire hydrant. Max pulled out a stool from under the workbench and sat down. He placed the Qube into a small docking device next to the computer. It began to glow a solid bright red.

"See, this is an exceptionally nasty one. The computer screen here shows the values inside it as a curve." Indeed, the display showed a grid with a series of icons horizontally along the middle. A shallow curve snaked along the bottom. The vertical scale went from negative one to positive one. The curve for this particular Qube was almost entirely at negative one.

"I would hate to meet this one in a dark ally," said Min.

"That's for sure. And we don't want to subject the virtual population to this negativity either. So we choose not to reintroduce these bad ones into the world."

"How do you reset them?"

"Unfortunately, that's a limitation of using quantum phenomenon. We can't clear the slate; the qubits have a permanent memory of their state. It can change over time, but can't be cleared."

"So what do you do with them then?" asked Min.

"Well, because they're still functional processing units, we need to destroy them. We don't want random people finding them in the trash. So this pillar here is a special incinerator we built." He lifted the lid of the red hydrant-looking thing, revealing a small depression with vertical slits all around it. He removed the Qube from the computer stand and placed it inside the device. After closing the lid, he reached for a rubbery button on the side which read 'Stop.' "We salvaged this button from an old table saw, my idea. I think it's an ironic play on words." He pressed it. There was a click, followed by a fierce whooshing sound like a blowtorch. A moment later the sound ended and the pillar clicked again. Max opened the lid showing that the compartment was once again empty. He then pulled out a small tray from the base of the column. It was full of powdered charcoal dust. This he dumped in the trashcan beneath the workbench.

"Yep, we destroy the bad ones. I guess in a way they burn for all eternity."

Min paused the video. "That was the good part."

"I have *no idea* what this guy is saying!" exclaimed Sheila. "He's a total whack job if you ask me."

"Really? I think he's hot," argued Min.

66

CHAPTER 8 - THE RIFT

They made camp next to the Rift. Sa·ma, using the pointy tip of his leg, traced a circle on the ground between them. Le·ma removed the small yellow shard she'd been carrying strapped to her underside. She laid it on the ground inside the circle. Then she sat on the other side, facing Sa·ma.

They silently watched the Source fade above them and the world darken around them. All seemed quiet, calm, and a slight bit ominous. Normally, they'd be in their hives or gathered around the Colony center. Being in a group gave them a feeling of safety. Out here at the edge of the world, in the dark, they both were vulnerable and unsettled.

Le·ma tried to relax by taking everything in. In the dim light, the other side of the world looked different, like a negative image. They could see the mountain ranges on the opposite hemisphere like blue lines. Their maze-like meanderings twinkled as the glow from the red rivers illuminated them. In one area, an unusual formation of mountains created a large perfect triangle, with no rivers inside. Le·ma knew this, as everyone learned as a child, to be the Valley of Three. It was a fixture in the sky at night, something that Soldiers used to navigate by when it was dark.

Le·ma pointed at it. "What's the Valley of Three?" she asked.

"Nobody knows for sure," replied Sa·ma. "It's said that the gods go there to play games, as there's not enough room for that in the Source. Sometimes, on certain nights, you can see them inside as flickering dots, moving about. What they're actually doing there nobody knows, since a Polyan has never set foot on the opposite side of the world. As large as that triangle is, however, it's tiny compared to the formation we came here to see."

Le·ma turned her focus to the Rift, looking over the edge into nothingness. She traced its path with her eyes as it curved upwards. From this position, she could see the entire chasm going off in two directions and circling the world. It divided it into two halves. It was insurmountably wide, about twenty times wider than the red river they'd crossed.

"Every time I see it up close, and I've seen it hundreds of times, it takes my breath away," said Sa·ma.

"I've never seen it up close like this. I heard many stories about the Rift, but none prepared me for its actual size. It makes me wonder how large the world is, and how small we are."

"These are typical feelings. This journey is one of learning and self-discovery. It's to help you come to know yourself. Only by knowing oneself may you focus on helping others."

Sa·ma fell silent. He watched as Le·ma mulled over his words, knowing this was part of the process. She said nothing more. He'd given her a ton of information for one day to think about. Yet, they still had to perform the ritual they'd journeyed to complete.

After what seemed like an eternity, Sa·ma broke the silence. All he said was, "It's time for the offering."

Le·ma, who'd become entranced by the yellow crystal, looked up. She nodded, rose to her feet and picked it up, as she had rehearsed. She walked to the edge of the Rift, and without hesitation, tossed it in.

Sa·ma appeared next to her. Together they watched the crystal fall, illuminating the walls below as it did so: brown rock, as far as the eye could see. It fell for a long distance, visible but getting smaller. It became just a dot, after which it grew too small and dim to see any longer. As far as Le·ma could tell, it hadn't reached the bottom.

Sa·ma began to hum. Le·ma joined him. Then together they intoned the ancient verse:

Deep into the Rift I go
Lighting the path to nothingness
Deep into the Rift I fall
Shining like a spark of hope
Deep into the Rift I plant
A seed of yellow, sprouting
Deep into the Rift I sprout
Bringing forth a bubble of charge

They were silent, staring down into the darkness as if expecting something to happen. Nothing did. Eventually, Sa·ma turned to Le·ma and said, "You're now a Lumen Seeker, bringer of life, counselor to others. The seed you planted will bring forth a yellow bubble, the rarest kind. It'll rise until it reaches the Source, thus turning it yellow for that day. When it radiates yellow light, all life crystals in the world will begin to fill from within. For that day, no creature will need to hunt or forage, and they can rest without having to fight for survival."

Le·ma shivered in the cold night, their source of comfort lost in the depths.

"Is it bottomless?" she asked. Le·ma imagined the crystal exiting their physical world, and in doing so, releasing a yellow bubble from the world without substance. Then it would begin its ascent toward the Source.

Sa·ma repeated the answer he'd been given long ago. For neither he nor any other living Polyan had any direct knowledge of what lay in the Rift. A few had fallen in, but none had ever returned. "It doesn't have a bottom for us, the living. But when a Polyan dies, her structure journeys below to dwell with all those who have left us. This place, which we call 'Qubessence,' has an endless supply of violet energy. The lands are violet, the mountains are violet, even the sky looks violet. Everyone dwells in peace, never needing to find food for survival. There, everyone spends their time doing what they enjoy: playing, talking... and making statues." He smiled at her.

"It sounds amazing. Why would I not just jump in the Rift and go there now?"

"Because, to go there, you must be pure. This is your final story and it'll answer your question. It's about how the Rift came to be, and why you wouldn't want to jump into it."

Le·ma sat back down next to the empty circle. "I'm ready."

Sa·ma paced around her, wanting to illustrate his story with motion. "Remember the Troaten we saw from the top of the mountain?"

"Yes."

"It plays a key role in this story. It's the story of how the Rift was made, and the Source for that matter."

"But nobody knows how the Rift was made, right?"

"Lumen Seekers do. It's the one story that's passed down only to us, never told to the others. There is no need for them to burden themselves with this knowledge. It's privileged to only us and our apprentices."

"I'm ready for the knowledge," she implored.

"A long while ago, just after the world was formed, the creatures did not yet know their bounds. At that time, the world was still a whole sphere; there was no Rift. If you could make it around the mountains and over the rivers, you could walk completely around the world and come back to the same spot from the opposite direction. The Rift changed all that.

"One day there was born a Troaten, larger than the rest. This Troaten needed more food to survive. It depleted its sources, growing quite large in the process. It had become large enough to push itself over the mountains with its gigantic tentacles. So it flopped into the next valley and consumed everything there, growing even larger. It was never satisfied, and in its greed, drained every creature in the entire world. Nothing could escape its reaching grasp.

"By now it had grown so large that its tentacles could reach across the whole world. It could push in all directions and suspend its center in the open middle, where the Source is now. Because it was so large, it was insatiable for more energy. Since no more creatures were alive, it did what no Troaten has done before or since; it began digging for buried crystals. It dug its tentacles into the ground and found the buried life crystals that feed the plants. It dug deeper and deeper, flailing more and more in a giant circle. It literally carved the chasm in the ground that we know today as the Rift.

"But still it grew. It dug deeper and deeper, growing and growing, stretching farther and farther. And then, it reached the Qubessence with its tentacles." Sa·ma tried his best to recall the story exactly as Go·ma had told him, but he embellished it slightly to connect it to the world without substance. "When the tentacles crossed the boundary into that world, the entry of physical matter caused a massive shockwave of energy. This flowed into the body of the Troaten. In a bright flash, its tentacles were shattered to dust, and the energy ignited its body radiant white. With its tentacles gone and its body in the exact center of the world, instead of falling, it just hung there."

Le·ma interrupted, "So it became the Source?"

"Indeed. The Source is what remains of that giant Troaten. Thanks to it and its greed, we now have something to give us guidance, and to illuminate our world. It's also said, and this part is common knowledge, that the gods now dwell inside the Source, because it gives them a view of all the lands."

"Why is the Rift story kept a secret?"

"Because some might be tempted to leap into the Rift, knowing the Qubessence lies beyond. But, as we learned with the Troaten, the Qubessence doesn't want your body, only your structure. The resulting death is agonizing, and it's suspected that the gods won't welcome you as readily."

"Has anyone ever jumped in?"

"Some have, I'm afraid, and I can only imagine the horrible death they received."

"That's awful."

"Yes, it is. Yes, it is. Now you have much to think about, so get some rest. Tomorrow we make the trip back, and you'll face the last trial of your journey."

CHAPTER 9 - FIRST DAY

"Every new beginning comes from some other beginning's end." -
Seneca

Min arrived at 10 a.m. as instructed and entered the door to the makeshift lobby. Max was sitting at the reception desk playing on his phone. Apparently, he didn't want to risk being late on her first day.

"Good morning!" she said.

"Welcome aboard the Spheria Project. You ready to begin?"

"Sure am. Where should I put my things?"

Max got up and stepped aside. "This is your desk," he said, motioning to the vacated seat.

Min looked at the reception desk. It did look comfortable and fancy with all the glass and contoured wood. But she was hoping for something more challenging than answering the phone and greeting people.

"I'm going to be a receptionist?"

"Um, no... I mean yes... uh... kind of..."

"Huh?"

"We get like one visitor a month. And we don't have that much space. So you'll be working at this desk, and if someone happens to come in, just say hello and offer to get him or her some coffee. That's all. I promise you we have cool projects for you to work on. But we need someone here, and all the other staff are, let's just say, socially awkward, being scientists and all."

"Got it, not a problem. I can deal with that."

She placed her bag on the desk and sat down. The chair was comfortable. Three big computer screens also, *awesome.*

Max grabbed one of the lobby chairs and pulled it up next to her. "Let me show you how to log in and get to the data files. We have a team meeting at eleven so you'll have a chance to meet everyone."

"Sounds good."

#

When Max and Min entered the conference room, there were only two vacant seats, so they each sat in one. The rest of the team had already arrived, and Max was late as usual by five minutes.

"Sorry everyone," he said.

The woman at the head of the table scowled at him, then turned to Min. "Hello, you must be our new intern."

Max answered, "Yes, this is Min. She starts today."

"Hi Min," everyone said, almost in unison.

"We'll do introductions in a second," the woman said. "First, I wanted to cover some administrative details, then I'll turn the meeting over to Max."

Max nodded.

"So the project is fully operational now, and Graham Neilson is pleased with that news. He's scheduling a visit with us and is excited to see everything firsthand. In case you're not aware, something like this was a dream of his since he was a kid. He just got a little distracted while becoming a billionaire. But, as they say, you're never too old to follow your dreams."

"True that," said a dark-skinned woman with an African accent. Others nodded in agreement.

"I'll let you all know exactly when he's coming so we can clean up any junk in the office. Some of you have a habit of accumulating soda cans and empty boxes, so we'll want to clear all that out. Maybe we can throw a cleaning party and bring in some pizza or something."

"Ugh," said an Indian man. "I am so sick of pizza. It's all we ever get. We should get some curried lamb."

"No way," said a small Italian-looking man. "I'm not eating any of your ethnic crap. We need to bring in pizza. American all the way!"

"Pizza is not American," said the Indian.

"Dude, pizza was invented in New Haven by Frank Pepe," he replied.

"Actually, that's not true at all," said a woman with glasses. "Folklore aside, it was indeed invented in Italy; Naples to be precise."

"Regardless," said the Italian man, "it emigrated here with my forebears and is American now, just like apple pie and Coca-Cola."

"Curried lamb is American then also," declared the Indian, folding his arms across his chest.

Max entered the debate. "As long as we've got alcohol, who cares?"

"I second that," said the Italian. "Give me a beer and I could care less about the food."

"Alcohol it is," said the woman at the head of the table, "and maybe some curried lamb *and* a cheeseburger pizza!"

This got a chuckle from a few people.

"One last thing," she said. "My goal for the next two months will be to get some public visibility for this project. So my focus is shifting from managing funding to marketing. I'll be contacting different trade publications, websites, news sources, etc. The purpose is to spread the word that our technology is functional, and we are collecting interesting data. I may be inviting the press to take a tour of the project. We'd like to get some articles written about us if possible."

"May I ask a question?" asked the Indian.

"Go ahead."

"Why do we care if the public sees this project?"

"Good question. Graham isn't the sole funding source. We also have a couple of government grants helping us out. At some point, the money will run out, and we'll be applying for extensions. The more publicity we can generate, and the more we can publish that adds value to the scientific community, the better our chances to keep going. Also, the grants we got require that the results be disclosed. I believe in doing that 'with a splash' in the media rather than just in specialized journals. We'll do both, but I'm starting with the press to build hype. You each are going to be required to publish your analysis and conclusions in your respective fields, those of you who are scientists that is."

"Understood," said the Indian.

"Well, that's all I have. Max, take it away."

Max cleared his throat. "Okay, so I have a bunch of boring statistics to go over, but first, let's help Min get to know us all better. I thought we could go around the table. Talk about your role on this team, and then to make it interesting tell us something about yourself that's not work related. Sound good?"

"Sure," a couple of people said. Others nodded. One shrugged.

"I'll go first. We've already met, but my full name is Maximilian Moreau. I was born in France, as you can probably tell by my accent. Actually, who here wasn't born in America?" He raised his hand.

Three other hands went up. The Indian man, the African woman, and Min.

"Four to six. So we're outnumbered. Min, where were you born?"

"Vietnam."

"Great. Well, that gets us closer to balancing things out. Anyway, I was one of the first two members of the team along with Dana." He motioned toward the woman at the head of the table. "I designed the Qube technology as my master's thesis in physics. But then I dropped out of college in order not to disclose how it works. Well worth it. So I should have a master's degree, but I don't. I don't care. What we're doing here is a blast, and better than any job I could get in the real world, no pun intended."

Groans, and nods of agreement.

"Like I said, I was born in France, Lyons specifically. I grew up on a vineyard, but it wasn't in my blood, and my older brother was taking it over anyway. I was more engaged by the hidden mysteries of the operation, like how particles of fertilizer managed to migrate up into a pouring watering can. So I discovered my love of physics at an early age. I came to the United States to attend undergraduate school at MIT and then I just stuck around because I liked it here. A little cold, but nothing I can't live with. Actually, there is a theory, not sure if it's true. All the great ideas come from colder regions because people are stuck indoors and need to invent stuff not to get bored or freeze to death. In warm areas, they just go hang out at the beach. Who wouldn't?"

The Indian man said, "India is very warm, and we are very progressive."

"Yeah, can you name one thing invented there?"

"Of course. Radio was invented there."

"Radio?"

"Yes. Jagadish Bose was the first person to demonstrate sound over radio waves in 1895 in Kolkata. That invention enables almost all wireless communications we have today. As Americans say, 'not too shabby.'"

"Touché," said Max, and bowed his head. "I didn't say it was my theory, but I heard that somewhere. Maybe there is a half-truth to it. Back to me. After I graduated, I got a job at this game company in Cambridge where I was working on coding artificial intelligence. While there, I got my citizenship, and conceived of some of the concepts that later became the Qube technology. I made some key observations while dealing with the deficiencies in how we did AI. What we did was make 'pseudo algorithms,' they just faked behaviors that one might think were intelligent by using state models and expression trees. I remember a magazine article about one of our games that lauded our AI because the enemy would hide behind barriers. But the code just told them to sidestep when they were getting shot at. And that happened to move them behind a barrier, so it was all just a misinterpretation of simple rules. Anyway, when the game company went out of business, I went back to grad school. I focused on inventing the Qube in the cold halls of the MIT Stata Center, and the rest is history. Next."

"You didn't tell us anything non-work related," said Dana.

"Oh yeah. Well, my entire life is kind of work-related. But I like to read, both fiction and non-fiction. I have a huge book collection at home. Although everything I get now is digital, so it's not growing, at least not physically. Other than that, work and video games."

Dana went next. "Hi Min, my name is Dana Carter. As Max mentioned, there were two of us at the beginning; I'm the other one. I used to run the American office of Aboriginal Accruals for Graham Neilson. He contributed most of the funding for this project. This project is so important to him that he wanted me to be engaged in its management. He wants me to make sure the core values are never compromised and that the data we get is pure and unbiased. So in other words, I manage the boring administrative part of the project. But I do also get to manage the semi-cool scientific side of it. The researchers here report to me. Max handles the technical staff — those building the hardware, software, and world elements. It's a good structure and works well."

Watching her speak, Min estimated she was in her early sixties. She was stocky and had short curly blond hair. The hairstyle probably made her look older than she was.

"I used to be in the U.S. Navy, so I'm very organized and

like things structured. But after living in nine different places over eight years, I decided to give civilian life a chance and apply the logistics skills I had acquired. I took some time off to travel the world and happened to meet Graham on a scuba diving expedition. At the time, he was looking for someone who had the ability to navigate the U.S. grants system for him, and we hit it off. I helped set up an office here for his firm and, fast forward a few years, here I am. So yes, as I mentioned, I'm an avid scuba diver, and have had more than a few close encounters with sharks."

"Hopefully not loan sharks?" asked an Asian man, who'd until now remained silent.

"No, I managed to avoid those so far." Dana looked at the person to her left, who was the Indian man.

"Hi, Min. My name is Ravi Rashtrakuta Reddy, but people just call me 'Rash.' I work as a sociologist here. My job is to study the society of the Polyans. How it developed and organized, and how it's evolving over time. When I was a child, my father ran a mental health facility, and I used to go there after school to do homework. Observing how people interacted there, admittedly not in a normal sense, fascinated me. It formulated my career interest. After grad school, I stayed on as an assistant professor. But when the program started performing research on lab monkeys, I decided to quit. I was friends with Max from school, and happened to bump into him at a 10k run, and mentioned I was unemployed. He was looking for my exact specialty so it was perfect timing. Having the ability to work with a species uncompromised by any other neighboring cultures is an opportunity that we seldom get, if ever. I jumped at the chance.

"Among my accomplishments was creating the Polyan language, which is based on English, so we can understand them. You will see that their names all have a dot in them between two syllables, like in the pronunciation keys in the dictionary. This dot is called an 'interpunct,' a symbol that joins things. In math, it's a logical 'and' operator. The Polyans use this to connect their given name (prefix) to their leg count (suffix). So there is a consistent suffix for each caste, and they are, starting with three legs: ·ni, ·ma, ·zo, ·sa, ·ro."

Rash took a sip from a mug, then added, "I like to run, a lot. It clears my head and lets me focus better afterward. So that is my hobby." Turning to his colleague, he said, "Jean?"

"Hello. I'm Jean Evens," said the woman with glasses. "I'm the team's anthropologist. So Rash's focus is on how Polyans form into groups. My focus is on how that organization affects them as individuals, how it manifests into a culture. Somehow I fell into a job after high school as a food inspector and used to go around surveying restaurant cleanliness. After a year of that, I couldn't stand how disgusting things were and wanted to know how our culture allowed for this. This led me to go back to school for anthropology. Otherwise, I have three young kids ages seven, three, and one, so they keep me busy. Unlike most of the staff, I'm never here working into the wee hours of the morning. Anyway, it's nice meeting you, Min." She threw Min a motherly smile.

The African women then spoke with a thick accent. "I am the biologist for the team, even though we are not actually doing biology, so my role is more of a consultant. I was born in Ghana..."

"You forgot your name," interrupted Max.

"Oh, sorry. My name is Abina Andam. As I was saying, I was born in Ghana to a poor family and spent many of my teenage and early adult years as a safari tour guide. That is where I learned much about animals and the environment. Over time, I saved some money and through the United States Embassy was able to get a sponsorship to come study in America. There, I met my husband, who is American, so I was able to stay here and become a citizen. Using my biology major and my hands-on learning, I design the creatures that populate Spheria. I never in my dreams expected to be working with computers rather than animals. But I am enjoying this experience. It allows me to express creativity."

"And if you get sick she can cure you," said the Italian man.

"Yes, that is true," agreed Abina. "I come from a long family tradition of practicing Vodun. Most Americans know this as the more famous Haitian version Voodoo. Here, this is for you."

She handed Min a small pouch on a string necklace.

"It's a gris-gris and will bring you luck and keep you safe. Wear it at all times except in the shower."

Min fondled the leather pouch and could feel a couple of small solid objects inside it. It was sewn shut so she was unable to see what they were. She looked around the room with a puzzled expression.

Rash pulled his out of his shirt, as did two others she hadn't yet met. Apparently, this was a common token for the team.

"Thank you," she said.

"You are welcome," said Abina. "If you are ever feeling sick, you come see me."

"I will," replied Min, not ever expecting to take her up on the offer. She did place the gris-gris over her head because... when in Rome.

Next up was a muscular, bald black man who looked like he could be a pro wrestler. He spoke in a deep but clear voice. "Hello, my name is Desmond. I'm a hardware engineer and report to Max." If you closed your eyes, you would think he was a radio announcer. "I built the computer system that the Qubes attach to. I also maintain the workstations that everyone has, which contain some specialized components. Something nobody knows about me. Hm. Well okay, I used to work for Apple in its consumer electronics department. It was disbanded by Steve Jobs when he came back as CEO. We designed a bunch of wacky products that had nothing to do with computers. My group was working on an electric razor, not kidding, that used ultrasonic waves to give the closest shave possible. I still have a prototype and use it on my head. That's why you'll never see any sign of hair up there."

"Either that," said Rash, "or you just made all that up to explain your low testosterone." Rash unconsciously combed his right fingers through his thick head of hair.

Desmond answered him in an even deeper voice. "What do you think?"

"I... get the point," added Rash.

"I guess I'm next," said a thin Caucasian with an acne covered face. He looked too young to actually be part of this project. "My name is Tim Feynman, and, fun fact, I'm actually related to Richard Feynman. Why's that cool you ask? Because he's the physicist who formulated the theory of quantum mechanics. So, if we go back far enough, he's the reason this project is possible. When I heard about it, which was just a random act of chance, I called Max and begged him to add me as a programmer. He wasn't at that stage yet, but he kept my contact information, and I bugged him enough that he ended up hiring me. That and he wanted some star power on his staff. Also, I'm very humble."

"I can tell," said Min. "That's a pretty cool claim to fame."

"Top that, pizza boy," he said, turning to the Italian man.

"I think I can do that. Min, my name is Frankie Pompeo, and I'm the 3D designer and world builder on this team. In contrast to how Richard Feynman *theorized* about how the world works, I actually *create* how a world works!" Turning to Tim, "Oh yeah, you're cowering now."

Tim countered with, "Nice try. But it's easier to know the rules when you make them up."

"Okay fine, you win," said Frankie. "So in case my title didn't give anything away, it was me that conceived of the virtual world as being on the inside surface of a sphere. It's mathematically called a Spherical Eversion, which is like a planet but inside out, and provides us a world with no out-of-bounds to deal with, except for the Rift. That was created to segregate the two halves so that we could someday run a second experiment on the other side. So I create the building blocks of the world. In the human universe, everything is comprised of atoms, which as you know are very small. In Spheria, everything is made from a 3D polygon or a polyhedron. These much larger building blocks allow us to construct a world relatively quickly. And with Lee's help we've got programs that can build forests, mountain ranges, and otherwise terraform an area. We can also reduce a polyhedron into smaller polyhedrons, so the size of things isn't limiting. So, say one of our inhabitants decided to dig a hole in the ground. We can take the large ground polyhedron and instantly subdivide it into smaller ones. This allows the smaller pieces to be removed thus allowing the hole to exist. So the world is always changing. Not only by the rules we set forth, their equivalent to laws of physics, but because we're constantly adding things. The work is rewarding, and I love adding little mysteries or obstacles for the Polyans to encounter. I could, of course, go on and on because this is super fun stuff."

"You certainly are passionate," commented Min.

"Yep, let's get together over the next couple of weeks and I'll show you how I do this."

Max added, "He loves showing it off. Actually, I've got to admit he exceeded my expectations. I'm glad we found Frankie's creative genius to make the world alien, but not so foreign that we can't understand it."

"Thanks, Max. Other than work, I have a passion for photography. So if I'm not here, chances are I'm outside photographing something. I sometimes work on the weekends taking photos at weddings for extra cash, since these research jobs don't pay as well as I'd like, hint hint. Max couldn't convince any of his game industry buddies to move to Connecticut, so here I am. Lucky me, and I don't mean that sarcastically. Oh yeah, and I like pizza."

Chuckles all around. Then the room fell silent.

"Lee?" asked Max.

The thin Asian man feigned waking up. "Oh, yeah, who? What? Right." He shook his head then turned to Min. "Nice to meet you Min. My name is Lee Chang and I am the software architect on this project – the glue that holds it all together. Before this, I worked at Raytheon designing missile guidance systems. The work and mathematics were complex and challenging, but not at all creative. I am pleased Max took a chance and brought me in. Like Max, I don't have any hobbies. I am either here working or at home sleeping. I love coding, and I help Abina give behaviors and actions to the creatures she creates."

Lee fell silent and looked around the room. Max finished with, "Short and sweet."

Min jumped in without prompting, "Thank you all. This

was most helpful and you sound like a great bunch of people to work with. I'm looking forward to my internship here."

"In case you don't know," said Max, "one of Frankie's professors gave Min glowing remarks, which is one of the reasons we selected her."

"Yeah," said Min. "I'm also a student at CCSU but am taking a semester off to get some work experience and to build my resume. This seems like an amazing opportunity and I'm thrilled to be able to join this project. After my interview, I did some research, and it's the coolest thing I've ever seen. As I said a little while ago, I was born in Vietnam, and my parents emigrated here when I was three years old. They ran a motel in Arkansas until I was eight and had saved enough money to get a loan for their own motel. They ended up buying one in New-ington, Connecticut, after a long national search. It's not the best area, but they've done well. So I'm going to school now for Data Analytics. I'm actually still a Vietnamese citizen. When I turned eighteen I kept it that way so that I could someday return to my homeland and try to make some positive changes there. I've got a permanent work visa, however, and consider myself to be completely American."

"Thank you, Min, we're happy to have you on board," said Max.

"Yes we are," said Dana.

"Hear, hear," said Frankie, raising his coffee mug. Most of the others made the same gesture.

Max closed with, "Sorry that went so long, everyone. I hope we old-timers even learned a thing or two about each other. I'll make the rest of the meeting quick. Does anyone have any significant progress to report? If it doesn't affect anyone, let's save it for next week."

"I do," said Lee.

"Go," said Max.

"Really quick. I added some code to auto recycle blue Qubes. When a Polyan dies and if the associated Qube is over 50 percent blue, the system will assign it to another Polyan. This will remove the need to manually monitor and reset them on the panels all the time. We only have to deal with the red ones that we decide we want to destroy."

"Awesome. That'll save me a ton of time," said Desmond.

"How fast does the recycle happen?" asked Jean.

"There is a slight delay before the restart sequence occurs. But it all completes within ninety seconds."

"Thanks. We won't have to go into the server room every day then," finished Max.

88

CHAPTER 10 - THE FERTILE FIELD

"Gold is a treasure, and he who possesses it does all he wishes to in this world, and succeeds in helping souls into paradise." - Christopher Columbus

When Sa·ma was young, he worked quicker than most his age. When he finished his daily routine, he liked to explore outside the Colony in his extra time. He never crossed the mountains, not yet having the knowledge to do so. But he'd venture farther each time, making mental maps of the region. It was a skill he was good at and was one of the reasons he was later selected to become a Lumen Seeker.

One day, when he was farther than ever before, he came upon a land formation that looked unnatural. It seemed like a hill that had been cut to have vertical sides. As he investigated it, he found an opening in one side, and, being brash, entered. Inside, in the center of a hexagonal room, lay a glowing yellow crystal. Seated beside it was an old and feeble Polyan who Sa·ma did not recognize.

"Come and sit," said the Polyan, "I've been expecting you."

Sa·ma did as he was told, choosing a spot on the other side of the yellow crystal. "Who are you and why were you expecting me?"

"This dwelling you are in is called the 'Lumen Grotto.' It's a resting place of sorts. As you know, it's quite a distance from the Colony. Normally, Polyans are much too insecure to venture this far. Only the excessively confident actually do so, and those are bound to eventually find me. When you do, you pass the first test."

The old Polyan fell silent and just stared at the yellow crystal. Sa·ma pondered the word 'test' and debated how to respond. *Who is this crazy one, and how could he possibly have been expecting me, and why would there be a test, and do I even care?* Somehow, he didn't exactly know why, but he felt that how he responded would affect the rest of his life.

"I came seeking you," he said.

The older Polyan looked up at him and paused for a long while. Then asked, "How do you seek that which do you not know exists?"

"Many things exist which I don't yet know. The reason I'm here is I'm seeking to learn about things, discover things, that I didn't know yesterday. That's why I sit before you. That's why I found you." The age of the Polyan before him was apparent, so he added, "I seek knowledge" for good measure.

"Then you've found some. A Lumenary firstly seeks knowledge, for only through knowledge can you then find solutions."

Sa·ma stared hard at the old Polyan. "Lumenary you say? Go·ma is our Lumen Master, and we don't have a Lumen Seeker yet under him. So who are you?"

"It's a misconception that a Lumen Seeker is promoted to Lumen Master only when the previous one is dead. That'd make the transition abrupt and unplanned. We don't like to leave such matters to chance. Therefore, as the Lumen Master gets old, he goes into seclusion and a Lumen Seeker takes his place. This isn't known to the Colony. Thus, you share the incorrect belief that the previous Master has died. I was the Master before Go·ma. I trained him. He was my Seeker. When my master died, I took his place here as Lumen Elder, and Go·ma became your current Master. In this way, we always have a backup in case the current Lumen Master meets an untimely death.

"Additionally, since Go·ma is in such high demand, he won't have the time to give you complete instruction. I will fill in the gaps. He'll focus on acclimating you to the ways of nature and the world. I'll give you the history and lore of our people."

"Wait, does this mean I'm a Lumen Seeker?"

"It does should this be the path you desire."

"It's been my dream since I first learned of this way, and my hope that it would someday open for me."

"Then that day is today. I'll inform Go·ma that he has a new apprentice. My name is Do·ma, and we can begin your training now."

#

And so it was that Sa·ma visited Do·ma every chance he could. He was taught how they used to have much greater freedom to wander this side of the world sphere. That was until the mountains grew thicker and the rivers widened. And there were far fewer Polyans, so moving from place to place was much easier. But the changing landscape forced them to form the Colony and build hives, giving them a central dwelling space to congregate for safety.

He learned that they used to only gather green crystals from the ground, digging under plants. Then they discovered how to bring down beasts by working as a team. And the energy of a single one could replenish many of them at once.

He also learned many tales and legends from the distant past. One, in particular, was a place called the Fertile Field. It was said to be a circular shaped clearing with violet crystals sticking out of the ground. These replenished themselves as if they grew there or rose up from some distant buried treasure trove. This mysterious place could provide an almost endless supply of energy for free. But that's why it was a legend, because such a place would never exist. *Or could it*?

That was what Sa·ma now intended to find out. Having seen the strange violet spot yesterday from the top of the mountain, he could only hope that this one legend could be true. So he rose and left the Rift before Le·ma awoke, as was the tradition. She was on her own from this point forward. Either she made it out alive, or she failed to become his successor. This was how the process worked from one Lumenary to another, generation after generation. It was just the way it had always been. The trials in the proving ground determined if you were worthy of receiving the responsibilities ahead.

He retraced the trail for a while, heading back to the red river that they'd crossed. At the bank, he veered to the right. The vegetation was thicker this way, and there was no natural path to follow. His pace slowed as he picked his way around obstacle after obstacle. This would be enough to make most lose their sense of direction, but after years of practice, he was able to keep a mental map. He made gradual progress toward his destination. After quite some distance, the plants thinned and Sa·ma stepped into a large clearing. In the center, forming a rough circle, were twenty large violet crystals protruding from the ground. He stood there in shock. He'd actually found the Fertile Field. The legend was real!

Then something else caught his eye. Something he hadn't seen at first, as if it had just materialized. Standing in the center of the circle, towering above him, stood a seven-legged Polyan with a red core.

CHAPTER 11 - MIN'S ASSIGNMENT

"Everything we see hides another thing, we always want to see what is hidden by what we see." - Rene Magritte

Min hung her wool jacket on the lobby coat rack and sat down at the reception desk. She paused for a moment, allowing the warmth of her Starbucks coffee to soak into her hands. It was still far too hot to drink. She moved the mouse and the computer lit up, prompting her to log in. She entered her username and password. As the authentication icon spun, she removed the cover to her coffee and began to blow on it.

As soon as the computer desktop appeared, an instant message popped up from Max: "See me please."

"Sure thing," she typed. "Where?"

"In my office."

#

Min entered Max's office but stopped just inside the doorway.

Max looked up, smiled at her, and said, "Just a moment, I need to get the files for you." He inserted a memory card into his computer and started clicking his mouse.

Min looked at the chairs but instead of sitting decided to browse Max's selection of books. The bottom three shelves contained dull looking textbooks. They were categorized into physics, astronomy, anthropology, and programming. The fifth shelf held more eclectic selections such as *In Search of Schrödinger's Cat* by Jon Gribbin, *Chaos* by James Gleick, and *The God Particle* by Leon Lederman. Min picked up one that looked fairly worn and started flipping through it. No pictures.

"Ah," said Max, "you found my favorite!"

She looked again at the cover. It was an unassuming blue. To one side was a small photo of Earth with an asterisk next to it. Large lettering gave the author's name: Bill Bryson. In small white lettering at the bottom, the meaning of the asterisk read, "A Short History of Nearly Everything."

"Amazing book. I read it at least once a year. I really wish Bryson would do a second addition that has a chapter on subatomic particles and quantum physics. History is always being created. We are creating history here, incredible history." Max motioned for Min to sit.

She placed the book back and noticed that the top shelf was apparently reserved for knickknacks: a crystal scarab, an R2D2 model, one of those things with the hanging balls that bounce from side to side, and an assortment of Smurf figures. The smart looking Smurf with glasses was on a stand in the middle, more prominent even than the old guy with the red hat.

Min turned and sat in the guest chair, facing Max.

"So I hired you because you had strong statistical experience on your resume," said Max, "something that we never have enough of. One thing about this project is it generates massive amounts of data. And I prefer that my senior scientists work on other problems than looking for trends. So your task is to run a first pass and find any significant correlations." He handed her the flash drive.

"What's this, data?" she asked.

He nodded. "Longitudinal data for population size, caste ratios, settlement density, and ethical alignment."

"Alignment?"

"Yes. Remember when you interviewed and I gave you a tour of the server room? I showed you how the colors of the Qubes change based on the characteristics of each Polyan. If we directly measure the values of each qubit, it'd collapse their quantum field, thus removing the ability for the Polyan to make a non-predefined decision. We don't want that to happen. We only want it to collapse when the actual Polyan is making a choice. Instead, color is a convenient shortcut for alignment: their tendency toward good or bad. So we end up with a value from -3 to +3. It's certainly enough data to find trends."

"I get it. Why red and blue? Is that based on Star Wars lightsabers?"

"One would think. It's actually just how it worked out. Dumb luck I guess. It simplifies things that it matches our pop culture interpretation of colors."

Min studied the flash drive as if she could see the data inside its steel exterior. "So what software should I use?"

"You know MatLab?"

"Yes."

"That should be installed on Olivia's, I mean, your machine." He blushed at his inadvertent use of the former intern's name. He didn't want Min knowing about her predecessor. "But if you need something else, let me know. We get an excellent academic discount on almost any software."

Min paused a second, apparently curious about Max's odd expression. Then she said, "I'm more familiar with SPSS, but I've wanted an excuse to dig into MatLab, so this is as good as any. After all, interning is meant to be a learning experience, right?"

"Yes, that's correct," said Max. "Let me know if you need anything else." He stood up abruptly, almost knocking over his chair. Min stood as well, albeit more gracefully.

"And Min…" Max smiled at her. "Good to have you on board."

#

Min returned to her computer. She inserted the flash drive and began copying the data file to her local storage. A progress bar appeared but didn't seem to move. She frowned and looked at the file size: 400GB.

"Jeez," she whispered to herself, "That's huge!"

She sat back and watched the green bar creep across the screen. She pondered how many hours of her life she'd lost watching progress bars. It was a disturbing thought. As she waited, her mind began to drift. She remembered Max's little slip-up about Olivia, who used to be the owner of this computer. She was aware of the intern's suicide from a story the local news media had run. It wasn't difficult to connect that with the job opening she now filled. This only bolstered her curiosity.

She opened the hard drive and navigated to the Users folder. Then she dug into the folder named "oholland," the username for Olivia Holland. It had the typical assortment of subfolders: Downloads, Desktop, Documents, etc. She looked inside the Documents folder and it was empty. Suspicious.

She looked in the Trash folder, and it was also empty.

Someone had cleaned out Olivia's file history.

This piqued Min's curiosity. It was either standard practice – something she doubted – or it was deliberate. Using her hacker skills, she downloaded an undelete program and ran a scan of the hard drive. Hundreds of files appeared that used to be in Olivia's Documents folder. Most were statistical data sets like the one Max had given her, but some were word documents. She immediately canceled the flash drive progress bar, not to risk overwriting any more hidden files. She then made the program restore all of the deleted documents, and it chugged along.

She scanned the files, which were all disorganized, and many had garbled file names. She sorted by type and then focused on the text documents. Most were status reports or analysis results. She read a few and they were, for the most part, formulaic and routine, with no abnormal findings. She knew she had a lot of these kinds of results in store for her, as well. Statistics wasn't always fun and games.

After about a half hour of scanning, nothing of any interest or value was found. So she gave up. Still, she couldn't help but wonder why Olivia's folder was deleted, but her entire user directory was not. It seemed amateurish.

She decided just for good measure to do a scan of wiped data. When a file is deleted from a hard drive, it's marked as hidden in a special table. The file doesn't show up anymore, but the data is still present. That's how the program she used was able to undelete the files. So, if someone wants to permanently remove a file, they need to wipe it by replacing the data where the file used to be with a bunch of zeros. Then the data is gone and can't be recovered. The problem with this technique, however, is it leaves detectable traces. Only a new hard drive would have continuous stretches of nothing.

Part of the program she'd downloaded contained a bit editor. This allowed her to see the actual ones and zeros stored on the drive. She used it to scan the area where Olivia's documents resided. There, like a homing beacon, was a single sequence of zeros.

To the amateur-level hacker, the data that used to be there would be irretrievable. But to a more seasoned professional and to the FBI, that's not the case. In reality, the positioning of the write head of a hard drive isn't 100 percent consistent. As it writes, it may be a little to the left or a little to the right of where it was last time. This doesn't affect data retrieval, because when it reads, it looks at a center slice, which will always be correct. It's the edges that can get fuzzy, but the read head doesn't normally go near those.

Min logged into her Pirate Bay account and downloaded a professional hacking tool. This tool allowed her to read that section of the drive over and over. Each read slightly shifted the drive's head to the left. The first three passes produced all zeros, as expected. Then on the fourth pass, a few ones sneaked in. After a couple more passes, she got a chunk of data that was about an even amount of ones and zeros. When the next pass showed the exact same sequence, she knew she had retrieved the ghost of the wiped file.

She directed the program to restore the lost data file to her desktop. It appeared there, titled "Intern's Log." Min opened the file and began reading.

CHAPTER 12 - RETURN JOURNEY

"It's ironic, but until you can free those final monsters within the jungle of yourself, your life, your soul is up for grabs." - Rona Barrett

Le·ma woke to find the camp deserted. Sa·ma had left her at some point during the night, and she was on her own. She looked up at the Source and it shined a bright white color, perfect traveling season. She peered down into the darkness of the Rift once more. The depths made her wonder what had become of the shard. Then she noticed a yellow bubble slowly rising. *Had the shard indeed turned into a bubble? Or was it just a coincidence?* Sa·ma's knowledge always impressed her. Even so, there was still much about their world that she suspected even he didn't understand. Or worse, that those who came before had made up to explain observed phenomena. She vowed to seek the truth when she became Master. Somehow.

She collected herself and searched the camp for a moment, finding the tracks Sa·ma and she had left when they entered the night before. Her plan was to return the way they'd come until she reached the mountain. Then she'd try to find another way over. Since they entered a fissure when coming, she'd begin by searching for a similar anomaly on this side.

She proceeded down the trail, and it was easy going, easier than when they came to the Rift. It was actually pleasant traveling alone, and it gave her a lot of time to think about everything that had transpired. She was learning quickly, both skills and history, and she felt that she'd soon be qualified to take Sa·ma's place. Not that she wanted to do that anytime soon, but she'd be ready when the time came.

She came to the red river. Their bridge was still in place, but she decided not to cross it. It occurred to her that she was moving too fast, not taking in the environment around her. Since she'd made such good time, she decided to slow down to observe more. She walked a little off the trail and stopped at a peculiar looking tree. It was scraggly and had facets that twisted around and through itself like a big net. It was kind of beautiful. A typical tree nearby had produced a small indigo shard up at the top: a sensor. This type of tree produced vision sensors, which Polyans attached to their bodies to see. Other plants produced hearing and speaking versions, as well. But most plants just produced yellow dots. These were used to create joints between body parts, or segments in a rope or whip. She looked longingly at the sensor hanging above her. She did have a free sensor port, but lacked the ability to climb the tree to get this one. She tapped on the tree with her leg, but the sensor wouldn't fall.

As if in response to her tapping, she heard a low grunting noise from a thick patch of vegetation nearby. She wondered what might make that kind of noise. Obviously some sort of creature, but one that she was unfamiliar with. Since the brush that concealed it was relatively short, it couldn't be too dangerous. She decided to take a look. Weaving between the brambles, she proceeded slowly in the direction of the sound.

She heard it again. "Grunt, grunt, grunt." Was something sick? Or trapped?

She got closer, and the grunting rose in pitch. It became a sort of whine. A small creature, with a long body and many short legs, sprang from the bush. It darted between her legs, carrying a yellow dot on its back.

"Hey there, slow down," she said, turning around to watch it scurry away.

There was a loud crunch behind her, and the world flipped upside down. She was thrown backward through the air, landed on her back with a crash, and lay there stunned. When she regained her awareness, she heard the unmistakable roar of a Zalisk. Then she saw it. It charged at her again, scooping her up with its tusks, and threw her over its body. She landed hard, but upright, and dodged behind a tree as the beast turned to swing at her again. The tree exploded into a bundle of shards, and the Zalisk fixed its gaze upon her once more.

Le·ma dashed through a low series of arched plants. She heard the Zalisk crashing through each one right behind her. Without warning, she fell into a shallow gully and sprawled onto the ground. The Zalisk loomed over her. It raised its enormous tusks high and readied to deliver a killing blow. There was no way for a Polyan to survive a Zalisk attack alone, and she knew this. She briefly thought how fleeting life is; that a beautiful day could have an utterly nightmarish ending; that her plans to change the world were all in vain. She waited for the blow to come.

104

CHAPTER 13 - HAPPY HOUR

"When you're surrounded by people who share a passionate commitment around a common purpose, anything is possible." - Howard Schultz

Min squinted at the rows of cells on her computer screen. The numbers all blurred together as her eyes watered. She made two fists and rubbed her eyes, trying to work out the strain. She looked at the clock on her computer, "6:12 p.m." To her, this meant happy hour.

As if on cue, the sound of a blender and crushing ice emanated through the office. She saved her document, locked her computer, and stood up. Leaning backward in a gentle arc, she reached her arms toward the ceiling. Three of her vertebrae cracked, one by one. "Ah," she said out loud.

Voices were beginning to get loud so she followed the commotion. A couple of folding tables had been set up in the space between the cubicles. An assortment of ethnic dishes were spread on top. Min headed toward the kitchen and pulled her tray out of the fridge. Translucent cigar shaped rolls formed an inviting circle around a bowl of sauce in the middle. She walked back to the crowd and placed it on the table.

"What is this unusual delicacy?" asked Max.

"This," said Min, "is Goi Cuon, which means 'salad rolls.'

One of my favorite Vietnamese appetizers. They're stuffed with greens and shrimp, and my family's secret concoction of herbs."

"Hmm," said Max as he grabbed one, raising it toward his mouth.

"Nah ah," exclaimed Min, "you've got to dip it! The sauce is the key – Nuoc cham."

"Newock who?"

"Cham! It's a staple in the sauce world."

Max looked at the thick yellow sauce, with what looked like seeds and red peppers floating in it. He shrugged, dipped his roll in, and bit into it.

"Yum!"

"You like?"

"Sure do. It's like sweet, sour, and spicy all at the same time. Delish..."

His words were drowned out by the sound of the blender again, this time much closer. They turned toward the opposite table where Tim was mixing a frozen concoction. "It's after five, time for Margaritas!" he shouted. He stopped the blender, poured four glasses, and began handing them to those who had yet to get one. Max accepted one, Min declined. "What, not your thing?" Tim asked.

"Okay, give me one," she said.

Tim handed her the last glass, and she took a small sip.

Dana appeared from the lab entrance. "Team, thanks for staying late tonight and bringing all these wonderful dishes." Everyone else stopped talking. "Tomorrow, assuming he's on schedule in that flying contraption of his, will be the visit from our esteemed sponsor: Graham Neilson! I do have an ulterior motive for arranging this potluck, and that is cleaning. Let's make this place look spotless for him."

"Food and Margaritas," commented Frankie. "We're more likely to trash the place!"

"Try to remain civilized," said Dana.

"Wait until I break out the Jello shots," said Tim.

"Great," said Dana. "But I don't mean food and waste. I mean empty boxes, extraneous papers, soda cans, etc. We're supposed to be high tech, that means 'paperless.' I had a plastic dumpster brought up and it's over by the windows. Please clean out your cubicles and throw everything in there. The cleaning staff will come get it tomorrow morning. I also replenished the cleaning chemicals in the kitchen, so we're good to go. Eat, enjoy, and clean!"

"Go team," seconded Max, allowing his voice to trail off. Then, turning to Tim, "You were joking about those Jello shots, right?"

"No way, would I joke about alcohol?" He pulled an aluminum foil covered tray out from under the table and peeled back the top. Small plastic shot glasses lined up with jiggly solids of varying colors. Max grabbed a red one and slurped it down, digging a couple of lingering pieces out with his tongue.

"Hey, they're for the after-party," protested Tim.

"That's past my bedtime. I need them now."

"Very well, help yourself." Tim nodded toward the tray, then added more ice to the blender.

Max grabbed a green Jello shot and walked away.

#

"So where's the pizza?" asked Desmond.

"I have to mix it up," answered Frankie. "I brought the next best thing, lasagna. Did you try it?"

"Not yet, I can't get enough of these Swedish meatballs."

"I made those," interjected Dana. "Don't tell anyone, I stole the recipe from Ikea."

Desmond raised an eyebrow. "The furniture place?"

"Yeah. You never had their Swedish meatballs?"

"Can't say I have."

"Well, now you know what you've been missing."

"So," said Frankie, "you just bought them. We were supposed to make stuff."

"Aw, what's the difference?"

"You told us all to make something, and you break your own rule?"

"Senior management privilege."

"Speaking of breaking," said Frankie, "my drone broke the other night."

"No way," said Desmond. "Your $1,200 drone?"

"Yeah, that one, but actually I added on a night vision camera so it was like $1,500 at the end of the day."

"How did it break?" asked Dana. "Did it get shot down?"

Desmond jumped to conclusions. "You entered restricted

air space and the feds fired their anti-aircraft missile at it?"

"Actually, that's not far from the truth," said Frankie. "It's kind of a strange incident. So with the night vision, I've been doing a lot of nighttime imagery. Basically, trying to capture nocturnal animals moving about, hunting and such. So last Wednesday night, I hiked up the bluffs near West Hartford reservoir to get some added height. At the first lookout, I set up my headset and launched the drone, flying it along the cliff and then up and over the trees."

"You don't have to see it to fly it?" asked Dana.

"No, my visor shows the view from the camera in real time. So it's as if I'm on the drone flying it. Pretty fun experience."

"So did you crash it then?" asked Desmond.

"No. I flew over a clearing that was filled with people walking single file around a flat rock. I thought this was strange so lowered down for a closer look. That's when one of them threw a stick at my drone and took out one of its props. I lost control and it crashed right onto the flat rock in their middle. The camera definitely smashed since it stopped transmitting."

"Damn!" said Max. They hadn't noticed him join them during the story.

"What did you do?" asked Dana.

"I snuck over to the clearing, and when I got there, which was no more than ten minutes later, the people were all gone. And my drone was lying there in pieces like it'd been smashed."

"That's messed up, dude," said Desmond.

"Too bad you didn't talk to me first," said Max.

"Why's that?" asked Frankie.

"Because I could've stopped the drone from crashing."

"How so?"

"Well, I've been reading a great book on anti-gravity... I can't put it down!"

"Ugh, Max," said Desmond. "Go find another group to test out your corny jokes on."

"I will." Max walked away sulking.

#

"I've been white-water rafting," said Jean, "but I'd never try that in a kayak."

"It's way more fun," said Lee. "You against the element of water. A total rush."

"But you can flip over and get stuck on a rock, right?" asked Rash.

"You can, but it's unlikely. The boat is sealed, so it's super buoyant. The biggest problem isn't getting stuck on a rock, but hitting your head on one. The guys that don't wear helmets are the crazy ones. But the worst that could happen is a few bumps and bruises."

"Still sounds dangerous to me," said Rash.

"What's the biggest rapid you'd go down?" asked Jean.

"I've gone over waterfalls," answered Lee.

"Waterfalls?"

"Yeah, it's not so bad if you know what you're doing. You can either land flat at the bottom or go straight in nose first. Depends on how deep the bottom is."

"You are a crazy man!" said Rash.

"Maybe. Heck, I'd consider going over Niagara Falls."

"People have died doing that," said Jean.

"So what is death, right? The way I see it, every single night when we go to sleep, when we're not dreaming, when we lose complete consciousness, we are effectively dead. What's the difference between a complete brain shutdown and death? Yet, somehow, nobody is ever afraid of going to sleep. You may not wake up and you'd never know the difference. You'd just... cease to exist. It's always puzzled me why we humans have such difficulty accepting this possibility. Yet we experience that state every single night."

"Whoa Lee," said Max, arriving at the group, "that's way too deep a discussion for a party with... Jello shots!" He waved his arms in the air as he said this. Somehow, wedged between his fingers, were four cups of Jello. He handed them around, keeping one for himself.

"You ready?" he asked.

"Ready?" said Rash. "I was born Reddy."

That got a chuckle, and they all downed their shots.

"Hey, want to hear a joke?" asked Max.

"Sure, Max," said Jean, humoring him.

"Well, this one ties in nicely with the whole ceasing to exist thing. So, why can't atheists do math with exponentials?"

"I don't know." Rash repeated, "Why can't atheists do

math with exponentials?"

"Because they don't believe in higher powers!"

This didn't get a chuckle, only groans. Max left toward the tray of Jello shots, shaking his head.

#

"What do you call this?" asked Min.

"It is called fufu," said Abina, "It is the national dish of my homeland."

"It's kind of sticky."

"I should have explained to everyone how to eat it. So you take that sticky white stuff and roll it into a ball, then dip it into the broth, which is groundnut soup."

"Actually sounds..." Min dipped her ball in the soup and popped it into her mouth, "and tastes..." she chewed a little, "pretty good. Kind of like fluffy peanuts."

"Yeah. The soup is made with peanut butter. Have you tried the fried chicken that Desmond brought?" asked Abina. "I never had it before."

"Yes," interjected Tim. "It's pretty good. But the best I ever had was from this small dive in New Orleans called Willie Mae's Scotch House. Amazing! I haven't had it since I was a kid, though. I'd love to go back and get some."

"It wouldn't be good," countered Min, crossing her arms.

"You've had it recently?" asked Abina.

"No, but Jorczak's Law would kick in."

"What's that?" asked Tim.

"Jorczak's Law states that 'Nothing is ever as good as you remember it to be. And the more time that passes, the more disappointing something becomes.'"

"I never heard that before," said Abina. "Why would that be true?"

"If I remember correctly there are three possible reasons. First, the quality may have actually declined. So Willie Mae may have cheapened the ingredients. The second possibility is that you've had fried chicken since then, since you were a kid, that was actually better than Willie Mae's. So when you try it again, you'll think it's no longer so good. The last possibility is that your memory of the chicken has been so exaggerated over the years that the real thing could never be that good."

"That's pessimistic," said Tim. "I want to experience that chicken again!"

"Don't confuse pessimism with reality."

Abina asked, "Is there anything that can defy Jorczak's Law?"

"If there were," answered Min, "then it wouldn't be a law."

"Actually, there is something," added Max as he returned to the table, focusing on the tray of cups.

"Jello shots, Max?" asked Tim.

"No, actually. What I was thinking of is In-N-Out Burger. I don't get out to the West Coast much, but whenever I'm there, I stop at one. I get a Double Double animal style and it's always better than I remembered it to be. Even the smell walking into that restaurant is better than memory would serve."

"I've never had it," they all said in unison.

"You gotta try it someday. Hey, Tim, hand me one of those Jello shots and I'll tell you a joke."

"That's even more of a reason to hide the tray from you."

Min grabbed one and gave it to him. "Thanks," he mumbled and slurped it down. He went to place the empty cup on the table but missed, and almost fell over. Abina caught him and propped him back up. Min's lips pressed tightly together, almost into a frown.

"So," said Max, as if nothing had happened, "an electron walks into a bar and says 'a round for everyone, on me.' The bartender asks, 'are you sure you want to do that?' He replies, 'of course, I'm positive.'"

They all laughed at this, but Min laughed a little bit louder than the others.

"Max, c'mon," she said, grabbing his arm and pulling him toward the exit. "I think you need a little fresh air."

CHAPTER 14 - EXTRA SENSE

"For by grace you have been saved through faith. And this is not your own doing; it is the gift of God."- Ephesians 2:8

The blow never came.

Le·ma looked up at the raised tusks of the Zalisk. But instead of pummeling her, it took a couple of steps backward and lowered its head to the ground. It was standing completely still, looking over and past her.

Then she heard a familiar voice. "Turn around, move forward twenty lengths, and forget we are here." It was Sa·ma.

The Zalisk, as if in complete obedience, turned around slowly. It shook in place, then lumbered through the brush into the distance.

Sa·ma lent a leg to Le·ma to help her up and out of the ditch. She climbed up on wobbly legs, shaken by her near-death experience. She could only muster one word: "How?"

Then she noticed something different about Sa·ma. He had a new sensor on his core. It was indigo, like most other sensors, but instead of having an eye, ear, or mouth, it had three triangles pointing in different directions.

"You're lucky to be alive," he said, not answering her question.

"Did you save me?" she asked, still puzzled with why either of them was still alive. A Zalisk doesn't just turn around and walk away like that.

"I did. Something extraordinary happened to me." Sa·ma quickly shifted his weight between legs, almost hopping. "This new sensor I have is an artifact, a gift from the gods, that gives me greater insight into the world around us. It's going to improve our ability to be Lumenaries and will be passed from me to you someday. I'm still learning what it can do, but so far it's quite impressive."

Gift from the gods? Being alive is a gift from the gods.

"After leaving you at the camp," he said, "I went in search of something I saw. As unbelievable as this sounds, I actually found the Fertile Field."

"The legendary field of endless energy?" asked Le·ma.

"The same. The reason I never saw it before turned out to be that it isn't always there. It only appears for a brief time to receive the splendor of a deity. I wandered out of the woods and ran into a god! Pi·ro, to be precise. Never before have I, or any Polyan for generations, had such an honor."

Le·ma sat down. *Pi·ro.* This was turning out to be a truly amazing day. "Please tell me while I get my legs back."

"Yes, so this is what happened..."

#

Sa·ma bowed before the god. He'd never dreamt of such an encounter happening in his lifetime.

"Stand!" ordered the god.

He did so.

"I am Pi·ro. What dares to bring you to my sanctuary?"

"Lord Pi·ro. I came in search of the Fertile Field, which I believed this circle of violet crystals to be. But I didn't expect to encounter one such as yourself here."

"You have indeed found the Fertile Field, but it is only here when I deem it to be." Pi·ro straightened his legs so that his body rose even higher, then relaxed and settled low to the ground. "I like how the violet colors complement my glowing red core. So tell me, Sa·ma, why should I not extinguish your life?"

"I can't suggest the actions of a god. But I've done nothing wrong, unless discovering your resting place here in our world is an offense."

"It is not. But there is a price to pay, regardless. You now have to pass my test. If you can answer a riddle for me, I will reward you with a valuable prize. If you fail, I will take your life as compensation for your incompetence."

This wasn't what Sa·ma expected from an encounter with a god. Pi·ro seemed completely unreasonable and was threatening him with death for stumbling upon him. But gods could do whatever they pleased, he presumed.

"I bow to your reverence," he said. "Please give me your riddle."

"Here it is. Good luck."

Pi·ro lay on the ground before Sa·ma so that their eye sensors were at the same level. Then, staring at him, Pi·ro presented the puzzle:

I can be any color,
But I don't get to choose.
I command all others,
In response to my hue.

Sa·ma repeated the riddle to himself. It was so simple; the answer couldn't be what he believed it was. He tried to think of other things to fit the puzzle, but he couldn't come up with a one.

"Answer!" commanded Pi·ro.

"The Source," said Sa·ma, expecting this to be a trick and his life about to end.

"You are correct!" boomed the god.

Sa·ma was shocked. "I am?"

"Indeed, and for your reward, I present to you this artifact. Attach this to your vacant sensor port. This will give you the power to peer just beneath the world we are in, to sense things a little beyond, and to manipulate things that should not be controllable. Use it wisely, as you have been instructed by me."

With that, the ground shook with a boom, and the god and the Fertile Field vanished without a trace.

In the center of the clearing where Pi·ro had been, lay a short three-sided rod of indigo material. Each side, on the end, contained a protruding tetrahedron. Sa·ma picked it up and examined it, then attached it to his core.

Immediately, he could see once more the god and the Fertile Field, but this time as faint glowing outlines. Were these shadows of where they'd been or were they invisible to all but him?

"Be gone now," said the god. "Your apprentice needs you. Quickly!"

And he truly vanished for good, although the Fertile Field remained a glowing outline.

#

"Heeding his words, I sped to you Le·ma without hesitation. Through the vegetation, I could see your outline, fleeing. I rushed forward and came upon you lying in a ditch, the Zalisk about to crush you. I had no time for fear, and I just thought about it stopping, and it did. Then, as you heard, I commanded it to leave, and it obeyed."

Le·ma looked again at the artifact on his core. No words would come to her. And Sa·ma stood there speechless as well, just now being able to consider the implications of his encounter. He began to shiver.

CHAPTER 15 - STARLIGHT WALK

"Aim for the moon. If you miss, you may hit a star." - W. Clement Stone

They exited the Academic Entrance into the cool night air and cut through the parking lot. It was far from full, but still contained a decent number of cars, probably those of nursing staff and physicians working late rounds. Max staggered and leaned on the trunk of a car. He stood there for a moment inhaling the damp darkness.

"This was a good idea," he said. "I feel a little less dizzy. I just wish these cars would stop driving around."

"Um, they're parked," said Min.

"Yeah, I suppose so. Actually, they look more like boats than cars."

"Just take your time. We're in no rush. Let's just walk down the hill and check out the pond."

"So, a nature walk?"

"You could say that."

Max pushed off and weaved between the rows of parked cars. Most of them were pretty nice with a disproportionate number of BMWs, Mercedes, and Lexuses. Obviously, the majority of the students had long gone home. Campus night life was pretty much nonexistent at the Health Center. Unless your definition of a good time was hanging out in the library.

Max lost his balance again and leaned his butt against a black Mercedes.

"You shouldn't be sitting on that," said Min, glancing up and down the road for security vehicles.

"What? This?" He looked through the driver's door at the fine tan leather and wood grain finish inside. He straightened his legs and shook the car; nothing happened, no alarm. He grabbed the driver's door handle and pulled. The door opened. Before Min could react, Max sat in the car and closed the door.

"Shit!" she said. She grabbed the handle, but he somehow had the wherewithal to lock the door. She ran around to the other side and tried the passenger door. It opened.

"What the hell, Max?"

"Get in," he said.

"No fucking way."

"Just do it."

"You're gonna get us both arrested. Get out."

"Okay... okay."

He unlocked the door and opened it, swinging his legs out. Then, before standing up, he reached his hand into the coin holder and pulled out a handful of quarters. As he stood, he dumped them into his pocket, dropping several. They rolled down the parking lot, cutting into the silence with clanging noises.

"What's wrong with you?" she asked as she closed the passenger door.

"Nothing is wrong with me. I'm actually super fine. I feel happy, and I just got tomorrow's lunch money."

"You just broke into a car and stole money."

"Hey, these doctors make a fortune. I don't. Let's just consider it a private donation to the Spheria project."

"No Max, it's not a donation unless they give it willingly. That's just wrong."

He ignored her. "I read once that LoJack did a study and found that 21 percent of drivers don't lock their cars. This might prove that result."

"Don't change the subject."

"Min, chill. When I agreed to give Graham an exclusive to the Qube technology, I did so because I believed in this project more than anything." Max began gesturing wildly with his hands, making his balance precarious. "I wanted to be a part of history – to be a participant in the long line of scientists contributing to the collective knowledge of the human race. We have physics down. We've got a handle on chemistry. We even know a good deal about the subatomic particle landscape. What's left? The mind. The mind is what we don't understand. Well, that and gravity. I'm gonna tackle gravity next."

"Impressive," said Min, approaching him closely.

"Anyway," continued Max, less animated. "I still believe in this project, but it pays crap. I could've owned this Mercedes if I'd sold the technology to the military, or marketed it to big data analytics companies. I would've made a fortune. Instead, I accepted the humble life of a crazy scientist. It's nights like this that a little piece of me regrets that decision. If Graham wasn't already a billionaire, I bet he would've invested and licensed. It's not fair he had his opportunity to make it big with technology, but he's depriving me of it."

They both fell silent for a minute. Then Min spoke in a hushed voice. "Stealing isn't a solution, Max. I'm going to believe it's your current lack of judgment at play here. Let's keep walking before security comes by."

"Sure."

They made it to the road and walked side by side, heading toward the lower campus. It was misting. The humidity collecting on the asphalt created a bright reflective sheen. The many lights around the Health Center looked like a city when doubled by their reflections in the pavement.

They strolled down the road and around some construction areas. Max stumbled a few times, and Min was more than pleased to help support and guide him. In more time than should have been required, the road ended, and they turned left down Main. The street entered a traffic circle, which they crossed. Then they went a short distance down Dowling Way before exiting onto a footpath.

The small pond was just to their left as the path meandered around it. The surface was dead calm. The trees obscured the lights, allowing Max and Min to glimpse some of the brighter stars. The water appeared to lead into a mirrored dimension through which they could fall into the sky. They came upon a stone bench, and Max plopped down upon it. Min sat next to him.

Max stared up at the sky for an extended time in complete silence. Min stared at the reflections off the pond's surface. She wondered if they were looking at the same stars but in completely different directions. Then a bright spot appeared as the moon began to creep over the trees.

"See," said Max. "Take the moon, for example."

"Example of what?"

"We landed a spacecraft with people on the moon. Multiple times."

"Sure. It's impressive."

"That's not what I mean. What did we get out of it? America put a flag and some footprints on the moon. So what? Seems like a waste of money just to be able to boast about beating the Russians. But wait. Is that all we got?"

"I don't know."

"I do. These are the things I pay attention to. We got a ton out of researching how to land a man on the moon."

"Like what?"

"CAT scanners, computer microchips, cordless tools, the ear thermometer, freeze-dried foods, insulation, joysticks, satellite television, scratch resistant lenses, and let's not forget memory foam. Do you have a memory foam mattress?"

"No, it's too expensive for me."

"Yeah, me too. But a lot of people have them. And all this cool stuff that helps us live better, richer lives is a product of these scientific missions. I don't even have time to list all the amazing things that came from the space shuttle program. The point is, if the military had my Qube technology, even if they were using it to develop advanced warships or new forms of weapons, what kind of byproducts would trickle into society and enrich our lives? I almost mourn the lost opportunities. It's the regret I feel, sometimes, that makes me second guess my decision. That's all."

Max quieted down and gazed up at the moon with droopy eyes. When he finally looked back at Min, her face was mere inches away from his. And then, as if magnets were somehow involved, their lips gently locked together.

CHAPTER 16 - CLIFFHANGER

"We gain our ends only with the laws of nature; we control her only by understanding her laws." - Jacob Bronowski

Le·ma and Sa·ma walked back together toward the blue mountains, side by side. Still shaken from their terrifying experiences, they weaved through the foliage. They headed in the general direction of the river.

"We've both been through a remarkable day today," said Sa·ma. "The Lumen Walk is meant to be a transitional experience, but this one has gone beyond any I've ever heard of. Traditionally, as I said before, you're left here to figure out how to get back home."

"Over the mountains?"

"Not quite. Look at them."

Le·ma had been, but she focused her full attention on the mountains now. For some reason, they looked larger than before, and more imposing.

Sa·ma watched her for a moment, then added, "How will you get over?"

"My plan was to look for an opening on this side, and

take the platforms up again."

"That's the problem, there is no opening or platforms on this side. The mountain looks different because it's nearly vertical. The way we got here isn't the way we return."

Le·ma mulled this over for a bit. "So how long does it take to find an alternative?"

"About three to four days. The reason is there is no way over that you can find. I don't want to risk having you wander out here that long after what you've been through. So I will assist you a bit. I have a feeling you'll figure it out in short order regardless."

"If I can't find it," said Le·ma without missing a beat, "then I have to make it."

"Exactly!" exclaimed Sa·ma. "You never fail to meet my expectations."

"Thank you."

They emerged from the foliage and stood on the edge of a river of red. They could see to the left, further down the river, the bridge they'd built on their journey out here. They headed along the shore in that direction.

"So tell me," Sa·ma said. "I mean, use what you know, to find a way to the other side."

"Aha. You let slip clues through your questions," said Le·ma, as Sa·ma stopped to study her. "There must be a way to the other side that doesn't involve going over the mountains."

"Go on."

"We could dig a passage under the mountains. But if that were possible we'd have arrived that way."

"Probable theory."

They reached the bridge and began crossing. Le·ma stopped in the center, peering at the red rock below. The textures covering it seemed to flow in a slow ooze toward the Rift in the distance.

"If we can't go over, and we can't go under, and we can't go through, then we've got to go around."

"Around?" mocked Sa·ma.

"Yes, around is the only remaining option. But I can see all of the mountains. They start at the Rift, curve around, and meet the Rift again at the other end, thus enclosing this valley. So the only possible place to go around is at the Rift itself."

"The mountains," countered Sa·ma, "flow into the Rift, so there is no ledge to stand on." Le·ma could see, even from this distance, that the mountains tapered toward the Rift. They hung over the edge like giant fingers. Scanning the Rift around the world sphere, she noticed for the first time that the mountains resembled gripping claws. They looked like a massively contorted creature pulling the Rift apart.

"I see. But I suspect there is some way to solve this, using what I've learned on this journey."

"What have you learned?"

"I've gained a deeper understanding of the properties of the rock. And how the different colors react. In the Colony and valley around it, we have brown rock and green plants, and a river that we never approach. So the extent of our experience is that they just are. They don't react, other than the green plants growing during a green Source. We're told the mountains are impassable, and until now, I believed it. So I never had a reason to approach them. We're also told the river is dangerous and never to approach it, so I always stayed away. It's not until now that I understood the exact nature of why these rules are in place. So I've learned that the blue rock repels everything and that the red rock attracts everything."

"Good. A simple lesson, but one reserved for us Lumenaries. The common Polyans never question the rules of nature that we lay forth."

"Why's that? Why is this knowledge reserved for us?"

"Tradition."

"Tradition? Like throwing the yellow shard into the Rift? Or the Polyans with the largest number of legs getting to feast first? We do these things because of tradition. But why?"

"We've always done these things," countered Sa·ma, as if there was no other necessary explanation.

"If that's your answer and the extent of your knowledge, then I think we have forgotten why we do these things." Le·ma leaned toward Sa·ma as if trying to peer into him. "I think there was an actual reason sometime in the past, but we've lost that, and still continue to do these things. The reason we started them might not even exist anymore, or even worse, might be wrong now."

Sa·ma considered what Le·ma had said. Never before had he heard a Polyan question the rules, and it gave him an uncomfortable feeling. Still, it reinforced his belief that there was something special about Le·ma. Her mind could quickly grasp things as they are, then take them a step forward, one that even he rarely took.

He countered the only way his training would allow. "Tradition exists to protect us. To allow us to operate without having to relearn lessons of the past."

"But that's my point. We need to know the lessons, or

they may not be correct anymore. Like how the mountains can rise, the rivers can widen, and the plants can grow. The one thing we know is true is that everything changes. Our culture, habits, lifestyle, are changing. We used to be nomads, now we live in a Colony. You and I are changing. We need to question, to move beyond restraints of the past."

"Who's teaching who here?" asked Sa·ma, shifting his weight between his legs.

"Sorry, Master. If I'm overstepping my bounds, please let me know."

"Between us, you may say anything. But be careful when among the others, especially the Leaders. They're stricter in enforcing the rules than I am."

"I bet with some creative persuasion the Council could bend the rules, as well."

"You may be correct," said Sa·ma. "But nobody has tried that, as far as I know, and certainly I haven't."

"Maybe you should? Maybe our Colony could improve with some creative interpretation of the rules."

Despite his age, Sa·ma had a surprisingly open mind. But even still, he was getting uncomfortable with the direction of the conversation. He decided to get back on task. "So, speaking of rules, how can we get around the mountains?"

"Okay, the only special rocks, as far as I can tell, are blue and red, mountain and river. The one thing you didn't show me is what happens when these two meet. The blue should repel the red. But at the same time, the red should attract the blue." Le·ma looked at Sa·ma for comment, but he didn't react. "I can see you're not going to tell me, but you already did."

"Really?"

"Yes. In your creation story. The river god Pi·ro, who today you met, stuck his red rock to the blue rock of Ju·ro, who created the mountains. And the red rock didn't turn the blue to red. We need to bring red rock to the mountains."

Without pausing, Le·ma grabbed a stalk of plant and laid it on the shore so that only the tip of one end touched the red river. Like before, it turned red along the length. Le·ma touched a segment of the former plant with one of her legs, and it stuck fast to her. She yanked back, and the red piece broke loose from the other segments and remained as a chunk on the end of her leg. She touched the ground with it, and it didn't stick. "Correction, red attracts everything except brown."

She played with the red stone for a while. There was more to it than she expected. She found she could move it to various parts of her body. It was hard to unstick, but not im-possible. When it stuck between two parts, such as two of her legs, pulling them apart would dislodge it from one. And she found that if she tipped it a certain way, she could control which one it detached from.

Le·ma repeated the whole process, this time salvaging seven more units of red rock. She attached four of these chunks to each of them, one to the side of each leg. Sa·ma just watched in silent amusement. She was still unable to read him, but she took the lack of feedback as a good sign.

"Come on," she said, "let's go to the mountains."

She took off in as straight a line as possible toward where the mountains met the Rift, and Sa·ma followed. On their way, they did encounter a trail heading in roughly the same direction, which made movement faster. By mid-day, they'd reached their goal.

Le·ma removed one of the chunks of red rock from her

leg. She reached toward the blue rock of the mountain wall next to them but hesitated a short distance before reaching it.

"Do it!" commanded Sa·ma. He wobbled with anticipation.

She pushed her leg forward. There was no feeling of repulsion from the blue, and then the two stones met. Immediately an audible sound emerged, something between a crackle and a hum. The point at which the two rocks touched pulsed with a pink glow. Startled, she yanked her leg back, but it stayed stuck. She watched the pulse, which continued, but the blue didn't turn to red. She found that with some effort, she could slide the red rock over the surface of the blue. She grabbed another red piece with the tip of her leg and attached it to the mountain. Sliding them up, she hung from them. Then she positioned the remaining two so that she was now connected to the mountain with all four legs. Using a combination of pressure and sliding, she worked out how to move, and was climbing up and along the mountain. She made a circle, coming back facing the ground where Sa·ma stood looking up at her.

"Well done," he said. "It took me three days to figure this out. Maybe you had a little help from me, but not much." He took the four red stones he had, attached them to the tip of his legs, and likewise to the mountain. Together, they shimmied over the Rift. From this vantage, they were afforded an imposing view of the darkness below. After taking it in for a moment, they continued, and in no time were on the other side of the mountain. They dismounted by tilting the red rock at an angle, which allowed it to detach from the blue.

Next to the mountain was a small pool of red. Sa·ma touched each red piece to this, where it stuck fast. He was then able to, with effort, remove his leg. The four chunks sank into the pool, completely hiding evidence of their existence. "This pool is the result of the many crossings that have come before us." Le·ma nodded and added her four pieces to the pool.

CHAPTER 17 - GOD FROM THE MACHINE

"Miracles occur naturally as expressions of love. The real miracle is the love that inspires them. In this sense everything that comes from love is a miracle." - Marianne Williamson

Jean returned from lunch ready to get some serious work done. Unlike many of her colleagues, a big meal energized her rather than made her want to take a nap. She sat at her computer and donned her virtual reality headset and glove. She placed her other hand on a 3D SpaceMouse, a specialized controller for moving around in three dimensions. It looked kind of like the towing ball on the back of a truck. Around the hand grip was a series of programmable buttons.

Her headset filled with light. She was floating in the center of the world inside the Source. She pushed down on the controller and dropped toward the landscape. Then she rotated it to the right until her view lined up with the Rift, which was the most prominent landmark. It looked like an artificial horizon, except vertical.

Jean pushed the controller forward and flew ahead in the world, staying level with the ground. In this way, she cruised along the Rift until the Polyan Colony became visible on her left. She dropped down more, turned, and crossed the forest until she was at the edge of the Colony. She could've jumped here directly using a preset, but she liked to use this entry ritual as a form of warm-up. Unlike most of the other team members, she wasn't a video game player.

The Polyans were constructing a new hive. Three-legged Drones approached pushing loose brown blocks, and two four-legged Builders were stacking them. The structure resembled an igloo, except more pointed.

Jean could see the ghostly outline of her gloved hand floating in the world. She had the desire to grab some blocks with it to help stack them. But she was forbidden to interact with the world in any way. Only the engineers were allowed to, and only away from the presence of any Polyan witnesses. The rule was like their version of the Prime Directive from Star Trek. "No identification of self or mission. No interference with the social development of said planet. No references to space or the fact that there are other worlds or civilizations." This prohibited personnel from interfering with the development of alien civilizations, in this case, Polyans.

She lowered her glove and wondered why she even bothered to put it on, since she couldn't use it for anything other than menus. Even her buttons were configured differently than the others. Theirs allowed selecting objects, raising and lowering terrain, and adding textures. Hers allowed the recording of data. She could take screen captures, record videos, tag a Polyan or a location, or jump around. These actions allowed her to capture behaviors and interactions as they occurred. The computer also had the ability to point out interesting or unusual occurrences. With a click, Jean's viewpoint could jump to that location as well.

She clicked the preset for the Council Chamber. Her view switched to just over the tallest building in the Colony. Polyans of every number of legs were scurrying about, performing their daily routines. It was always amazing that these beings were 'alive' in the sense of intelligence and free will. But it was more amazing that they had, in a short span of time, formed a cooperative and functional society.

Jean entered the Council Chamber, but it was empty. "I guess the six-legs must be taking a break," she said.

"What?" asked Rash from the adjacent cubicle.

"Sorry, I was talking to myself."

It was odd that the Leaders weren't in the Council Chamber. Typically, they just hung out there and talked all day. *They must be taking a field trip or something.*

She pressed a button which opened a floating menu of Polyan names. Using her glove, she touched a filter to narrow it down only to six-legged ones. The list shrank to eight names all ending with the suffix 'sa.' She swiped her finger down the entire list, selecting them all. Then her view rotated to face the encroaching red river at the edge of the Colony. There she saw eight outlines highlighted in blue. *Yep, a field trip to the river. I wonder why?*

She tagged one of them to zoom over and watch what they were doing. But before she could click jump, an alarm appeared in the center of her vision. "Polyan Death," it said in red flashing letters.

She instinctively hit a different button. Her view immediately zoomed out to the Source. Then it dove all the way back to a different part of the world. It was a bit far from the Colony, in a jagged area of the landscape. In the center of her vision lay the smashed core of a Drone, its three legs scattered near the body. It had apparently fallen off a ledge. Such a distance wouldn't have been fatal, but it had the misfortune of landing on a pointed brown rock. This shattered the core of the creature, releasing its life energy in the space around it.

Jean wanted to observe its reaction as it was falling to see if, or when, it knew its death was imminent. She positioned her view so she could see the entire cliff from the top to the bottom. Then she dialed a replay timeframe using the controller. The computer began to calculate backward. The sheer amount of data in the world precluded the recording of its state over time. It did allow calculating what had happened from the current moment backward. It just took a little while. In other words, the replay wasn't immediate like on Monday Night Football. As she was waiting for something to happen, something did. Another Polyan came running into view and fell on the cracked corpse.

Jean canceled the replay and instead hit the video record button. She zoomed in to have a closer look. Her screen told her the new arrival was Po·ni, and the deceased was Ti·ni. Jean was trying to figure out what Po·ni was doing. She could make out some faint sounds, so she boosted the volume to hear better. Po·ni wasn't speaking, but emitting a kind of whine that changed in pitch from low to high over and over. Jean cocked her head to hear better in just one ear, although it made no difference. She swore that it sounded like a sob. Never before had she seen a Polyan display remorse, if indeed that's what this was. Polyans felt basic emotions, but they never seemed to get attached enough to mourn the dead. Then Po·ni spoke, which confirmed Jean's theory.

"Ti·ni! No! Not Ti·ni. You're my best friend," cried Po·ni. Her sobbing began again.

Jean confirmed the video stream was recording. This was anthropological gold. She watched and recorded. She created several viewpoint presets around the scene and kept flipping between them to make a more dramatic movie. This was the most exciting thing that had happened in weeks.

"Ti·ni," cried Po·ni again. "Please don't die!" Sob. Sob. Sob. "You can't be dead!" Sob.

Without getting up, Po·ni reached out and pulled the three scattered legs back to the body. She attempted to reconnect them, but they wouldn't stick. A slow and drawn-out whine emanated from her defeated form.

Then Po·ni raised one leg toward the Source and said, "Gods above, if you can hear me, please help. Please save my friend, Ti·ni. She's new to this world and hasn't learned its ways yet. She is my best friend, and it's my fault she fell. I forgot to tell her the ledge was in front of her. Please take me instead of her!"

Jean's jaw dropped. This was way beyond mere remorse. This was recognition and respect for a higher power. The Polyans had their legends about the gods, some of which were based on real encounters. But never before had she seen them ask the gods for help. She had to work fast. Without thinking of the consequences, she acted. It wouldn't take long before Lee's improvement prepared Ti·ni's Qube for reassignment to a new Polyan.

#

The world around Po·ni bent in an odd way, almost as if it was curved! She saw something that astounded her. Towering above, on seven large legs, stood a Polyan with a green core.

"Child," spoke the tall Polyan. "I am Ca·ro, god of plants, but I have heard your plea and have come to help you."

Unable to believe what she was seeing, Po·ni fell speechless.

"Step aside!" commanded Ca·ro.

Po·ni attempted to stand but stumbled, then rolled off Ti·ni's body.

Ca·ro leaped into action. She picked up the shattered core of Ti·ni and rubbed each facet, one by one mending their cracks. Once that was complete, she placed Ti·ni's core on the ground. She touched three of her legs to it, one on each leg joint. Po·ni watched as Ca·ro's entire body began to glow violet. Soon the same color was filling the clear cavity of Ti·ni's core. As soon as it turned opaque, Ca·ro grabbed Ti·ni's three legs and attached them to the joints. Then she vanished.

Nothing happened for a few seconds. Slowly, Ti·ni's limbs began to move. Then they moved faster. Ti·ni lurched over and stood on her legs. She glanced around and saw Po·ni with a look of disbelief and extreme joy.

"Wh-what happened?" Ti·ni stammered.

Po·ni ran over and wrapped two legs around Ti·ni. "Thank the gods! You're alive!"

Ti·ni looked up at the cliff. Then she saw the pointed brown rock on the ground next to her.

"How?" she asked.

"It's a miracle," answered Po·ni.

And Po·ni bowed her body and spoke in a whisper, "Thank you Ca·ro. I'm forever in your debt. May I repay the favor someday when I visit you in the Qubessence?"

#

Jean stopped the video stream. She not only had footage of the best event ever to happen, but the footage would get her fired in an instant. She archived it with the name "Zalisk foraging." Too bad she'd never be able to tell anyone about the amazing events the file really contained.

CHAPTER 18 - PRIME DIRECTIVE

"All of us make mistakes. The key is to acknowledge them, learn, and move on. The real sin is ignoring mistakes, or worse, seeking to hide them." - Robert Zoellick

Dana closed the blinds in her office. The sun was setting, and the glare made reading her computer monitor difficult. She sat back down at her desk and returned to scanning the logs from the previous week. Activity had increased, which was a good thing, although it now took longer to get through it. The trend was showing more and more unusual incidents inside their experiment. This was a sure way to build a strong case for additional funding.

The engineering team always led in terms of productivity. They continued to crank out new routines, geometry, code, and other incomprehensible stuff. It always amazed Dana how much they got done, week after week, with just a few people. Rarely would they fall into a rut where she would have to push them. If she did, they usually responded with some rhetoric about 'writing code being the equivalent of creating art,' and that it was unpredictable. She didn't believe it for an instant. Computers were concrete and well understood; it was just a matter of doing the same things over and over. Needless to say, this week they were true to form, although it wasn't their best week ever.

What caught her attention, however, was the number of entries in the anthropology log. For the first time ever, they exceeded that of engineering. She opened the list and it was full of videos and notes of unusual Polyan behavior and incidents. They were on the rise. Something was happening in their society, something the researchers did not yet understand, a kind of mind shift. One note from Jean summarized her observations particularly well:

All the recent Polyan behaviors seem to indicate they are moving toward a new social zeitgeist or a "new age." More and more, the most interesting things they have been doing, they are doing for the first time, and without any external stimulus. Examples consist of questioning traditions, trying new behaviors, exploring new regions, interacting outside their castes, etc. The biggest one that I have seen is their gaining an awareness, or rather a respect, for a higher power. Granted their folklore is ripe with mentions of "the gods," due to our interactions in their formative phase when we helped them kick off a baseline culture. But since interactions from us are now forbidden, they have little cause to gain this heightened respect, other than to fill some kind of void. What this void is, we do not yet know. But once we figure it out, it may help us explain some of our own cultural evolution as humans. This is the point of this experiment, after all, and it is exciting to see us on the brink of rapid discovery.

Dana looked out her doorway at the other offices in Building 20. They'd all been deserted long ago for the night. Her team, which was way up on the 7th floor, would still be working hard past dinnertime. Soon, someone would start circulating a takeout menu. She texted Max that her vote was for Subway; she wasn't in the mood for anything healthy. He said it'd probably be Thai food again. They seem to be hooked on it now that someone discovered the King & I restaurant. She said she would have the Lemongrass Chicken and would be up there soon.

She returned her attention to the daily logs. The new volatility Jean had written about in the Polyans' culture intrigued her. This was an important insight, and it made her curious about the particular observations. So she drilled deeper into Jean's video recordings and began looking through them. Most were labeled quite mundane titles such as "Building a new shelter" or "Searching for crystals." A few were more interesting such as "Soldier patrols a new route" and "Lumenaries journey to the Rift."

Dana played the latter video recording, watching the progression of Sa·ma and Le·ma with particular interest. Their entire journey wasn't captured, as it didn't in and of itself constitute anything unusual. What was captured was a discussion on the edge of the Rift. Here Le·ma questioned the purpose of the tradition of the shard throwing. Then again on the way back, she questioned the exclusivity of their knowledge. *It's just the typical younger generation questioning authority*, she thought. That was the bulk of it. There were no entries for anything more intense than those discussions.

She started scanning the list of mundane entries. She stopped when she saw one titled, "Zalisk foraging." This struck her as too boring to even bother recording. She opened it and began watching.

#

An instant message popped up on Jean's screen. It was from Dana, and said simply, "Come to my office."

Jean groaned. *What now?* she thought.

She locked her workstation, grabbed her mug, and headed to the kitchen. Max was there getting a refill of coffee, saw Jean's empty cup, and motioned to fill it.

"Please," said Jean.

Max poured the rest of the coffee into it and began making a new pot.

"So I get the high-test stuff, huh?"

"Yep, with the amount of time you spend jacked into the system, you need it," commented Max. He placed a new filter in the coffee machine, tore open a pouch of grounds, and poured them in.

Jean looked at the floor. "I'm on my way to Dana's office," she stated, slouching her shoulders.

"Oh?"

"Got the dreaded instant message."

"I'm sorry. Always a crapshoot. Either you did something great, or you're in big trouble."

"Well, I can think of things that could qualify for both, so wish me luck."

"Sure, good luck!"

#

"Close the door," Dana ordered.

Jean shut the office door slowly, as if not wanting to cut off her only way of escape. She turned the handle so it wouldn't make a click when the latch engaged.

"Sit," Dana commanded.

Jean sat in the chair opposite Dana's meeting table and smiled at her. "So what's up?" She sipped her coffee, waiting for the answer.

Dana stared at her for a while in silence. Her eyes seemed to be squinting.

This made Jean uneasy. Trying not to show it, she took another sip which did not hide her fidgeting. Dana's office was much sparser than Max's. She had two bookcases, but only a couple books. The most prominent feature was a bronze figure of Atlas holding up the world, which stood on her desk. Jean fixed her gaze on the statue, avoiding eye contact with Dana.

"I know you're a Star Trek fan, Jean," Dana finally said. "And I'm sure you can quote the Prime Directive, as we all can. But there is one particularly great quote from Jean Luc Piccard which I would like to read to you." She looked at her screen where it was apparently displayed. "'The Prime Directive is not just a set of rules. It is a philosophy, and a very correct one. History has proven again and again that whenever mankind interferes with a less developed civilization, no matter how well intentioned that interference may be, the results are invariably disastrous'."

Shit, Jean thought, *she knows*. "I agree with that," she said.

"Do you?" Dana stared, unblinking.

Jean nodded.

"Of course. As an anthropologist, you, of everyone on our team, should be ultra-sensitive to this. You're trained to know the kind of damage that can be caused by breaking these rules. The effect of interfering with the development of the Polyan culture. So tell me, please, why you would resurrect a dead Polyan? And even worse, while in the presence of another Polyan to witness it?" Dana's volume increased a bit. "Please let me know why you'd jeopardize the entire intent of this experiment and the efforts of everyone who's worked so hard?"

Jean looked at the floor, searching for the words to answer. She took a deep breath, then let it out with a sigh. She finally whispered, "I know. I am truly sorry. With the new auto recycle program, I had to make a snap decision. In hindsight, I know I made the wrong one. But at the time, I was caught up in the moment. To me, this was the most wonderful social outlier I'd ever seen, and I wanted to reinforce that. I know it was stupid. I know I broke the rules, and I know how you're going to react. Again, I'm sorry, and I'll go pack my stuff."

"Wait," Dana snapped. "What you did was unacceptable. You broke not only my rules but the agreed upon rules of the team. You may well have biased the results of this entire experiment. We can't make meaningful observations of change if we're in there pulling the strings. Your purpose of being on this team, as an anthropologist, is to make observations. Never before have we been able to observe an intelligent culture without influencing it." Dana seemed to notice Jean's blank expression. "But I'm preaching to the choir. You know this."

"Yes, I do, which makes it all the more wrong that it was me."

"I believe this was a terrible mistake, but one that you won't repeat. I'm going to give you a second chance, but not a third. If I find another such infraction, you'll be off this project. You'll be off any meaningful research projects for the remainder of your career. Do I make myself clear?"

"Yes, crystal clear. It won't happen again."

"Good. Don't make me regret this decision."

Jean began to stand.

"Wait," Dana snapped again.

Jean sat back down.

"Another reason I'm willing to let you off is that none of us are infallible. Certainly I could make a mistake like this along the way, as doubtful as that may seem. So should that happen, you'll look the other way, or I won't be able to keep this incident hidden from an investigation."

Am I being blackmailed? Not quite sure, she replied, "I understand." She rose and exited the office.

CHAPTER 19 - CROSSING OVER

"There is an orderliness in the universe, there is an unalterable law governing everything and every being that exists or lives. It is no blind law; for no blind law can govern the conduct of living beings." - Mahatma Gandhi

Max pulled off of Route 9 onto Route 84, heading east. He was late again. *When am I going to learn to stop snoozing my alarm clock?* he thought to himself. Sometime during the night, Graham was supposed to have arrived. He'd be waiting to see the fruits of their labor firsthand. It was going to be an exciting day and Max wasn't the least bit concerned. The project was going better than he expected and it still blew him away even after seeing it every day.

As the highway turned toward the UConn Health Center's main building, Max was shocked by what he saw. Perched atop the building, like a giant yellow whale, was the enormous frame of an airship. One of Graham's stipulations in the grant to the institution was to build a mooring mast on the roof. To most, it appeared to be a cell tower antenna, and indeed, it doubled as such. The nose of the airship was anchored to this.

Max had seen photos of Graham's personal luxury airship before, but he didn't expect it to look so big. Then again, from this location, the Health Center building appeared much larger that it actually was. This was due to the Ponzo Illusion, the same perspective trick that makes the moon look twice as large when it's next to the horizon. Because the building's edges were obscured by trees along the road, the brain confused the relative sizes of the objects. This caused the sensation that they were much larger than they actually were (or much closer than they actually were). Max waited until he was close enough for the building to emerge from the obscurity of the trees, and as expected, it shrank in size, as did the airship. Max loved this effect, especially since it was his mind playing tricks on him. *Every single time.*

Even at this smaller scale, the airship was impressive. It sat on the building and was almost as long. The airship had a tapered nose that arched upwards to a hump and then downward to a long sloping tail. The side had two protrusions resembling fins. The tail swooped downward into a flared solid structure that was both a thrust exhaust port and downward facing turbofans. The side fins contained turbofans as well. The body was essentially shaped like the cross-section of an airplane wing. Underneath the bottom, which was flat, hung the living area. It was completely surrounded by reflective windows. The view must've been breathtaking.

Traffic on Route 84 was heavy because all the other drivers were also gawking at the airship. Max laughed to himself. Everyone probably thought it was a UFO making first contact with the human race. Of course, there were better places to make first contact than at the Health Center. *Crap.* He was going to be really late.

He called Min from his phone.

"Hello?" she answered.

"Min."

"Yes?"

"Can you prep the Experience Room for me please? Set it to a roaming view of Spheria."

\#

Max opened the door but stepped aside, allowing Graham to enter first for the full effect. Graham stepped into a room that looked like the bridge of the original Enterprise. It was completely circular and the walls supported giant curved monitors. They connected seamlessly, except for across the door area, and were all on. In the center was a round table, matching the shape of the room, surrounded by wooden stools. Circling the table, outside the chairs, were segments of curved railing. Clearly, they had an issue with people losing their balance. Either that or they held crazy cosplay parties here.

"Welcome to the Experience Room," said Max.

Displayed on the monitors, in a 360-degree view, was the landscape of Spheria. Their viewpoint was in motion, flying over it. Graham grabbed the nearest railing for stability. There were jagged mountains of blue and vast expanses of brown fragmented by red veins and scatterings of green vegetation.

Max joined Graham at the railing. "Isn't it spectacular?"

Graham continued to look around, his eyes wide with rapt amazement. "Strewth," he finally responded. "I think I need to sit down."

"Of course. I keep forgetting with first timers," replied Max. "Just look at the floor and you'll regain your balance. Pick a stool and then look up once you're sitting."

Graham did as instructed and was soon sitting at the table. The stool rotated, so he was able to spin around slowly, taking it all in from every direction. The immersion was breathtaking. As they soared over the plains, a herd of six-legged creatures meandered across, not aware that they were being watched from above. "This is a beaut! So this is where you view all the action?"

"Well, this is where we do that as a group when we want to discuss something together. Normally we enter at our own workstations, where we get a full 3D view with a headset. But sometimes this is better because you can move around. It almost feels like you're standing inside the world. For the most part, this is where we bring guests. It's much more approachable than attaching something to your head, and we can actually see each other while watching."

Max closed the door, then retrieved a video game controller from a rack hung on the inside of the door. The same rack also, oddly enough, held six pool cues. Graham watched Max walk toward the table and sit next to him.

Graham nudged his chin toward the rack and asked, "What's up with the pool sticks?"

"Oh," Max said, suppressing a grin. "I thought we needed a little something to let the team burn off some steam. So we can take off the top of this table and underneath is a pool table." Max was expecting to get scolded for inappropriate usage of funds.

Instead, Graham blurted out, "I love billiards! But this is round?"

"Yeah. We're not the conforming types. You can play real pool anywhere. This is a custom table made by a company called JM Billiard. It's not like any game of pool you've ever played. It's like starting from scratch, which makes it a whole new experience. Anyway, I probably shouldn't have said that in case I wanted to hustle you."

"Hustling a billionaire isn't such a bad idea. Definitely work a game into your tour at some point."

"Sure. I can do that." Max grinned like a child having just gotten away with sneaking a cookie. But Graham seemed to buy the whole morale-boosting argument. You don't get to be one of the top companies with unhappy employees.

Turning to the screens, Max continued. "This controller lets us select what is shown on these monitors. See, I can use the directional sticks to maneuver and rotate the camera."

"There is a camera?" asked Graham.

"Not an actual camera, a virtual one. So inside the world of Spheria, we have virtual constructs that simulate what a camera would do in the real world. It's really just a coordinate. But from that point, it gathers an image in every direction and displays them on these screens. So we can look all around us."

"I see."

"It's like one of those fancy 360-degree cameras that Google uses for street views. But in this case, it's all fake."

"I get it."

"Okay. So this thumb stick," Max lifted the controller and indicated his left thumb by wiggling it in the air. "This lets me move us north, east, south, or west." Max moved it in each direction and their view moved the same way. "And this stick," Max indicated his right thumb, "will rotate the camera, letting us look left or right. It'll also tilt the camera, but it's disabled right now because that motion tends to make a lot of people sick. So instead we've got it configured to change the elevation of the camera. Also, the triggers will let me scale the view in or out."

"Very cool, may I try it?"

"Of course!" Max chuckled. "You paid for it."

Graham nodded at Max as he took the controller. He spent some time moving the view about. He observed how the camera always stayed level even when it approached a mountain. The view would rise automatically so it didn't penetrate the blue rock. Then Graham could use the stick to lower them on the other side. He zoomed out, which caused a little bit of distortion as the curvature of the world became visible. He pressed the stick fully forward which made the world around the room spin wildly. The dark stripe of the Rift repeatedly flashed by, showing that they traversed the entire world over and over. Graham released the stick and zoomed in on the Rift. He attempted to lower them into it. Several meters down, the camera stopped descending.

"Yeah," Max answered the unasked question. "We're still working on building what's down there so you can't go any lower just yet."

"She'll be right," countered Graham. Max wasn't quite sure what he meant.

"Try this," said Max. "Hit the menu button. That'll open a list of preset viewpoints."

Graham did so, and a box appeared in the middle of each monitor with a list of destination names.

"Pick the one near the top that says 'exclamation Polyan Colony Center.'"

The second item on the list was "!Polyan Colony Center." Graham asked, "Why the exclamation mark?"

"Oh, we haven't gotten around to programming labels yet, so that's just a hack to sort the most frequent destinations to the top."

Graham nodded in understanding, having used this technique himself in his younger days. He selected the item and hit the enter button. The view rotated and flew down to ground level landing in the midst of structures resembling huts.

"So this is the center of the civilization that was built by the Polyans," said Max. "For a long time, they used to wander from place to place, harvesting and exhausting buried crystals. But since they learned to hunt, they settled down in this place and have built quite a community. We call it the 'Colony' because, um, they're like insects. Each individual dwelling structure is a 'hive.'"

Since the camera was no longer moving, Graham jumped up and began walking around the room. He stopped to look at each monitor. There was a flurry of activity between the hives as the Polyans went about their business. Each had a violet central body, surrounded by pointy orange legs. Graham immediately noticed their resemblance to insects and was pleased. Some had three legs, some had four, and a couple had five. Their legs were evenly distributed around their bodies, so they didn't seem to have a front or back. The only thing that gave them any sort of variation were small indigo protrusions on top of their bodies.

The five-legged Polyans were stationary and appeared to be watching what the others were doing. "Why are those guys standing there?" asked Graham.

"Those are the Soldiers; basically guards. They make sure everyone is doing their jobs. They also hunt to get food crystals from other creatures. So their responsibility isn't without significant risk. Polyans have different roles depending on their number of legs. As a whole, everyone is essential to keep the Colony functioning as a unified community."

"How do they get designated as guards?"

"Well, it turns out there is a direct correlation between

the number of legs and deadliness or fighting ability. So the rankings just kind of worked themselves out. Also, it takes greater energy and more coordination to produce Polyans with more limbs. So the more they have, the fewer of them there are."

"I wonder if this classification by body structure has any resemblance to actual creatures here on Earth?"

"Not that we have found. But it's something we're looking into. We're trying to relate these behaviors to the real world as a means to help explain natural phenomena."

"What's that?" Graham pointed to a large structure rising above the other hives, sloped on three sides like an ancient flat pyramid with steps on each side. On the top stood a perimeter of columns supporting horizontal rocks, like a triangular Stonehenge.

"That's the Council Chamber. The Polyans with six legs have taken on the role of the government. They meet on the top of that structure and discuss what to do as a collective, when to hunt, or when to relocate. There are only eight of them, so that adds to their prestige."

"So they've self-organized this way?"

"Yes, they have."

"This is fascinating. What a fantastic opportunity this experiment is. The results so far have surpassed my expectations. I mean, I was optimistic that with your technology we'd do something brand new. But I didn't know you'd pull it off so well."

"Hey!" Max frowned at Graham. "I only do things first-rate."

"I see that. Keep up the good work."

Graham turned silent for a bit. He continued to walk around the room, studying the behaviors of the Polyans. Max let him take it all in. He took the opportunity to check the email on his phone, since he'd not had a chance to do so since arriving. As Graham watched, one four-legged Polyan walked up to them and stopped. It stood there as if it was studying them. Slowly it began to circle them, all the while looking directly at them.

"Hey," commented Graham. Max looked up. "Can this one see us?"

"No, they can't see us." Max followed Graham's gaze and watched the strange movement of Sa·ma circling their position. "What the hell?" he asked himself out loud. "Take us to the 'Knoll View' preset. It's near the top of the list."

Graham brought up the menu and picked "!Colony Knoll View." Immediately their viewpoint changed to an area close to, but outside, the mass of buildings. They must've been perched on a hill, judging by the name of the location. That and the fact that the view seemed to be overlooking the Colony. From this perspective, all the hives could be seen. There was definitely some kind of organizational logic to the layout of the Colony. Graham loved this. He sat on a stool across from Max and just stared at the hives.

"So what do they do at night?" he asked.

"Oh, I almost forgot," said Max. "We don't use this often so it's easy to overlook. It's just become a pool bumper to me." He stood and went over to the door, and on a switch panel he pressed some buttons. The recessed ceiling lights went off and a dome projector rose from the center of the table. It lit up the sky, which also showed the other side of the world above them, projected onto the ceiling.

"Stone the crows!" exclaimed Graham.

"If you say so. We built this because we thought it'd be necessary to see a complete domed view of the environment. In reality, it's not very useful because seeing what's above isn't important, at least not until the Polyans develop flight." Max grinned at his own joke. Seeing that Graham either didn't find it funny or thought he was serious, Max ended with, "Damn impressive, though."

"That's an understatement." Graham leaned back against the table, rolling his head from side to side, taking in the vast expanse of the entire world. Since they were inside a sphere, the entire landscape was visible aside from the patch of ground this room was perched on. Had the floor been able to replicate the actual ground, it would be as seamless as if they were there. Directly above them, obscuring part of the other side, was a bright spot glowing green.

"That's The Source?" Graham asked.

"Yes, it is. The Source of light, life, gravity, everything."

"Gravity?"

"Yes. Making the world inside a sphere allowed us to get creative with some laws of physics. It works like the opposite of our universe. The ground we're on isn't creating the gravity, not pulling us down, like the Earth does. Instead, The Source creates a 'push force,' which increases the closer you get to it. At ground level where we are, it's exerting one unit of push. As you approach the Source, the push gets exponentially stronger, becoming infinity at the center. So nothing would ever be able to contact it directly. Not that we expect anything to actually fly, but the higher something goes, the harder it gets to go higher until it becomes impossible. The Polyans think The Source is the dwelling place of the gods, so the fact that it's unreachable might someday reinforce that mystique."

"Interesting. Why is it green?"

"Look over there at the Rift." Max pointed to the left side of the room. From the Rift, very slowly, a shimmering violet bubble was emerging. "Those bubbles rise out of the Rift and, since they're not affected by gravity, will eventually contact The Source. When they do, it'll change to match that color. This is analogous to seasons. The color of The Source governs the behavior of the creatures inhabiting Spheria. The current color, green, is a growth color, so the vegetation is able to grow new branches. When The Source turns violet, the breeding color, any creatures capable of reproduction will begin to procreate. We control what color rises and when. Recently a large group of three-legged Drones foraging for buried crystals was killed, so we want to replenish them. The slow rising of the bubble gives everyone a small warning for what's going to happen; hence, they can prepare."

"Different. Alien in fact. But smart."

"Yes. We didn't want to just re-create Earth or the rules of our universe. We wanted something foreign, yet understandable. This lets us correlate developmental differences, if any, with actual differences in the environment."

"So what other colors are there?" asked Graham.

"Some of the others are rarer and cause the environment to change. Blue causes the mountains to rise and spread. Everywhere there is an open blue polyhedron face, a blue tetrahedron will sprout. Red has a similar effect on the rivers, causing them to widen. We don't deploy blue and red often because the world would just become mountains and rivers. Also, to the inhabitants, these are equivalent to natural disasters, so we get to see how they react. And since the Polyans see it coming, in the form of a rising bubble, we get to see how they prepare for the calamity."

"This just keeps getting better and better."

"Yeah, there is a bunch of stuff. I could go on and on but it'd take days to cover everything."

"Good, because I'll be here for a few weeks. I want to see everything. I couldn't..."

Just then, a thudding sound filled the room and the viewpoint actually shuttered.

"What was that?" asked Graham.

Max looked around in confusion. "I'm not sure. That's never happened before. Maybe some kind of glitch."

Bam. Shake, shake, shake.

Max caught some motion out of the corner of his eye and spun around toward the Colony. Standing just before them was Sa·ma. And he was hitting the virtual camera with one of his legs.

"Not only can he see us," commented Graham, "but he can touch us also!"

"This isn't possible," said Max, shaking his head. "The camera is invisible. There's nothing to see, let alone touch."

Bam, bam, bam. The camera spun and slid down the hill. Sa·ma followed.

"Can we talk to him?" asked Graham.

"We could, but it's highly discouraged. Dana is anal about us not interfering inside their world."

"Well Dana reports to me, doesn't she? How can we talk to him?"

"Are you sure you want to do that?"

"Yes. Let's find out how this is possible since you say it's not."

"I agree this is puzzling, but it must be some kind of software glitch. We can troubleshoot it offline."

"No, I want to do this. Patch me in."

"Alright, fine. To do so, we need to manifest as a seven-legged Polyan, which will appear to this one as a god."

"Great. I can fulfill my delusions of godhood. Do it."

"Give me the controller," said Max. Graham handed it to him. Max brought up the menu and navigated a series of panels, bringing up a list of odd names. "Which god do you want to be?"

"Not sure. What're the options?"

"Well, there is one for each color."

"Give me... blue then."

"Done." Max picked "Ju·ro," entered a passcode, and the room darkened. The view lifted up slightly and was perched atop a blue crystalline core, with seven legs protruding in various directions. Sa·ma jumped back, startled by the sudden appearance of the god. Then he bowed low before Max and Graham appearing as Ju·ro, god of the mountains.

"On the count of three," said Max, "he'll be able to hear you. 1..2..3!"

Graham cleared his throat. Sa·ma cocked his head at the odd sound. Then Graham said, "Rise." Sa·ma did so. "What is your name?"

"Blessed Ju·ro, I am your humble servant, Sa·ma."

"How did you find me here?"

"I sensed a disturbance like one that I've felt before and followed it. I wasn't sure what was here but didn't think it was a god. My apologies for hitting you. I was just trying to figure out what you were, as I couldn't see anything with my eye sensors."

"I forgive you," said Graham as Ju·ro. "Tell me, how do you have the ability to sense me?"

Max started to fidget in his seat, but Graham was too focused on the screen to notice.

"It was a gift from your sister, Pi·ro," said Sa·ma. "She gave me a sensor that allows me to feel that which cannot be seen."

Graham mimed cutting his throat with his hand, and Max muted the conversation.

"What the hell, Max? Who controls Pi·ro and how did this level of interference happen? You said interference was prohibited."

Max swallowed and a bead of sweat formed on his forehead. "I don't know. We can appear as any of the gods. They don't actually belong to any one person, so there is no way to tell unless it was recorded. But I doubt what he says is true. It must be a software glitch of some kind. I'll have Tim look into it immediately. Somehow this Polyan must have a connection to the glitch and thinks that a god gave it to him. We'll fix this."

"I hope so. Otherwise, I'll have to take back what I said about this project being perfect."

"Murphy's law," said Max.

"Just fix it."

Max nodded.

Sa·ma said, "Please, my lord. May I ask a question?"

Graham flicked his head at Max. Max un-muted the microphone.

"What is it?" said Graham.

"Ju·ro, please tell me if there is a way to prevent the red rivers from growing toward our Colony?"

Graham pointed at Max, indicating that he should take over. Then he nodded as if to say, "Answer him."

Max said, "Sa·ma, you have long been a valuable member of your Colony. Trusted by all, even by gods. I will answer you this one question: A single blue polyhedron will not grow when under a blue Source. Place two close together but not touching. The red rivers may only approach them but not grow between or through them. But, touch the two blue together, and you will have the makings of a new mountain. Continue the pattern, and you may create a barrier of any desired length."

Sa·ma understood. In fact, now it was obvious to him. He realized there was still a lot his Colony didn't understand, that Le·ma was right. He vowed to experiment more as part of her training. "Thank you, my lord. I am forever in your debt." Sa·ma bowed.

Max pressed a button and the monitor turned off.

"What happened?" asked Graham.

"I shut off the camera. We, I mean Ju·ro, has vanished from Sa·ma."

"Fix the glitch, and don't tell Dana what we did. This is

between you and me. What kind of effect will it have?”

“As far as I see it, best case, no effect. Worst case, it allows the Colony to remain where it is when the red river encroaches on their hives. Not necessarily a bad thing.”

“Maybe we should play god more often.”

“I’m on the fence on that one.”

“Keep me informed on what develops.”

“Will do.”

CHAPTER 20 - RUNNING OUT

"Obviously any group that has to have funding also needs to get attention to their issues." - Bjorn Lomborg

There was no elevator to the roof. Dana and Max had to figure out which stairway led beyond the seventh floor. The security officer who gave them the key merely said, "Use the emergency exit." After a couple of dead-end stairwells, they found it, although the 'Exit' sign above was unlit. The sterile white metal ladder led to a locked door. The key worked, and they stepped onto the roof of the Health Center. The view was impressive. The entire Farmington Valley unfolded before them.

But even more amazing than the view was the hulking form above them. The yellow airship overwhelmed all other visual stimuli. It sat silently before them, like an 8th floor of the building. Emblazoned across the bow in red script lettering were the words 'Buruwa Gunya.'

"Unbelievable!" said Max.

"Truly," responded Dana.

"I thought it looked large from the ground. But it's enormous up close."

A slanted gangway led up to a side plug entrance, and a guard stood there keeping watch. He nodded at them with recognition and opened the hatch. As they approached, he said, "Please walk up the steps and one of the staff will assist you."

"Thank you," said Dana.

They entered the hatch and walked up five shiny wood-grained steps. These led to the platform of the suspended gondola. The interior was massive, just smaller than the entire dimensions of the ship. It had an open floor plan, with slanted windows wrapping almost all the way around. The exception being toward the rear, which was walled off, probably containing private rooms. Flanking the entrance was a set of sunken booths, three on each side. These consisted of bench seats with tables suspended from the ceiling by thick cables. To their left was the kitchen, with an assortment of stainless steel appliances, countertops, and bar stools. To their right was another sunken area with sectional couches, coffee tables, and a panoramic view out the windows. The decor was all stainless steel and white acrylic with nautical wood accents. It looked ultra-modern but inviting.

"How in the world can this fly?" asked Dana.

"No idea," said Max. "But imagine being in it while it was?"

"I think I'd get vertigo."

"You're probably right."

"I don't even like looking out the small windows on airplanes. When I have a window seat I always close the shades."

"Well, it's a good thing you can see the building roof, otherwise it wouldn't be much different."

A stunningly attractive woman appeared from the kitchen and approached them. "Hello," she said, "is Graham expecting you?"

"Not exactly," said Dana, "but he said we could stop up anytime we wanted. Is this a bad time?"

"He's about to start his daily exercise program. Please take a seat in the living area," she motioned to their right, "and you can watch. Would you like anything to drink?"

"Sure," said Max, "what have you got?"

"This layout was built for entertaining. We have a full kitchen and bar. So almost anything."

"Could I have an iced tea, then?"

"Yes, sweetened or unsweetened?"

"Unsweetened please?"

"Of course." Turning to Dana, "and you?"

"Tea does sound good." Dana looked toward the windows and shivered. "Do you have hot tea?"

"Of course. How would you like it?"

"Just plain is fine."

The woman nodded and walked back toward the kitchen. She could easily be a supermodel

"Tell me that isn't a Bond girl," whispered Max.

"I've worked with Graham a long time. He always has one or two of them around. Kind of degrading if you ask me, like his personal sex slaves."

"Looks like they've got much better perks than a typical slave would have."

"I suppose there are a few. And he's not such a bad-looking guy either."

"Playboy of the year, right?"

"So said GQ Magazine."

Max and Dana descended the three steps to the leisure platform and took a seat on the couches. It was hard not to stare out at the expansive view. They heard voices from the back of the ship. Graham emerged from a hallway accompanied by two scantily clad supermodels. They were all wearing padded headgear and carrying long black poles.

They did some kind of quick warm-up exercises. Then, exchanging bows, the women began swinging at Graham. Their staves moved in a blur, creating an impressive whistling sound. He deftly blocked each thrust and poke, moving like a man half his age. He swung at one, and she ducked. His staff spun over his head like helicopter blades then swung low as he turned toward the woman behind him. She jumped and his staff passed beneath her feet. She attacked downward, but he blocked it with both hands. The other woman lunged at his back, but he anticipated it and stepped to the side. As her staff passed him, he grabbed it and pulled her, sending her careening into the other woman. They collapsed on the floor, which had a layer of padding. They arose unharmed to attack again.

"Here you go," said a voice, startling them. The woman from the kitchen placed their drinks on a table beside them. They thanked her, sipped, and focused again on the action.

The battle between Graham and his beautiful adversaries went on for about twenty more minutes. Graham bested the women most of the time. But occasionally they got the better of him and sent him rolling onto the mat. After a particularly long volley, he managed to get his staff between both of their legs. Pulling upwards, he flipped them over. They grabbed him and they all fell together into a pile of flailing limbs. As they sat there laughing, he noticed for the first time his audience.

"Good run, ladies," he said. They stood. He bowed to each of them. "Thank you. Now please excuse me." They left back down the hallway they had arrived through.

Graham popped off his headgear and grabbed a towel from a hook on the wall. He approached Max and Dana, wiping the sweat from his forehead. "So what do you think?" he asked.

"Impressive. Is that kung fu?" asked Max.

"I was referring to my ship, but yes and no." Graham sat in a recliner facing them. "Kung fu literally means 'hard work.' So yes, it was kung fu. The opposite of which would be luck, and there was a good amount of that in there also. What you were watching was Wushu, the Chinese martial art. The staff is my favored weapon."

"Well, you're good at it," commented Dana.

"I do it every day, so I would hope so. My assistants keep me young." Then he winked at Max and added, "In more ways than one."

Max grinned. Dana gagged on her tea.

"So what do you think of my ship?"

"It's quite amazing," said Max. "I've never been in any-thing even remotely like it."

"Of course not. There *is* nothing else like it. It's the first prototype from Aboriginal Airships, and she's a beauty. The airfoil design allows an enormous living space, unlike traditional airships."

"Max and I were wondering how this can fly?" asked Dana.

"I don't want to bore you, but since you asked, it's a new category of aircraft known as a 'hybrid airship.' Hybrid because it has characteristics of both a lighter than air craft and a heavier than air craft. This is actually heavier than air even though the large cavity above us is filled with helium. It's not enough, however, so the craft is slightly negatively buoyant. To take off, we use a technique called 'rotostat.' It's like a helicopter, where the turbofans on the sides and back create a downward thrust. Once it has lifted off and begins moving forward, the shape of the body acts like a wing. This keeps it aloft through a principle called 'dynostat.' Combining these together, you get a pretty bonza piece of technology. We're going to sell tons of them to wealthy individuals who feel too water-restricted by their yachts. We already have more than thirty orders, and I'm showing it off everywhere I go."

"Can we take it for a spin?" asked Max.

"No way!" exclaimed Dana. "Not with me on it."

"Aw, c'mon, Dana," taunted Max, "it's perfectly safe."

"Nope. Let me off first."

"Actually," interjected Graham, "it's not the easiest thing to land, so we don't just take it for a spin. Unless you're wealthy and about to buy one. I doubt that's the case here."

"Darn," said Max.

"So anyway, enough about my toy. What can I do for you?"

Dana cleared her throat. "I heard you got a firsthand

taste of Spheria in the Experience Room."

"I did. I couldn't be more pleased with what you all have built." Graham grinned ear to ear at Max. "Observing the interactions of virtual life forms was definitely on my bucket list. Now I'm able to check that one off."

"Does that mean you're done with the project?" asked Dana.

"Done? By no means. I think it's just getting started."

"We agree," she said.

Max added, "There's still a ton we can learn from this."

"We're all in agreement then," said Graham. "So keep going."

"That's the thing," said Dana. "To pull this off we had to double the staff from what we'd originally planned. We can only make payroll for three more months."

"That's not much time."

"No, it's not. Are you able to provide some additional funding?"

"Dana," said Graham, "we've been over this several times! It's your job to get more funding."

"The problem," said Max, "is the exclusivity. Nobody seems to care about the research we're doing. They want the technology for other purposes."

"Mate. Are you telling me no other organizations or wealthy individuals want to move us light-years ahead in the fields of anthropology and sociology? That they don't want to provide inroads into how our brains actually work?"

"None that we've found."

"Then you're not looking hard enough. Do a TED talk or something. Get some press. This isn't a secret. We need people to know about it, and to know that they can be a part of it. They can be a part of helping us understand how the mind works."

"But I'm actively working on the project," said Max. "I don't have time to market it."

"Max," said Graham, "if you want this project to survive, you've got to do what is necessary. Wear many hats. Do you think I have a business empire because I focused only on programming algorithms, or on a single company? No. I build. And I take the earnings and build more. I build upon success after success after success. This is what you have to do. Dana can help you. That's why I hired her. Dana, this is your specialty. Get out there and drum up funding, and teach Max how to market."

"We're trying," said Dana, "we really are."

"Well, try harder."

Max sat there dumbfounded. Graham just looked back and forth at them.

Finally, Dana asked, "So you won't give us anything?"

"Listen, I'm reasonable, and I do care about this project. How about I match any funding you get? This way it will go further, but you still need to get funding on your own. It's up to you both to make this project work. I have faith you can pull this off. You are two of the most talented individuals I know. You just need to apply some kung fu!"

"Kung fu, indeed," said Max.

"So we have an understanding. Thank you for stopping by, but I must excuse myself now, I have some work to do. Tammy will show you out."

As if on cue, the woman from the kitchen appeared beside them.

As they walked down the plank, Max paused and turned to Dana. "That didn't go the way I had hoped."

"No, but it could've been worse. At least he's willing to put more money in. We just have to come up with a strategy to get new investors."

"I've got a couple of ideas," said Max.

"We need all the ideas we can get, or we both will be looking for new jobs before we know it."

174

CHAPTER 21 - CAT AND MOUSE

"I shall argue that strong men, conversely, know when to compromise and that all principles can be compromised to serve a greater principle." -
Andrew Carnegie

Rain pelted the windshield as the black sedan approached the slick pier. The headlights shut off as the car rolled through the darkness. The incandescent glow of New London on the horizon and the marina at Shaw Cove were the only light sources. As such, they barely provided enough to avoid driving into the river. The northern horizon was completely obscured by the hulking silhouette of a Virginia-class submarine docked next to the pier.

The driver leaned to the right for a better look. The blurry photonics mast waved through the raindrop covered window. It was one of the new smaller low-profile masts, designed to resemble a traditional periscope. This eliminated the previous towering mast that rendered them easily identifiable to enemies.

This mast was unique in submarine design. It consisted of an array of cameras connected to the body by fiber optic cables. The connection eliminated the need to have a hole penetrate the hull, thus strengthening the structural integrity of the entire craft. The driver wondered if this one had a 360-

degree camera installed.

The driver glanced at the car's navigation display again. It read, "Pier 3, Electric Boat, Groton, CT," confirming the destination. Toward the end of the pier was an enormous yellow crane designed to lift massive cargo, from submarine parts to shipping containers. Next to this was a haphazard assortment of cargo containers. The car came to a stop beneath the crane. A couple of small bulbs illuminated the area, making the darkness even more imposing.

The door opened, and the driver emerged, pulling on a dark green hooded rain jacket. The concealed figure skulked around the car toward the containers. There were several types and colors, but all were the standard twenty-foot-long variety.

The driver wandered among them, finally finding, by feel, a corrugated container. A quick illumination by cell phone revealed that this container was red. It was the one.

Looking at an email on the phone display for reference, the hooded driver tapped the pattern on the end of the crate: dot-dot-dash-dot, dot-dash-dot, dot, dot, dash-dot-dot, dash-dash-dash, dash-dash.

Immediately, the squeaking sound of a bolt sliding sideways was audible. The door of the crate creaked open a sliver. A dim gray light spilled onto the pavement and the figure outside. The driver tightened the hood, providing even better facial concealment.

"In. Now!" came a booming voice from inside.

The driver darted through, and the door immediately closed. A hulking figure in a Navy uniform latched the bolt, then turned to face the newcomer. The four stars on his shoulder indicated his rank.

"You idiot! Why the hell is your cell phone on? And

parking under the crane's light was a moronic thing to do!" The man glared at the shrouded figure, the hood making eye contact impossible. Admiral Troy Miller was an imposing man. Standing at almost 7 feet tall and with a torso like a redwood, he was enough to scare the ghost out of anyone. He used his physique frequently to his advantage.

"Sorry, I couldn't see anything," a nervous and fearful voice returned.

"That's the point. You aren't the only person out there with eyes."

"Sorry."

The admiral pointed at a chair. "Sit," he commanded.

The visitor's gaze followed his finger to the chair, which was one of two in the cargo container. The remainder of the space was lined with tables and glowing monitor screens. They all displayed animated data or video feeds of some kind. Several showed clearly the area around the container in infrared. One table was dedicated to projecting weather maps from around the world. Others presented what appeared to be star constellations with lines streaking by. Yet others showed maps of the oceans with red and green blips, followed by dotted yellow trails. The chairs, currently, were positioned in front of a rather large 60-inch display.

The visitor sat, as instructed, and looked up at an imposing wire diagram of some sort of cannon. It gently rotated on the large display.

"What's this?"

The admiral sat in the other chair. "Project Disintegration," he said matter of fact. He leaned toward the display, and slowly added, "This... is... our... future." He picked something up off the table resembling an old-school joystick, and began moving it. The cannon stopped rotating and zoomed out a bit. "Watch this."

He hit a button and the display began to animate. The accompanying outline of a Navy Destroyer appeared. It had a cannon mounted on the front. The gun swiveled around rapidly, tracking something in motion. The ship deployed what appeared to be large metal plates underwater. They created an inverted 'V' shape to about twice the ship's original depth. Then the cannon fired.

Although this was just an animation, the result was impressive. A spinning blue vortex of energy inside the cannon barrel instantaneously accelerated a cylindrical slug. It shot out and off the screen. The resulting kickback rocked the Destroyer, almost capsizing it. The purpose of the metal plates now become apparent as they dampened the shock.

The view zoomed out and panned to follow the flying slug. It was moving upwards at a tremendous speed. The horizon began to curve, and the outline of continents became visible. Then the screen was filled with thousands of fragmented triangles.

The admiral looked at the visitor's puzzled expression and laughed. "Too fast for you? Watch it again." He fiddled with the joystick and the slug was once again rising up over the earth, but slower. Then, from the side of the screen approached a satellite in orbit. The slug impacted it and the satellite was obliterated. Within three frames, it was replaced by a thousand tiny particles.

"Holy shit!" exclaimed the visitor.

"Yes, that's some holy shit, indeed. Angel fire! Even the gods aren't safe from us anymore."

"How's that possible?"

"It's a rail gun. A giant rail gun. The largest we've ever designed. It will be deployed on every Destroyer in the fleet. It will allow us to wipe out any target from a fail-safe distance, even hitting targets in space. Nothing is capable of stopping one of these in motion. It will secure the dominance of the United States military for the next 30 years."

The visitor turned to the admiral. "That's an astounding weapon. And I'm glad you're keeping us all safe, but what does it have to do with our battery?"

"Well, this cannon is based on sound and proven technology – only bigger than anything we've ever done before. Yet, there is a slight problem with it."

"What kind of problem?"

"Power. It needs more delivered to it at once than we have the means to provide. I'm not talking about the amount of energy; the nuclear reactor on the boat can create more than enough. It just can't deliver enough of it all at once as fast as needed. What we need is some means of storing a massive amount and delivering it immediately, like a giant capacitor. That's where you come in."

"Hold on here. You told me this project didn't involve developing a weapon. That was the stipulation of our arrangement. Our main benefactor, Graham Neilson, forbade us from taking funding that could contribute to weaponization. This is a violation of our agreement."

"Listen, I know you academic research types all think alike. I've heard your talks before. 'Stop construction to save the flat-tailed horny lizard!' you say. 'Stop funding the military, but keep us safe,' you say. Well, you can't have it both ways. Our might is what keeps us and you safe. The battery we're making will guarantee generations of peace. I'm funding peace, not a weapon. The weapon just happens to be the means to the end."

"This is blatant deception. You tricked and misled me. I would never have done this to begin with. I'll shut down the project."

"I don't think that'd be a good idea."

"Why not?"

"You've just violated a top-secret clearance by viewing extremely confidential security assets. I'm the only one protecting you now. If you complete the project on time, you get a windfall and can retire and do whatever you please without the constraints of any funders. You'll be free to run your own scientific experiments if that's what floats your boat. If you fail... well, let's not even discuss that option because it isn't one."

"Wait, what do you mean? You never said anything about guaranteed success. How do I even know if your equations are correct?"

"They're correct. That much we know. Our best minds put them together. We just don't have a computer fast enough to find a solution in a reasonable amount of time. The best traditional computer we've got will take an estimated 19,000 years to find a solution. We don't have that much time. That's where your little experiment fills the gap. The massively parallel quantum computing of the Qube technology is just what we need. And thanks to you, the decree of Graham is no longer a barrier. Don't be so hard on yourself. You're a true patriot.

"When the calculations are complete we'll have the molecular formula for a new composite battery compound. It'll store the required energy and release it as quickly as a traditional capacitor. This will be like nothing built before. We'll have to come up with a new name for it. Something like 'capattery.' So tell me, is the second site functional?"

The visitor slumped in the chair, displaying a posture of defeat. "It is."

"Is it online now?"

"Yes. It's been running and is 30 percent populated and has begun crunching your equations. The current metrics tell us that it could be within 90 days of providing a solution. It'll be even faster if we can increase the number of Qubes working on the problem."

"I need a solution in 45 days. Find a way to get more Qubes working on the problem. You get your money as soon as the solution is delivered. Then you can forget Graham Neilson and his pet projects and do whatever you want with the rest of your life!"

"Okay, I can accelerate it. I've already laid the groundwork to get more Qubes. I just need to influence a few more… things… and we should have a windfall of calculation engines."

"That's the best news I've heard all day!"

Once again the cannon was spinning on the screen. The visitor knew time was running out and there was only one acceptable outcome.

182

CHAPTER 22 - IN OUR IMAGE

"In any moment of decision, the best thing you can do is the right thing, the next best thing is the wrong thing, and the worst thing you can do is nothing." - Theodore Roosevelt

Sa·ma walked to the edge of the Council Chamber and peered out through the vertical columns. In the distance, he could see the red bubble rising past the edge of the Rift, starting its slow ascent toward the Source shining above it.

"It's past," he said, facing the others in the chamber.

Gathered in a circle were the eight Leaders, the totality of the six-legged caste. By name, they were Wu·sa, Yo·sa, Me·sa, Ju·sa, Ki·sa, Co·sa, Pi·sa, and Vu·sa. They looked concerned hearing Sa·ma's news.

"This is the fourth red bubble in a row," said Co·sa.

"The river is getting too close to the Colony," said Me·sa. "When this bubble joins the Source, the river will widen again and consume several of our hives."

"We need to move the Colony," said Wu·sa and Pi·sa, in unison.

"Yes, we need to move it," agreed Vu·sa.

"But we haven't had to move for eighty seasons," object-
ed Ki·sa. "Red bubbles are rare."

"Then why have we had four of them in a row?" asked
Co·sa.

"The gods are angry," declared Me·sa.

"Sa·ma," intoned Ju·sa. He searched the columns, fixing
on the Lumen Master, who stood motionless observing them.
"Can you tell us why the gods are angry?"

"I can't," he replied. "There could be many reasons,
which all remain a mystery to us, even to me. I may have many
insights into the workings of nature, but I can't speak with the
gods." He dared not reveal his encounters with the gods Pi·ro or
Ju·ro, lest the Council try to force him to attempt something
that was beyond his powers.

"Regardless, speaking with the gods or not, we still have
to address the immediate problem," said Wu·sa. "We have to
move. We can try to find out what we did wrong later, but we're
going to lose dwellings at dawn tomorrow."

Le·ma's insightful words popped into Sa·ma's mind. *I
bet, with some creative persuasion, the Council could bend the
rules as well.* He thought back to the solution Ju·ro had given
him. But could he convince the Council it was his idea?

"There might be another way," he said. He pretended to
think hard. "No, there definitely is another way."

"Do tell," said Co·sa.

"I know how we can stop the expansion of the river
permanently," answered Sa·ma. "We can use blue stone to
make a wall. The red stone of the river won't cross that boundary. The Colony can stay here forever after that."

A hum rose as the Leaders began discussing this piece of information. Finally, Ju·sa turned to Sa·ma and asked, "Never has such a thing been built. You're a great architect, but you can't perform magic."

"It's not magic. It's creative manipulation of the rules. I can do it. I can instruct the Workers right now, and before dawn, we'll have it done and the Colony will be saved."

There was more quiet debate with hushed voices. Ju·sa stood up and said, "It seems like we have two options. One, move the Colony, which we've traditionally done many times as the rivers grew. Two, do what's never been tried, build a fence to stop the advance of the river. Let's vote." He then sat.

More noise as they discussed again. This went on for some time, and several swapped positions to talk to others. Sa·ma watched with interest as they actively debated, trying to convince others to vote in a similar fashion. He could only hope that the wall would be accepted unanimously.

Finally, Co·sa raised three of his legs. The others followed suit, and the hall fell silent. "Those of you who vote for the wall, stand. Those of you who vote for moving, remain seated. Do so now."

Co·sa stood. So did Wu·sa, Me·sa, and Ju·sa.

"Four to four," said Co·sa. "A tie."

Sa·ma couldn't believe the outcome. When the Council members reached a tie, the rule was not to do anything. In this case, the result was catastrophic. "If we do nothing, the Colony will be wounded," he said.

"But we have a tie," said Ju·sa.

"We need to break the tie," said Pi·sa. "We need a sign from the gods."

"There will be no sign from the gods," said Vu·sa.

"What are we to do?" asked Wu·sa.

"We can no longer tolerate ties," Co·sa stated, looking from member to member. "We need another to break them. We need a god among us."

"A god among us?" asked Wu·sa.

"Yes, it has never been attempted before, but I am suggesting we make a Polyan with… seven legs!"

Several exclaimed in unison, "Seven!" followed by hushed murmurs. More movement and debate.

"Let's take a vote," said Ju·sa. "Stand if you are for making a seven-legged Polyan, sit if you are opposed."

All stood. Sa·ma watched this with puzzlement. How could making a god be less controversial than building a fence? But such was the way of the Council; it didn't always make logical decisions. Maybe it did need someone higher to help the Leaders think rationally.

"Then it is decided," said Co·sa. "On the next violet Source, we will attempt what's never been done."

"Ahem," said Sa·ma. "I have the sincerest respect for this Council and its decisions. But the river is our immediate concern. If you can do the unimaginable trying to make a god, surely you can do the trivial and allow me to build a wall."

"I say we let Sa·ma be the tiebreaker this time," responded Wu·sa.

"I second that," said Pi·sa.

"Me, too," said Co·sa, Ju·sa, and Vu·sa.

"Then it is decided," said Me·sa. "What is your vote, Sa·ma?"

Wasn't it obvious? "I vote to build the wall."

"For the Colony!" said Me·sa.

"For the Colony!" said everyone. And thus, the decision was made.

188

CHAPTER 23 - NOURISHMENT

"When confronted with the order and beauty of the universe and the strange coincidences of nature, it's very tempting to take the leap of faith from science into religion. I am sure many physicists want to. I only wish they would admit it." - Tony Rothman

Max watched Min finish her drink as the waiter cleared the dinner plates from their table.

"You certainly have an interesting background, Min," Max said. "What else should I know about you?"

"Well, what do you want to know? Ask me anything."

"Do you believe in a supreme being?"

"That's generally off limits for a first date," Min resisted.

"Well, I don't get out much. Plus, it's something I ponder a lot. I just like to hear what other people think about it."

"Okay. My parents emigrated to America and converted to Christianity just after I was born. I believe they did it as a way of fitting in better with their community. I'm not sure they believe the theology, but regardless I was raised Catholic. I went to Mass every week, religiously, pun intended. I learned all the proper words to recite, and the history and stories from the Bible. Overall, I believe what I was taught. Religion gives us hope, gives us a reason to go on. It gives us something to look forward to when our physical bodies fail us. But I don't get too wrapped up in it these days. I like to go to church once in a while, just to keep things fresh, but other than that I don't dwell on it. How about you, are you religious?"

"Not really. The way I see it, this physical world is too mathematical. We see repeating patterns everywhere. It's like the universe is just some algorithm being executed. Dissolve Epsom Salt in hot water until it's saturated, then drop a grain in. The grain grows into a crystal with a repeating structure. It self-assembles. If there is a God, I believe he just created some fundamental rules, and everything else just formed from that over time. He's just sitting back watching the elegance of his creation from a tiny spark to the grand expanse of the cosmos, all on its own."

"That sounds like our little project. Do you think we're playing God?"

"Definitely. I think what we're doing to the Polyans, something else much more powerful is doing to us. And something more powerful still is doing it to that thing, and on and on. Maybe it's the angels messing around with us, and what we consider to be God messing around with the angels. Whatever it is or isn't, the exact nature is beyond our comprehension. Just like the Polyans would have no way of comprehending the complexity of the world we live in. The true nature of God, or God's God, is something we can't ever understand. We're not capable of it. So we draw analogies, like streets paved with gold, but it's not even close to reality."

"That's too deep for my brain; you make my head hurt. Either that or I've had one too many Cosmopolitans. Or maybe not enough." Min waved to the bartender for another.

"Sorry, let me put it this way. Have you ever heard of the Game of Life?"

"Yeah, I love that game. My sister and I played it all time when we were kids. I loved driving my plastic car around the board picking up family members. We used to dream of being doctors or lawyers and ending up with two kids and a mansion. We didn't care who won because at the end we'd visit each other's houses."

"Ha, I remember that! But that's Milton Bradley's board game. I'm talking about Conway's Game of Life. You're a CS major, you must've heard of it."

The bartender began mixing another drink. He poured it into a martini glass and brought it over. "Another beer?" he asked Max, delivering one, having assumed the answer.

"Sure, since the lady is having another."

Min took a sip, then remembering the question, answered, "Not sure who Conway is?"

Max took a sip, mimicking Min's behavior. "Conway was a mathematician. Around 1970 he invented an algorithm that would simulate bacteria-like life spreading on a two-dimensional grid."

"I remember now. That was discussed briefly in my Intro to AI class. They built computer programs that could run these simulations over and over creating many generations in a span of minutes. It was a primitive simulation of life and death."

"Exactly!" Max was pleased she'd heard of it. He loved smart, geeky women, especially if they were sexy. *Or maybe it was the geekiness that made them sexy.* He shrugged at the thought and continued. "But the relevant idea is Conway created just a few simple rules that governed how his universe worked. Look." Max found a pen on the bar and grabbed a napkin. He drew a grid of lines on the back. He colored in a couple of the squares randomly. "The filled in ones represent living cells, and others empty spaces. The first rule was that living cells need friends, but not too many. So any with less than two neighbors would die of loneliness. And any with more than three would die of overcrowding." He pointed at spots on the napkin where each of these rules applied. "The second rule was a new living cell would be born into any empty space that had exactly three neighbors, as if by reproduction." He put the pen down.

"That's it?" asked Min.

"That's it," repeated Max. "Apply the rules and the magic happens. Cells live or die, multiply and spread, wither away, move around, even replicate. It's like looking at a microscope slide of bacteria. What makes this even more interesting is, since then, others have created different sets of rules for their versions. Many, many different sets. Some sets result in simulations that thrive with interesting patterns and life. Other sets of rules lead to outcomes that are either too chaotic or too desolate to be of interest."

"I think I was sleeping through that part of the lecture. It certainly sounds more interesting when you describe it," said Min.

"That's because you're smitten by my charm and charisma!"

"Yeah, or something." Min smiled and rolled her eyes. "But you can't explain why the rules of our universe are so perfect. I mean, they're exactly balanced to support life. Plank's constant, Avogadro's number, the speed of light, the gravitational constant, etc. All these are balanced perfectly, just too perfectly, for chance. If the constant of gravity were just a slight bit less, then the planets in our solar system would fly into space. Or if the atomic bond strengths weren't the exact amount they are, atoms wouldn't stick together into molecules. There must be a God to have set all this up in equilibrium."

"I don't disagree. It makes sense for only God to have the ability to establish the parameters of our universe. But we could be the one experiment that worked, among many that did not. It's like the many universes theory: that out there in some higher dimension, there are a bunch of universes. Each has a random set of laws of physics, rules if you will. Some universes can self-assemble into something fantastic, something that can spawn life. Others merely have drifting dust because nothing coalesces.

"The catch is, only the universes that produce life, and intelligent life at that, develop the ability to ask the question, 'Is there a God?' You say 'because things are just too perfect.' I say, they've got to be perfect or we wouldn't be here to ask the question. So we happen to be in the one, maybe the only one, that happened to have just the right random mix of rules. That doesn't prove the balance was intentional."

Min processed this. "I guess that makes sense. I wouldn't expect aliens living on another planet to be struggling to stand because their gravity was too strong. They wouldn't have developed there expecting any other amount of gravity. Yet their planet could be twice as massive as Earth."

"Yea that's a good analogy. I will add this: We barely know anything about how the universe works. In 100 years, people will look back on what we now know like we look back on the ancients. It was only a short time ago we thought the sun orbited the earth. And we had no clue why birds didn't fall from the sky."

"We've come a long way," said Min. "I can't even imagine the world without the Internet."

"The trap is that at any given point in time, many think we've reached the end. That there's nothing else to discover. But history has shown us that we've merely scratched the surface and that anything is possible. Ghosts are possible. Telekinesis is possible. Life after death is possible. We just don't know and thus can't dispute anything. The best we can do is to keep looking."

"Life after death. Then you're not an atheist?"

"Technically, I'm not. I just don't think we have proof of God, but similarly, we'll never have proof that there isn't a God. I guess you'd call me Deist. I believe that a higher power exists, but the nature or intentions of such can never be understood. In other words, I'm hedging my bets." Max mimed rolling dice.

"Does that mean you'll come to church with me on Sunday?"

"Let me get back to you on that." Max cracked a smile. "Anyway, if there is a God, we are so minute and insignificant that there is no way any individual matters."

"Not true. He cares about all His children equally."

"Maybe so. But I think we'd be like bacteria on the bottom of His shoe, praying that He doesn't take another step. We're so small and invisible; He's not even aware that we exist."

"Are the creatures in Spheria so tiny they're invisible?"

"No, but that's not the same kind of experiment. We did 'create' Spheria, true. And I agree we handcrafted much of the land, and even the initial set of beings and their behaviors. But it was in the interest of time. We could've created a pure procedural experiment, but we would've had to iterate it until we got one that worked. That'd have taken much more time, just like that failed universe theory. We may not have found an interaction that worked. But when you've got infinite time, that's no longer an issue."

"Well, maybe the same applies to God. Maybe He didn't want to make infinite universes until one worked. Maybe he just decided it'd be easier to handcraft things and He did create all this, and us. And He is aware of us and watches us, just like we watch the beings in Spheria."

"It's possible. One thing I know for sure, we'll never know, as long as we're alive, what the actual answer to that question is."

Min yawned. Max yawned too as if it were contagious.

"It's getting late. Want to call it a night?" he asked.

"Yep. Will you drive me home?"

"Sure. Where do you live?"

"Well, I was hoping you'd show me your place."

#

Meanwhile, in Spheria, a violet bubble was rising. The next Source would trigger a mating season. The Council members took notice and began preparations to implement their plan.

196

CHAPTER 24 - PRO CREATION

"Being made in the image of God, man was the crown of creation." - Walter Lang

Max held the door open for Min, and she slipped into his apartment. It was stereotypically minimalist, with beige walls, void of any artwork or decorations. A maroon couch, a coffee table, and a couple of floor lamps surrounded the focal point of the room: an impressive entertainment center complete with several modern video game systems. There was no doubt where Max's priorities lay.

The rest of the apartment consisted of an open kitchen off the living room, a small bathroom, and a bedroom. Peeking into the latter, Min could see the walls were covered by many filled bookcases. Max's bed was also made. Odd for a single guy, unless he was either expecting her or was actually that anal.

"What kind of games do you like?" asked Max.

"I'm not very coordinated," replied Min, "so I usually go for the building kind."

"So you're a Minecraft fan?"

She chuckled. "Who isn't?"

"I tried to get my dad to play it," said Max, "but he said he doesn't like it because it has no story. He doesn't get that the point is to build your own story."

"That's too bad. Although I wish my dad were cool enough to play *any* video games."

"Yeah, true. I never thought of it that way. You want something to drink?" he asked.

"Yeah, but I can get it. You have stuff in the fridge?"

"I do. I'll have a beer. Help yourself to anything in there. I'll get the game loaded while you're getting that."

Min walked over to the fridge, opened it, and was surprised at the healthy selections. She'd expected to see it full of beer, and maybe some soda, but it was quite the opposite. An assortment of juice and iced teas took up the majority of the space. Only a small corner held some micro-brewed beers.

"What kind do you want?" she asked.

"Blue Moon," he answered. "There are oranges in the drawer."

"Sure." She grabbed two of them and garnished each with a slice of orange. She walked to the living room and handed one to Max.

"Thanks," he said.

"Cheers, to video games and beer!" she said, clanking her bottle against his.

"Hear, hear." He quickly sipped the foam off the top before it overflowed. "So, you want to play survival mode or build mode?"

"Let's do survival. We can see how well we work as a

team."

"Perfect."

He handed her a controller, and they started a new game. They were spawned in an Ice Plains biome, which was a crappy place to begin.

"Looks like we have our work cut out for us," she said.

"Yeah, we need a shelter before nightfall."

"That goes without saying. Why don't you find or build a shelter and I'll begin crafting some supplies?"

"Sounds like a plan!"

#

The meeting chamber had been converted into a secluded breeding room. Never before had a seven-legged Polyan been created. The Council didn't want any disruptions, knowing how the act of creation would leave the members. Wu·sa paced, waiting for the others to arrive. He walked to the center of the room and checked on the seven-sided body crystal they'd placed there. It was clear, save for three sensors already attached, one each for seeing, hearing, and speaking.

Ga·zo, the head five-legged Soldier, watched from the doorway.

Noticing him, Wu·sa asked, "Is the perimeter secured?"

"Yes, we have a Soldier at each entrance. Nobody but the other Leaders can gain access."

"Good. Please see to it that it remains that way."

"I have my best Soldiers on it. You can trust us. We never fail."

"I know. It's just my nature to worry."

"Is that why they left you here?"

Wu·sa hadn't made the connection but slumped, knowing it was probably true. *Maybe so*, he thought. "I'm here to ensure things are set up right," he said. "Can you let me know when the Source turns violet?"

Ga·zo replied, "As you wish." After which he left, knowing full well everyone would be able to 'feel' when the season started. It was just an excuse to get rid of him.

#

Max moved his avatar toward the nearest mountain and walked along it. It was relatively standard, but at the edge of a frozen lake, he found an indented area, like a wide open cave. "Check this out. What do you think about this?"

Min looked at his side of the screen. "That'll make a perfect shelter."

"Agreed."

He began mining some rock from a nearby hill, then returned to the cave to close it with walls. He left a space to walk through.

"I need a door," he said.

"I'm on it," replied Min, who was crafting materials out of wood.

She had cut down the few trees and had managed to build a workbench. On this, she crafted torches, and also was able to create a door. She carried all this over to Max's location and installed the door in the opening that he'd left. Then their avatars met inside the cave. It grew dark.

She hung up 4 torches and lit them. The hollow filled with light but was cold and barren. The hiss of a creeper could be heard outside.

"This isn't a home!" she exclaimed.

"What do you mean?" he asked.

"We need some rugs, some plants, and some lovely wall hangings or pictures."

Max looked at her, then he looked around his apartment. "Are you insinuating something here?"

"Only that you could use a woman's touch. I'd be happy to help."

"Okay, show me how nicely you can decorate our cave, then maybe, just maybe, I'll let you decorate my man cave!"

"Challenge accepted." They both chuckled at this, excessively so.

#

One by one the other seven absent Council members arrived. Each carried an elongated orange shard, about the size of a large leg. These they placed on the floor, equidistant around the clear central body crystal. Then they each took a position straddling one.

It was dead quiet in the chamber as if unspoken apprehension filled their minds.

Ki·sa broke the silence. "I know we're all anxious over what we are about to do – to bring forth a god to live among us in our Colony." Ju·sa, Me·sa, and Vu·sa nodded in agreement. The others glanced around, shifting their weight from leg to leg. "We should all feel amazed and empowered by this honor.

They'll tell stories about this day for many generations."

"If it actually works," mumbled Co·sa.

"True. This has never been done. How could we not be worried about it?" asked Pi·sa.

Ki·sa countered with, "As far as we *know*, nobody has ever tried to do this before. Only recently have we found some seven-sided body crystals. There is no reason to believe that this wouldn't work the same way as creating any other Polyan. The number of legs shouldn't be a factor, assuming we can provide enough initial energy."

"Except that the result is a god!" Co·sa took a couple of steps backward. "The world was created by the seven-legged ones, not the other way around. We're messing with things beyond our authority. This could affect the stability of our world, change things in a way the seed god Ra·ju never intended."

Silence once again filled the chamber as they considered Co·sa's skepticism.

"Speaking of the gods," said Pi·sa, "how are they going to feel about a new addition to their ranks? It could trigger a battle that affects the structure of our world."

"Listen," said Wu·sa, "we agreed to this at the last Council meeting. It was unanimous that we needed someone to look to for guidance, someone who has a connection to the gods. This creation will be the solution. He'll be one of us, but also a god. A bridge between our two worlds: Spheria and the Qubessence. This will give us insight we've never before had. The benefits completely outweigh the risks."

"Simple for you to say," said Co·sa. "You don't have to take part in the making."

"I'm ensuring everything goes as planned, not a trivial task."

Just then Wu·sa felt a tingling sensation in the core of his body. The others did also, as they began to stir.

Ga·zo appeared in the doorway. "It is time."

\#

Min proceeded to create some nice beds, right next to each other. She added a window, created four paintings, placed the workbench, and added a furnace. The place was looking quite livable now.

Meanwhile, Max had been crafting some weapons and gave her a bow, and for himself, he made a sword and some armor.

"Did we just stereotype ourselves?" he asked.

"I think so. Even in a virtual world, we play the roles society dictates to us."

"Hmm," mused Max. "Next time, I'm going to be the woman."

"Great, I get to kill things. Just what I'm good at."

"Okay, maybe not. But I like the place. Feel free to spruce up my apartment if you want."

"Tomorrow," said Min. She moved her avatar to the bed and went to sleep. Max followed her and lay down next to her. The screen dimmed.

\#

"The Source is violet," Ga·zo said.

"Thank you," replied Wu·sa, although they already knew it.

Wu·sa was about to tell everyone to begin, but nature took its course.

The others began to gyrate in slow circles, first clockwise and then counterclockwise. The more they moved, the more glow their cores emitted, filling the room with a soft violet light. They could feel the mounting sensation as if their life force was exceeding its capacity. They *needed* a vessel to deposit the excess.

Each Polyan, when the time felt right, touched the base of its body onto a point of the orange shard below. Their energy flowed into the crystals, making them glow. With the little bit of strength they had left, they each attached these legs to the large body core. Then they collapsed upside down, exhausted. The life force in each leg was drawn into the transparent core, turning it solid with violet color.

The ritual was complete. *But nothing happened.*

#

Max paused the game, placed his controller on the coffee table and leaned back on the couch. Min did the same. They watched their avatars lying in bed. Min turned to Max to ask him why he had paused it, but before she could speak, his lips were upon hers. They made out for a while on the couch, giddy and tingling sensations coursing through their bodies.

Eventually, they stopped to take a natural break. Max stared at Min with wide eyes and shuddered. She stared back, then glanced sideways toward the bedroom. Taking a deep breath, he reached out, cradled her in his arms, and stood up. She giggled.

He carried her through the bedroom door, and, had she

not ducked, would've whacked her head on the molding.

"Oops!" said Max, breaking the tension.

"It's fine." She tightened her arms around him.

#

Their seven-legged creation lay there, motionless. It was evident that the new body core wasn't full enough to ignite life.

"More, brothers!" shouted Wu·sa.

But the others lay on their backs, twitching their legs, unable to stand.

Wu·sa ran up and shook the potential god. *No response.* He ran around checking each Leader, but they were all exhausted and incapable of giving any more.

Co·sa summoned the energy to speak. "We are done. We'll die if we give more." Then, looking at the lifeless god, he added, "We have failed."

"No!" exclaimed Wu·sa. The rule was one Polyan per leg. That was how their breeding worked. So what he was about to try was extremely unorthodox, but there was no other option.

Wu·sa leaped upon the central core, impaling himself upon one of its points. His energy began draining quickly into the heart of the being. He was committing suicide.

#

Max lay Min onto his real mattress, leaned over, and kissed her passionately. Then he gave her a relaxing massage, as a pile of clothes formed next to the bed. He kissed up and down her body, while she moaned intermittently with approval. Then, when she was fully relaxed, she returned the favor to him.

Gradually, their bodies entwined into an embrace, and the warmth between them was inviting. As they indulged in each other's comfort, the box spring began to gently squeak.

Suddenly, Max's whole body stiffened, and he started moaning.

"Yes," Min whispered in his ear.

"Nooo!" he grunted.

"No?" she asked, furrowing her eyebrows.

"No… it's a charley horse… in my leg… ahhhhh!"

Min giggled. Max grimaced.

They both laughed together. Min sympathized, "Sorry, I don't mean to laugh. I just thought you were doing something else."

"I know. That's what made it funny."

They both chuckled some more, and Max flipped over. Min lay on top of him. The feeling of skin on skin was indulgent. When they both were exhausted and satisfied, Min rested her head on his chest. The warm feeling inside carried her off to sleep.

#

The opaque core of the new Polyan brightened and lit up the room as if a spark had been ignited. The violet glow was so intense that Ga·zo, standing guard outside, peeked in. Two other Soldiers also entered, drawn to the light.

The new Polyan's body seemed to shudder. Its seven legs began to twitch. Then they touched the floor of the chamber and the Polyan stood abruptly. Wu·sa lost contact and tumbled to the ground, where he lay unmoving. Ga·zo ran over to check on him. He was drained, but not completely, so it seemed he would live.

The new Polyan towered large, impressive, and godlike. It stood there unmoving, waiting for its brain to be assigned to an inactive Qube. This took only a couple of seconds, and its visual sensors came to life. It looked down upon the inverted six-legged Polyans and the standing five-legged ones and said, "My name is Fa·ro."

The Soldiers bowed in reverence to the new god that stood before them.

Outside, the number of Polyans had increased by 28 percent. It was a productive night.

208

/ PART TWO /

DYNASTY

210

CHAPTER 25 - START THE PRESS

"The media's the most powerful entity on earth. They have the power to make the innocent guilty and to make the guilty innocent, and that's power. Because they control the minds of the masses." - Malcolm X

Scientists Play God In This Virtual Experiment

Gizmodo *- 3 hours ago*

By Moses Diego

Filed to: QUANTUM SOUL

After exploring the halls of the University of Connecticut Health Center in Farmington, I entered an unassuming door bearing the cryptic label "L7E04 Intelligence". The modern lobby, with smoked acrylic sheets and recessed lighting, was tempered by a dead fern and an old copy of *Popular Science.* I thumbed through this antiquated form of publishing as I waiting to meet Max Moreau, creator of the Qube technology I reported on last year.

Max greeted me with his usual charming self, although he appeared older and more tired than I remembered him. After exchanging pleasantries, he got right down to business showing me to the wonders in his lab.

Hall of Monsters

The first stop was a hallway that could have been right out of a Hollywood movie studio. It was lined with posters depicting polygonal creatures that resembled crabs. Max explained that these creatures, called Polyans because they were comprised of polygons, were a sentient life form existing in a virtual world. I pressed Max on his definition of "sentient", and he assured me they actually have true self-awareness.

As proof, he explained that these Polyans had developed a pecking order based on their number of legs, ranging from three to six. Apparently, the number is correlated to fighting ability, so a caste system naturally emerged. Recently, they've managed to create one of their kind with seven legs. This one was revered as a god. The level of anthropomorphic behavior sounded truly astounding, far greater than any AI I have ever heard of, and engaged a diverse team of researchers in studying their development.

Spheria

My next stop was a place called the Experience Room, where I could see into the virtual world, and this was equally strange. The Polyans occupied the inside surface of a sphere. The way Max described it to me, it sounded like a Dyson sphere, with the sun in the middle. The key point is it is a finite space, equivalent to an electronic terrarium. It holds resources both rich and hostile, presenting a playground for the Polyans to live, die, and explore.

So the Spheria Project, ultimately, is a study in how societies develop. Nowhere else could scientists watch a culture form and stabilize in real time, from scratch, without outside influence. It's the perfect scenario for anthropologists.

Max pointed out two special Polyans, who call themselves Luminaries. These two have begun to question their own existence. One, in particular, was described as their version of a Renaissance man. He and his apprentice have been seeking answers beyond what they can merely observe. But what is outside their world? Our world. I found this both mind-bending and intriguing.

Most of us humans go along accepting everything we're told,

whether from a religious or scientific perspective. Or we don't even give any thought to it at all. Few bother questioning or testing to separate what's true from what's conjecture. That's fine; it works. We need the majority to go along with the way things are, keeping the social machinery intact. But we also need the rare individual to poke things, to move everyone as a group to the next level. If societal intelligence is a bell curve, these activists are outliers. They move the entire curve to the right. This is where the real progress is made, and it only happens once in a great while.

Witnessing this happen faster compared to Earth is the real magic of this project.

The Death Star

My last stop was the Server Room. This over-sized closet was lined with seemingly meaningless glowing lights like the command deck of a 1970's spaceship. They were either red, blue, or some in-between pinkish hue. This is where I connected the dots.

Max explained that each light was actually one of the Qubes that I had written about previously. In case you missed that article, a Qube, or Quantum Uncertainty Binary Engine, uses the unpredictability of quantum particles to allow seemingly random calculations. As it turns out, a separate physical Qube is connected to every Polyan, and these govern their personality, while still enabling them to make non-deterministic choices.

In essence, each Qube contains a set of characteristics, like emotional DNA, or the ability scores on a player sheet from Dungeons and Dragons. These characteristics – honesty, courage, loyalty, empathy, etc. – describe a tendency to make a decision, but the roll of a dice is the actual decider. If you roll higher than your value, you succeed, if you roll lower, you fail.

This probabilistic behavior is rather difficult to accept in our own universe. Even Albert Einstein resisted it, countering with his famous statement: 'God doesn't play dice with the world.' But as it turns out, reality isn't an absolute, but a 'maybe.' Quantum physicists use the term superposition, which is defined as something being in two states at once. But in actuality, it is neither a 1 or a 0 until you look at it, and then it picks one.

The easiest way to imagine this is to picture one of those lottery machines with the circulating air – the ones filled with ping pong balls, each with a unique number. When a flap is opened at the top, one lucky ball pops up, and that's the winning number. Now picture such a machine, but all the balls have either a 1 or a 0 on them, and we don't know how many of each are in there. That is how a quantum bit works.

But unlike Dungeons and Dragons, the value of each characteristic in Spheria can change over time. A Polyan that makes positive decisions will tend to make more positive ones. Those that make negative ones will tend to make more negative choices. This provides a feedback loop to control the emotional development of each personality. Consider a person robbing a bank. If they succeed, they will tend to rob more banks. If they are caught and go to jail, they will be less inclined to rob a bank again.

So the characteristics inside a Qube do not make up a Polyan's brain, but more its individuality. Buddhists have a concept for this called the 'germ of consciousness' which is essentially the same idea. It's what makes us humans self-aware and not predetermined.

As my visit came to an end, I had one last question for Max. If each of these Qubes makes a Polyan self-aware, why not use one in an actual robot to give it consciousness? The answer, it turns out, is simple: they cheat in Spheria. Our brains are much more than just consciousness. About 85% of our neurons are used to process sensory data, to interpret the world around us. Making a robot adequately see, hear, and feel are still unsolved problems. Since the computer of Spheria knows where everything is, it feeds that knowledge to the Polyans, and they don't need to have the capacity to detect sensory data on their own. Thus, Polyans are much more primitive than what would be required of a robot.

I guess we will have to wait a few more years to get an actual R2 unit.

CHAPTER 26 - CONSPIRACY

"I want you to watch out for the adversary. Guard yourself from any spirit of entitlement. Restrain any and all subtle temptation to gain attention or to find ways to promote yourself." - Charles R. Swindoll

Fa·ro strolled through the Colony center. The open circle was quiet for this time of day. Apparently, his Drones were hard at work somewhere else or taking a break. This possibility displeased him. He stopped at the central dais and glanced around. Still nobody. He climbed onto the platform and stood tall, like a statue.

A Drone entered the clearing, noticed him, and changed direction. It vanished into the maze of hives that formed the Colony's dwellings. Fa·ro faced the direction of the Rift and stretched tall. He could barely see over the tops of the hives. It was unbelievable how large the Colony had grown since he was created. To his right, hive structures spread all the way to the edge of the red river. Along the river, a wall of blue rock had been constructed. This prevented the river from reaching the Colony and destroying the bordering hives. The wall was one of Sa·ma's insightful designs. *I'll have to keep my sensors on that one*, he thought to himself.

Nearby, the hive buildings sprawled up to and around the base of the Council structure. Soldiers stationed at the top of each of the three faces meant the Council was in session. No one was allowed to approach during this time. *Why am I not looking down on the Leaders?* This disturbed Fa·ro; he was a god after all. But they treated him like a servant, only calling on him to break a stalemate.

He turned around on the dais and assumed a prominent pose, flailing four legs out while balancing on only three. He noticed a Drone watching him from the window of a hive. *Yes,* he thought, *I do look imposing, don't I? They should build a statue of me so I will always be remembered. I wonder if Sa·ma is capable of doing that?*

He lost interest in acting tough, stepped off the platform, and walked to his hive. He had nothing better to do but rest until, or rather if, the Council summoned him. It occurred to him that he should find out what the Drones were up to. But lethargy settled in and he decided it wasn't worth his time.

His hive was similar to the others. But instead of housing five Drones, three Workers, or two Soldiers, it was his alone. This was due to both his size, and that he was the only one of his kind. He had to crouch a little to enter the arched doorway, but the inside was plenty big enough for him. He walked to the window and looked up at the Council structure. He had a clear view, as if the Leaders gave him this hive to taunt him incessantly.

"You want to be up there," said a deep voice behind him, "don't you?"

Fa·ro whirled around. *How dare someone enters his hive uninvited?* He swung a leg to smack whoever it was. But his leg passed right through the trespasser and Fa·ro almost fell over.

"It is forbidden to strike a god, even by another god," said the intruder.

Fa·ro focused until he was sure of what he was seeing. Standing there before him in his hive was another seven-legged Polyan; indeed, a god.

"Who are you?" demanded Fa·ro.

"You should know your brethren. Has the Council not taught you anything about the gods?"

The creature before Fa·ro had a red core, unlike his violet one, which was the same as all the other castes of Polyan. "Pi·ro," answered Fa·ro. "I know the name of each color well. Tell me, will I get a new color when I join you in the Source?"

"Ah, the Source. Yes, of course you will. You can't very well have the same one as Wi·ro. Plus you are special, so you should look different than the common Polyans that grovel at your feet."

"Give me my color, brother."

"Not quite yet, I'm afraid."

"What do you mean 'not yet?'"

"Well, you see, you are a demi, not a god."

Fa·ro scratched his legs on the floor. He wasn't receiving happy news. He did not expect his first encounter with another god to go this way. "What's a demi?"

"A demi is a... pre-god. You have the shape and abilities of a god, but you have not yet earned your place beside the others. To join us, you must prove yourself. You must pass a test."

Bad news, but good news also. Hope.

Pi·ro continued, "You see, all of us were here when the

world, Spheria, was created. We participated in its creation. You have not done anything as magnificent. Frankly, you have not done anything at all, and you must earn your title. You must prove you are worthy of becoming a god."

Fa·ro remembered the story of the creation, of how the gods all formed from the legs of Ra·ju. And one by one they created a feature of this world. "How could I ever do anything as impressive as what you all have done?"

"We're in a new period: the era of life. The world is formed and stable; you can't create the mountains or the rivers. But you can develop... your Colony. You can shape the minds of your species."

"How might I do this? I'm merely a pawn, waiting to assist the Council. I have no influence over anyone, except when asked."

"Don't wait to be asked. To all of them, you are a god. Nobody will dare oppose you for fear of the wrath from us all. The Council is naive and doesn't realize this. The Leaders have been in power too long and are blinded by tradition. It's time for a new structure. Look at yourself."

Fa·ro took this literally and began scanning his legs one by one.

"Yes, you have seven legs, but you dwell here on the ground with the other lower castes. Meanwhile, the Leaders sit atop their structure high above. It's time for you to take your rightful place at the top, to make the Council bow before *you*. Only by this path will you prove you are worthy to be a god."

"The Council will never allow this. The members barely interact with me, let alone allow me to influence their activities."

"I'm not saying you convince them through discussions.

There are other ways, other options.”

“Like what?”

“You are large, powerful, intimidating... I saw you posing in the center. No other Polyan would approach you. Use this to your advantage. Begin with the Soldiers. They have unyielding respect for authority, and they will never oppose you. Win them over, and the Colony is yours. Earn the Colony, and earn your place beside us.”

Fa·ro turned back to the window and glanced up at the Council structure. Ga·zo stood guard at the top, scanning the horizon. “I will start with him,” said Fa·ro

There was no response.

Fa·ro turned back, but the room was empty. As magically as Pi·ro had appeared, so had he vanished.

220

CHAPTER 27 - THE WORLD BUILDER

"Texture is something we forget - it makes outfits look very expensive. You can do a monochromatic outfit, if you're afraid of things that are more colorful and printed, and still create interest." - Stacy London

Min leaned in close to her screen and squinted through her glasses at lists of similar numbers. She scrutinized them all, trying not to let the zeros blur together: 0.00009, 0.00008, 0.00006, 0.00010, 0.00009, 0.00009, 0.000008.

Aha! "That one has an extra zero in it," she muttered.

"So now you talk to your computer?" The voice made her jump. "Sorry, I didn't mean to scare you."

Min turned around to see Frankie standing behind her, looking over her shoulder. "Yes, you did!" she proclaimed.

"Maybe a little," he replied, winking at her. "You get so serious about numbers. I don't know how you math types can stare at that stuff all day. It makes no sense."

"It makes a lot of sense. More sense than anything else, actually. Numbers are concrete. Combining them gives you tangible results. There is no..." she paused looking for the right word, *"nonsense* about it."

He grunted at her. "I think it's all nonsense. What makes sense is the beauty of life. The colors in the world, how they mix and blend. And how the patterns in nature create a magical beauty that can't be replicated elsewhere, I mean, anywhere."

"You know," said Min, "the world you speak of is just one big mathematical formula. The repeating patterns of the nautilus shell are like the layers of a sheep's horn which is like the leaves on a cabbage. These patterns all follow a set of numbers that means, in essence, we're all just equations."

Frankie glanced at the ceiling and almost, but not quite, rolled his eyes. Then he squinted at Min. "Are you talking about us, or Spheria?"

"Us!" she squealed.

"C'mon. I'm heading out to get some textures. Let me show you the real beauty that lies out there in random patterns. It's not all as cut and dried as you make it seem."

"Um." Min fidgeted a little in her seat. "I'm supposed to be working on these numbers."

"Enough with the numbers already! You were hired to assist us all, you know. Max and Dana have been monopolizing your time. I need some help today accomplishing something real."

"Real?"

"Yes. We're done with the entire surface modeling of Spheria. Lee and I have begun work on constructing some subterranean caverns. But we want to use some new textures. Something less smooth and grittier for this, so it looks different than the stuff above ground. This will give the Polyans, when they find these caverns, something new to ponder. All part of the 'creating wonder' part of our agenda. So I need a fresh set of eyes to help me find interesting, well like you said, mathematical patterns out there in nature. So let's go." Frankie nodded toward the door.

Min looked back at her screen, frowned, sighed, then said, "Okay, I could use a little fresh air anyway." She stood up and grabbed her jacket off the coat rack behind her. "Lead the way."

#

Except for an occasional patch, the snow had melted, but the trees were barren. The grass was a far shade from green. Frankie and Min strolled around the main Health Center building. They were looking for interesting patterns, both natural and man-made. Frankie had his tablet, which had a good enough built-in camera to get some decent images. The wireless connection allowed him to work on the Spheria world from outside as long as he was close enough to the building.

"How about this truck?" Min pointed at a beat-up pickup from the 70s parked along the road. It was a faded powder blue, almost white, and riddled with rust patches. There seemed to be more rust than paint. It looked a little like a cow.

"Ooh, that's good!" praised Frankie. He ran up to the truck and began photographing the rust patches. He was so close, in fact, that the bumps and divots looked like an alien landscape. "I don't want the caverns to be red, so I can color shift these images blue to make them look more neutral. See."

He handed her the tablet and she looked at the screen. What was displayed indeed looked like the interior of a cave — an ice cave, because most of the triangular panels that formed the shape were pure white except for a couple of segments that looked like rusty stone.

"Why are these white?"

"The white ones don't have a texture yet. We start by building the geometry with basic colorless triangles. These connect to form surfaces. It's like one of those geodesic domes or the Spaceship Earth attraction at Epcot. We create surfaces in two stages: modeling and texturing. Lee and I finished the modeling back at the office. You've got to be sitting at a desk with all the 3D controllers to efficiently build things like this. But the second stage, texturing, can be done anywhere. That's what we're doing now. We are 'painting' these white surfaces with images that I'm taking with this camera. Check this out."

Frankie took back the tablet and touched a toolbar icon labeled "Position." He began changing the angle of the tablet, left then right, forward then back. As he did so, the viewpoint of the inside of the virtual cave changed, as if they were looking around. He held the tablet at arm's length and raised it over-head. They were looking at the ceiling of the cave. Then he lowered it and they were looking at the floor. He spun around slowly enough for Min to stay with him, and the view panned around the cave walls.

"So what I do is get the view to be centered on the area I want to texture, like so." The view settled on a patch of white wall. "Then I touch 'Freeze,' so it won't move anymore. I can play with distance by pinching my fingers in or out." He did so until part of the wall had grown to encompass the entire screen on the tablet. "Now I touch 'Camera,' and voila, what the camera is shooting is projected onto the surface." He handed the tablet to Min.

As she moved it around, the image from the camera — the road, the building, the sky, a stop sign — all were displayed on the fake wall inside the tablet. It was pretty cool how the image seemed to automatically wrap and cling to the curved surfaces of the cave. It was as if the image were on a big sheet of plastic that was melted onto the walls with a hair dryer.

"Now hit the 'Paint' icon," instructed Frankie.

Min did, and the image of some trees froze in place on the wall. Moving the tablet no longer changed the texture.

Frankie took back the tablet. "And that's how we paint the world! Makes you feel like a god, right? Like we can command a volcano and spew forth creation itself."

"Yeah sure Frankie. It's fun, I'll give you that much."

He clicked 'undo' and the texture of the trees disappeared. "This is going on live," he said, "so we don't want to put any textures in there that wouldn't make sense in the Polyan's world. Otherwise, we'd tear a rift in the space-time continuum."

"Really?"

"No, I'm kidding. But it would certainly confuse some of them, and that's not within the parameters of our experiment."

As they talked, they resumed their walk up the road. It traced the curve of the building to the left and started up an incline. As they got to the top of the road, they arrived at a rather odd art sculpture. A bronze family of four stood in a circle atop a marble base, holding hands. The mother and father faced each other, lifting their youngest child between them, while the older child stood opposite the younger, laughing. The thing that made this sculpture odd was that all the people were completely naked, and anatomically correct.

Min pretended not to notice and glanced away. Frankie said, "Oooh, look at that," after which he left the road and walked up to the people. Min assumed he was ogling their nakedness and her cheeks blushed. Following his gaze, she realized he was taking a texture from their tarnished surface. She joined him and indeed the mottled bronze had some interesting patterns when viewed up close.

Frankie got a good number of usable shots from their

backs and behinds but failed to get anything useful from the father's penis. "I don't think this is big enough to actually use," he said. "What do you think?"

Min chuckled and countered with, "Certainly not big enough for me!"

Frankie grinned at her response. "You do have a sense of humor after all!"

"What do you mean?" she snapped back, not hearing this type of comment for the first time.

"Well, you always seem so serious. Maybe the fresh air is doing you some good after all."

Before Min could formulate a comeback, Frankie's eyes locked onto something behind her. She turned to follow what he was looking at. Across the street the Health Center was building a parking garage. A group of construction workers walked out carrying lunchboxes. Min and Frankie watched them get into a couple of trucks and drive off.

"This is our chance! C'mon." He grabbed her hand and quickly pulled her across the street, darting into the new structure. They ducked under a barricade that said "construction zone." The garage was far from complete, having rough surfaces and layers of rebar crisscrossing all over the place. "This is perfect! Just what I was hoping to find. This is a windfall of cave textures – alien enough to not look like stone, but with enough texture and variation to make an interesting surface."

Frankie led her down a level as the garage wound underground, presumably to get out of view from the street. It was a little bit darker, but not so much that the camera wouldn't be able to get some good shots. He went to work, positioning the virtual view, then snapping texture after texture. He layered some over what he'd taken outside, so they blended together, forming even more interesting variations. Finally, the walls and floor of the virtual cave were complete. Only the ceiling remained.

Frankie raised the tablet over his head and zoomed the view out until the entire cave ceiling was on the screen. Then he froze the position once more and activated the camera. "I need a nice texture for the ceiling. I think I can get most of it in one shot, then it'll look completely seamless." Frankie wandered around the area some more, aiming the camera at different things, but didn't find anything that satisfied him. Eventually, they found an open yellow door that led into a storage room. Frankie was trying to get an image off the door when they heard footsteps approaching.

"Shit," whispered Frankie and he darted into the room. Min did as well. They stood there listening as the footsteps grew louder.

"Is it a guard?" Min murmured.

"Probably."

"Do you think he saw us?"

"I hope not. Now hush."

They stood as still as possible. Min could literally feel her heart beat in her chest. Not that they'd be in super trouble anyway, but the adrenalin rush of being where they weren't supposed to be was ramping up her system. The footsteps stopped. As their eyes adjusted to the dim light, the room became visible. It was covered on every wall and the ceiling with rolls of pink fiberglass insulation. This meant it was probably not intended for storage but would become some kind of an office. In the corner was a set of work lights on a tripod, currently turned off.

"You think he's gone?" she whispered.

"Not sure," Frankie replied in a hushed voice. "I didn't hear the footsteps leave."

Suddenly, they were blinded by bright light as the work light came on. "You there," said a loud voice from the door. "What're you doing here?" A security guard stood in the doorway, looking stern, and blocking their exit. *Oh great*, Min thought, *just what we need, a rent-a-cop with an attitude.*

"I'm taking some photos for a project we're working on," answered Frankie. As he answered, he hid the tablet behind his back. Although it might reinforce his statement, it technically wasn't a camera.

The guard squinted and scanned them up and down. "This area is a construction zone and is for employees only."

"We work at the Health Center, so we're employees. Are we good?" It was a lame attempt by Frankie. The guard obviously meant 'construction crew' rather than 'employees.'

"Not quite. It's for workers only." So that confirmed it.

Changing tactics, Frankie replied with, "Can you make an exception for us? We won't be long."

"I get what you're saying, but you can't remain here. You need to leave immediately."

"Why?"

"Regulations require it for your safety. You don't even have any protection on."

"Like a hard hat? C'mon, nothing is going to fall on us right now."

"There's plenty that can fall. Things aren't fully secured yet." The guard glanced at the insulation in the ceiling. It didn't look like it was going anywhere.

"Is there a time when we can come back?"

"You can come back when it's done."

"Okay then, thank you," Frankie breathed. He decided it was better to leave than make a scene, especially since they were blatantly in violation of the rules.

The guard stepped to the side so they could exit. Frankie and Min left and rushed up the cement incline beneath the crisscross of girders. Frankie took a look at his tablet and realized it was still filming textures and displaying them on the cave ceiling in real time. Worse, a flashing indicator showed something he never expected to see. "Shit," he exclaimed. He quickly took a photo of the cement floor and hit the 'Paint' icon, locking that image in place.

230

CHAPTER 28 - STREETS OF GOLD

"Vision is the art of seeing what is invisible to others." - Jonathan Swift

Sa·ma stumbled into the Colony. He wandered to the center, lost in a daze. An assortment of Drones swerved around him, not wanting to run into him. He sat on the edge of the celebratory staging, staring toward the mountains.

"You alright?" asked Ti·ni, who was too new to have developed a proper respect for, or fear of, the higher castes.

Sa·ma turned to face her but said nothing. A few other three-legged Drones stopped as well, and in an instant, Sa·ma had an audience. He scanned the crowd. The Drones gathered before him looked expectantly, as if he'd come to impart some knowledge upon them. Indeed, this is something that Lumen Masters were known to do from time to time.

A few Drones sat down, and he took this as a sign that he needed to share his experience. He began.

"The Colony is at full capacity. The last remaining hive, which could hold five of you Drones, was given to Fa·ro. We need to increase our dwellings before the next breeding season. We Workers spread into the wilderness in search of more building material. I headed toward the mountains but was blocked by the river. Something compelled me to follow it, and I moved deeper into the wilderness, forgetting my original intent.

"I noticed something different, or rather felt it, ahead. Not just ahead, but *below the ground.*"

"Below the ground?" repeated Ti·ni, in a hushed tone of wonderment.

"Indeed. I could feel it getting stronger and stronger. I could see it there, shapes changing beneath the ground. Then I found it on the side of a hill – a hole. A large hole... the entrance to a cave."

"Mmmm," said several of the Drones in unison as they fidgeted. Caves were a fantasy to most of them, although quite real to the Workers.

"I entered the cave. But it was unlike any cave I'd ever been in."

"How so?" asked Po·ni, forgetting her manners. Ti·ni stood next to her admiringly.

"It wasn't a room. It was a tunnel. It sloped down, and I descended. It got dark fast, but I could see a light ahead. After quite a while, the tunnel ended, and a large room appeared. At least I think it was a room, although it was more like a maze interwoven tunnels. Scattered about were glowing protrusions, emitting a faint green light. I'm not sure what they were. They almost seemed like a plant.

"I tapped one with my foot, and it seemed brittle. I hit it, and the tip broke off, and a beam shone out from it, sending light down a passage. I followed the light until it ended on the side of a wall. I smashed another of the plants, and a new beam of light emerged in a new direction. And so I followed the beams, making new ones when each one ended. I could feel I was getting closer to the thing that drew me forward.

"Suddenly, I no longer needed a beam. I stumbled upon a room bright as the Source. It was a perfect octagon, and the ceiling was pure yellow. It was not rock like the previous caverns and wasn't like any material I'd ever seen. I could only assume it was from out of our world."

The Drones began talking among themselves. This experience was way beyond their comprehension, and they tried to make sense of it to each other.

"Then I saw it," said Sa·ma.

The Drones immediately fell silent, watching him with rapt attention.

"The ceiling of the room… changed. I could see… movement. Blurry shifting patterns until it went entirely… violet!"

"Violet?" they all repeated, astonished.

"Yes. There I was, looking through a window into the Qubessence. I was gazing into the world of the gods. And every surface, every single object, was an energy crystal. In such a place, there would never be a need to forage or hunt ever again."

More whispers spread through the crowd. Sa·ma noticed the gathering of Drones had grown as he relayed his experience.

"And I know this to be true," he said, "because a god spoke to me."

Ti·ni couldn't control her excitement. "What did it say?"

#

"What're you doing here?" asked the voice from beyond the ceiling. It echoed throughout the chamber.

Sa·ma wasn't prepared to address a god, although it wouldn't be the first time. He apologized and relayed the truth, as he had done before. "I sensed something and followed it."

"This area is a construction zone," said the voice, "and is for employees only."

Employees? That was a word Sa·ma had never heard before. He had no idea what it meant. He did understand the first part. "Construction zone?" he asked. "Are you saying that this cave is being built right now?"

"Not quite. It's for Workers only."

"I'm a Worker," explained Sa·ma, realizing the stupidity in trying to explain anything to a god. He tried to recover by adding, "I guide all the Workers."

"I get what you're saying," responded the god, "but you can't remain here. You need to leave immediately."

"Understood. I'm going now." He turned to exit the room.

"Regulations require it for your safety. You don't even have any protection on."

Sa·ma stopped. Apparently, the god wasn't finished with him. "What do you mean by protection?" He looked around the barren cave. "What can harm me here?"

"There's plenty that can fall. Things aren't fully secured yet."

Sa·ma looked upwards into the billowing violet Qubessence. He imagined a piece of that breaking off, falling through into the room, and crushing him. The irony of being killed by a giant life crystal made him uneasy. He didn't want his life to be extinguished that abruptly. "Okay, I'm leaving."

This time, he moved quickly into the passage and found the light beam that would guide him out.

"You can come back when it's done," said the god.

"Thank you, supreme one," he responded. But instead of heading down the tunnel, his curiosity got the better of him. He peeked into the room and stared at the ceiling. What he saw then was beyond description.

#

"What did you see? What did you see?" squealed Ti·ni.

But Sa·ma knew she wouldn't understand. None of them would. He barely did. He could still see it in his mind. For a brief moment, the Qubessence shifted and changed. The billowing violet walls were replaced with straight red beams. They connected in a zigzag pattern, forming flat but open geometrical surfaces. They established a structure larger than the materials present. This structure clicked in his mind, and he immediately understood the elegance of its strength. It was incredible: a glimpse of arcane knowledge not meant for him to see. He felt a combination of shame and bewilderment. He was still in shock even after having relayed his story.

"What did you see?" chimed in Po·ni. "Yea what did you see?" said others, eager to hear the mysteries of their universe.

Sa·ma declared, "How to make larger and stronger structures than anything we've ever built before."

"Most interesting," came a voice from behind Sa·ma.

The Drones cowered, then scattered among the hives.

Sa·ma slowly turned around. Fa·ro was standing behind him. "Take me to this cave," he demanded. "Now!"

236

CHAPTER 29 - THE DELETED FILE

"What is a diary as a rule? A document useful to the person who keeps it. Dull to the contemporary who reads it and invaluable to the student, centuries afterwards, who treasures it." - Walter Scott

INTERN'S LOG BY OLIVIA HOLLAND

5/30: First day on the job. Everyone seems very nice. My boss Max is a little intense, but the rest of the staff seems normal. Everyone is super dedicated to this project, and I'm happy to be part of the team. It appears that they'll have me doing a statistical analysis of data all summer, but it's better than working at McDonald's. Since this is my first "real job" I've decided to keep this work journal, and this is the first entry. I'll try to update it weekly when things aren't too busy.

6/02: Loser! That's what he is. I'm sitting here preparing a nonlinear regression on a data set Max sent me, and I get an email from Randy. The bastard broke up with me! I get that the long distance thing wasn't working, but that's spine- less. Six years of emotional investment down the drain. His loss. I need to drag Ashley out for a drink tonight. Maybe I can head home sick. I don't feel like working right now.

6/03: Oh my head! I can't believe it's like my fourth day, and I'm at work hungover. I hope nobody can tell, although it's hard to act awake. Max was way too cheerful when he arrived, and I tried to be pleasant as much I could, which was hard. He seems a bit nervous around me, which is cute. Eventually, he's going to realize I've not produced anything meaningful, and with days like this… ugh. Luckily I don't have any deadlines yet, so I'm just going to browse the web today rather than look at spreadsheets. My eyes just can't take it.

6/09: Okay, so I'm over Randy. Finally, I think. I've at least stopped dwelling on it while at work. Ashley has been great. We hang out every night now, and it's been a real help. I think we're much closer roommates now, which is great since my family is in Boston. Our relationship helps me get through the evenings. At work, I've found that I can get lost in data and have no room for outside thoughts to creep in. I meditate on this a lot. It's been therapeutic, and I'm enjoying it. Ashley would call me a nerd. Maybe she's right.

6/14: Really, I need to take back what I wrote last time. I think I'm losing my vision, or going cross-eyed, or both. There is so much data from this project; it's unfathomable. It's amazing how much is produced. And they're only key level metrics, not every piece of data from the simulation, which would be incomprehensible. Speaking of that, sometimes I feel like I'm that guy on the Matrix that can look at the green numbers flowing down the screen and see a world there. I even installed a Matrix screen saver that looks like that. I crack myself up.

6/16: 6 past one isn't late. I got back from my lunch break, and Lee was standing near my desk. I asked him what's up, and he said he liked my screen saver. He said it's a nice reminder about how science fiction foreshadows reality. What if we are a simulation, and Spheria is a simulation in a simulation? What if the Polyans evolved sufficiently to run their own simulation? What if we could have simulations of simulations of simulations and it went to infinity? My head hurts thinking about it. It's crazy working with all these people who are way smarter than me.

6/24: Curious. Now and then I notice some strange glitch, some unusual piece of data in the sea of numbers. It's not something that I've been able to correlate into a meaningful trend, at least not yet. I mentioned this to Max, and he said it's probably just some random noise in the system and that I should ignore drastic outliers. This comment seems a little odd to me coming from someone who is so much of a perfectionist.

7/04: Only one here working on Independence day. :(Ashley says I need to get a new boyfriend. I think she's right. Work is fun, but it's not contributing to my social life at all. If I didn't enjoy crunching numbers so much, I'd never have worked so many consecutive days even forgetting there was a weekend in there somewhere. But I'm not unique. Most of the team is here on weekends. I'm it today, though. It's lonely and eerie also. I swear there are new electronic noises I've never heard before. A ghost in the machine?

7/08: Datasets are my life! I was analyzing yet another, and I noticed more noise. But I swear I've seen this before. I did some digging through old datasets, and I found two more with the same sequence. Something is off here. If it was noise, the probability of this happening more than once, according to my calculations, is 0.0006 percent. Spock would be proud of me. My only explanation is there is some kind of data "leak" from another system into the metrics accumulator. But that shouldn't be possible. The Spheria Project has its own isolated network for the specific purpose of preventing contamination, and hackers.

7/09: Eccentricities abound in these files. Yet, there is some organization to their randomness. It's as if there is a very low level of data bleed, and at a consistent rate. It only appears when sampling the data at a certain scale. The odd thing is I think I started to make sense of the noise, like there are actually patterns within it.

7/10: 2. That's the number of days I've been focused on investigating this… noise? Dana and Max both asked for updates, and I had to tell them my machine was too slow, and Excel kept crashing, which was perfectly believable. Dana said if I see anything unusual, she wanted to be the first to know, even before I tell Max. Her manner made me suspicious, as if she knew something but wasn't letting on. I wonder if she thinks Max is doing something inappropriate.

7/14: 4 days with no progress. I had to get some real work done this last week, so I finally got a breather. I'm going to spend the remainder of the day digging into these anomalies. Wish me luck. Right, now I'm talking to myself.

7/15: 6 more pages of numbers and Eureka! I found a pattern in the data. Nothing complete, but I figured out how to decrypt the data into human readable form. It's definitely not random noise. In fact, it has got to be bleed from some other system. Time to wear my hacker hat. I have enough information to follow the white rabbit down the hole.

7/17: 5 more hours of digging and I'm in! Maybe I should have minded my own business. If the records I found aren't fake, then I might be in a serious breach of national security. I need to tell someone at once, but I don't know who to tell first. I know Dana would want to know first, but I think I should tell Max. I don't know who to trust. In case something happens to me, I hacked their password database and added my own. Wow! is the passcode. Ashley, keep this safe and give this to the police if I disappear.

CHAPTER 30 - GOD LIKE YOU

"Leroy bet me I couldn't find a pot of gold at the end, and I told him that was a stupid bet because the rainbow was enough." - Rita Mae Brown

The Source dimmed by the time they reached the opening. Sa·ma peered in, and could almost see the glow of the strange plants below, or at least he believed so.

"You first," commanded Fa·ro.

Sa·ma entered the passage. Ga·zo came next, followed by Fa·ro, and last, by Za·zo. They felt their way forward in the darkness. The floor seemed rougher than Sa·ma remembered. Maybe he took less time to pay attention before. He wasn't in a huge hurry now. He didn't want to encounter the cave god again this soon, who clearly had said, "Come back when it's done." And he didn't say to bring others.

"I don't think this is a good idea," Sa·ma mumbled for the fifth time.

"Say that again and I will have your legs removed," said Fa·ro. "If what you claim is true, then I must reunite with my brethren. It's my destiny to take a place next to the other gods."

"I know you have seven legs, but you..." Sa·ma thought better of it and didn't finish.

"But you, what?"

"I meant... 'so you,' so you... are... the only one worthy to pass through the portal to the Qubessence."

"Exactly. More than worthy. Required. I must join the gods. I'm not meant to be here among you lower castes. It's a disgrace being trapped on the surface of Spheria."

They emerged into the twisting maze of passages with the glowing plants. The ones that Sa·ma had broken had healed themselves, as the light beams were no longer shining. He concentrated on his artifact, but couldn't sense anything unusual ahead. The portal must be closed, and this was bad news. Fa·ro wouldn't be pleased, assuming Sa·ma could even find the same room again.

"Stop stalling and take me there."

Sa·ma thought he remembered which plant he broke, and hit it with his leg. A light beam shot out and illuminated the wall next to them. It was the wrong one.

Fa·ro glared at him. "If... you... stall... again... I... will... kill... you... myself."

"I don't mean to delay; it's hard to remember."

"The first time you came you didn't have to remember. You said you were drawn to the god. How?"

"It was a feeling."

"What kind of feeling? Why would *you* have this feeling and not *me*?"

"I don't know." Sa·ma focused on his artifact. He couldn't sense the way to the cavern. He did notice, almost imperceptibly, a slight difference in one of the plants. He hit it.

A light beam shined down a corridor.

"This way," he said.

They followed the beam down the passage. The hulking form of Fa·ro behind Sa·ma cast eerie shadows in the distance. It was as if a giant Polyan was swooping down to consume Sa·ma. He shivered.

When the light beam ended on a wall, Sa·ma stopped and concentrated once more on the artifact. Again, one of the plants was different, and he hit it. A new light beam emerged. In this manner, they continued five more times. At the seventh intersection, Fa·ro, having watched Sa·ma pause and focus at each turn, made the connection. He grabbed the artifact and ripped it off Sa·ma's core.

"Nooo," groaned Sa·ma, and reached for it. Fa·ro slapped him and flung him against the wall, from which he fell upside down. Ga·zo and Za·zo jumped on Sa·ma, pinning his legs to the ground.

Fa·ro attached the artifact to his own core. Immediately he saw the world shift and become strange. The shapes forming the world became distinct, like they all had outlines around them. He looked about, and the heightened sensation made him dizzy. He sat and took in the subtle differences.

"Should we kill him?" asked Ga·zo.

"No," answered Fa·ro. "Not yet. Let's find this room."

The others waited while he took in every shape, every polygon, every surface and every plant. Then he noticed it. One plant was different: more jagged rather than pristine and smooth. He reached over and plucked it from the wall. A bright light pointed the way down the final passage.

Fa·ro bolted down it.

Ga·zo and Za·zo lifted Sa·ma to his feet and prodded him to move. He reluctantly made his way forward. The world seemed sterile and bland without his artifact. He'd grown accustomed to its imagery, desensitized to it even. Now he realized how things were without it, and how much he'd come to rely on it. He felt as sick as Fa·ro, but for opposite reasons. He shuddered again. Ga·zo pushed him, and he staggered and fell. Then got to his feet and continued, all the while prodded from behind.

Finally, they emerged into the octagonal chamber. The walls were brown stone, and the ceiling was black. Fa·ro stood in the center peering intently upwards. He was using the artifact to inspect every surface, every seam. He extended a leg up, which was large enough to touch the ceiling. He tapped on it in a few places, then turned to Sa·ma.

"Where is it?"

"The Qubessence?"

"Yes, the Qubessence!"

"The cave must be finished. The portal is closed."

Fa·ro stomped in place. He stomped around the perimeter of the room. He stomped into the passage and returned carrying a stone. He hurled this at Sa·ma, knocking him over. Sa·ma began to stand and another stone send him rolling. He felt as if his core might've cracked and he lay there flat, his legs splayed out. Then Ga·zo was upon him, pinning his four legs and lowering his core onto the top of Sa·ma's body. The point made contact, and Sa·ma felt a searing pain as his life force began to drain into Ga·zo.

"Stop," commanded Fa·ro.

Ga·zo pulled away. The pain subsided.

"I want to rip each of his legs off one by one. I want to throw his core into a river. No, that'd be too easy. I want to throw him into the Rift where he can fall to eternity. But, the Workers obey him. And he is the Lumen Master; he's got useful information that I do not yet possess."

Sa·ma wasn't so sure life among the brutality of Fa·ro and Ga·zo was the best option. He didn't yet know how, but he swore to himself to spend the rest of his days finding a way to correct this path they were on.

248

CHAPTER 31 - THE EXCHANGE

"Our sun is one of 100 billion stars in our galaxy. Our galaxy is one of billions of galaxies populating the universe. It would be the height of presumption to think we are the only living things in this enormous immensity." - Wernher von Braun

Ashley removed a beaker from the cabinet and filled it halfway with ice crystals. She placed it gingerly on the granite counter, knowing from experience that it would shatter if placed too hard. She turned her attention to the aluminum cylinder that had already been set there. Examining the top, she rotated it to face her. Taking care not to break a nail, she grabbed a small metal lever that had been crafted onto the top and pried it upward. The cylinder made a short popping sound followed by a whoosh of rushing gas, as an opening in the top formed. Ashley picked up the can and poured its contents into the beaker, making sure not to let the foam bubble over. The sweet smell of Dr. Pepper rose to meet her nostrils.

A flash illuminated the dark kitchen as lightning streaked across the sky outside the window. Ashley took a sip, and as the bubbles danced on her tongue, she waited: one one-thousand, two one-thousand. Boom! *Guess the storm is two miles away,* she thought, *a perfect night for some scary TV. Alone!*

She returned to the couch, took a seat, and put the beaker on the end table next to her. Grabbing her favorite crocheted blanket and the remote, she unpaused the show. *The Walking Dead* resumed playing a particularly dark scene. She pulled the blanket over her, tucking her feet inside.

On the TV, Rick Grimes was sneaking through a warehouse riddled with zombies. Old crates stacked to the ceiling filled the space. Chains hung here and there, painting the perfect setting for any imaginable horror scene. Rick bent low and slipped between the crates, being careful not to make any noise. Suddenly there was a knocking sound, but Rick didn't seem to react. *Odd.* Nor did the zombies seem to hear it. The scene changed to another character walking outside. The knocking continued. The sound made Ashley jump, even though she was watching a daylight shot.

Then she realized, the knocking was coming from her actual door!

She threw the blanket aside and paused the show before depositing the remote on the coffee table. She scampered to the door, a bit annoyed, but curious to see who'd be visiting her in the middle of a thunderstorm. She looked through the peephole. A short, thin Asian woman with glasses stood in the hallway. Ashley didn't recognize her, but she looked harmless.

Turning the deadbolt, she opened the door. "Can I help you?"

"I hope so," said the woman outside who looked at a Post-it note with some writing. "Are you Ashley Swanson?"

"Yes, I am. Are you here to see the apartment?"

"Um, no. Not exactly. Was Olivia Holland your roommate?"

Ashley made a slight but distinct frown. "Yes, were you

a friend of hers?"

"No, although I feel like I knew her. I'm the intern that replaced her at the Health Center. My name is Min."

Ashley's eyes glazed over for few seconds as she took this in. "So what do you want?"

Min felt she had to disarm Ashley, or this conversation was going to end abruptly. "I'm really sorry to bring up any painful memories. But I think I may have some information about Olivia's death. I found her deleted journal on a computer at work."

"Really?" Ashley's voice got higher, and her eyes widened. "Does it say why she committed suicide?"

"Well, that's the thing, I don't think she committed suicide."

Ashley just stood there in disbelief as her eyes began to water.

Min continued, "You mean you never saw her work journal?" She knew the answer but wanted confirmation.

"No," Ashley replied with a quivering voice, "how would I have seen it?"

"Look," said Min glancing down the hallway, "I don't want to say too much out here in the open."

"Yes, sorry. Where are my manners? Please come in." Ashley turned away from the doorway, trying to obscure her hand brushing the tears from her eyes. She flicked on the lights. The dark apartment now seemed warm and inviting.

Min entered and closed the door behind her. Turning, she found herself standing in the living room, which was small but cozy. It had decent furniture and a bunch of framed photos on the walls. To the right was a breakfast bar separating the room from the open kitchen. Straight ahead were two doors, one open, leading into a bedroom. It occurred to Min that she could easily live here, had she not had six months remaining on her lease with Sheila. Then she pushed the irony of that thought out of her mind. "Nice place," she commented.

"Thanks," said Ashley. "Please have a seat."

Ashley moved into the kitchen and turned on some recessed lighting. "Would you like something to drink? I've got water, soda, milk, juice, and," she opened the fridge, "yep, a fairly old beer. Probably still good. I could also make some coffee or tea."

"Water is fine, thanks. I drink coffee all day so water would be nice for a change."

"Sure thing."

Ashley proceeded to fill another laboratory beaker with water as Min looked at the photos on the wall. Shot in interesting places, they all were of Ashley and another woman her age.

"Those are all Olivia and me," said Ashley as she returned to the room, handing the water to Min. "We used to take a lot of road trips together, and hung a photo after each one. I should take them down before people start showing up to rent the other bedroom, but I haven't had the heart to yet."

"You two were close?"

"Well, yes, you could definitely say that."

"Did she show any signs of depression or unhappiness before, well, you know?"

"No, the police asked the same thing. I told them definitely no. Olivia was always happy and loved her job. She did mention there were some strange things happening that she didn't want to tell me about 'just in case.' She'd never elaborate. I figured it was just office politics and brushed it off. Now I wished I'd persisted."

"I've got a feeling she was trying to protect you. Whatever she discovered, I'm convinced it cost her her life."

A glazed look entered Ashley's eyes. They began to water but she managed to suppress a tear. "I knew it," she said softly. "I tried to get the police to investigate, but they said this was a cut and dried case." Ashley removed one of the photos from the wall and gazed at it. It was her and Olivia at the Statue of Liberty. "What did she discover?"

"That's just it; I don't know. I decoded a hidden file that Olivia had on my, um, her computer. It's a work journal that she kept, but it gets sort of weird toward the end."

"Weird? How?"

"Well, she talks about something she did 'in case something happens' to her."

"In case something happens to her," Ashley repeated. "That could be planning a suicide."

"No, I don't believe so. It's the way she phrased it and led up to it. I think she was preparing to email this file to you since you're mentioned by name at the end. I suspected she didn't get the chance. If it were a suicide, she would've completed sending it. It took a lot of work for me to get the journal. Someone went to great lengths to ensure that it couldn't be found."

"Do you have a copy of it?"

"I have a printout of it here." Min reached into her purse

and pulled out some folded pieces of paper, handing them to Ashley. "It's only three pages."

Ashley sat on the couch and read them.

Min sat next to her. She sipped her water, watching for a reaction.

Ashley completed reading and began again from the top.

"Ashley," Min interrupted. "I'm curious about the passcode she set using the characters 'w-o-w-!', most systems don't allow passwords with only four…"

"Screw the password!" Ashley scowled. "We need to go to the police immediately. She even says so. This journal is new evidence."

"Not so fast. I had the same thought, but it's not enough evidence. The police will only tip off whoever is behind this that there is a leak. That person will fix it, and will get away with murder. I want to find out what Olivia knew, from the inside. Then we'll have the evidence we need to redeem her."

Ashley stared at the frozen image on the TV screen, mulling over this new information. "Yes… Yes, that sounds like the best approach. But it's putting you at risk just like Olivia. And whoever is behind this is probably even more observant than before."

"I know, but I'm good at covering my tracks. As long as I can be sure this password works, I think I'll be able to find this hidden system and get in. Then I can dump all the data onto a flash drive and go to the police with hard evidence."

Ashley reread the last entry in the journal. "I know what this is, this 'Wow!' passcode. Olivia didn't mean it literally. She phrased it that way for me. So when her boyfriend broke up with her, she was, she was depressed for a few weeks.

To cheer her up we started hanging out a lot and became close friends. I like to sightsee, so she joined me on road trips every weekend. That's when we took all these photos.

"Sometimes, we'd go as far as a ten-hour drive to whatever destination we chose. To pass the time in the car, we'd listen to podcasts. There were several we listened to, but she seemed to take a liking to one in particular. *Stuff You Should Know*, hosted by Josh Clark and Charles Bryant. These two guys just talk about some random topic each week, as if they're having a chat about it over a beer. It's both fun and informative. I dug the format, she dug the information, and it worked for us both.

"So there was this one episode, not too long ago, about something called the 'wow signal.' It's a radio signal from space that many believe came from an alien planet. It had a hidden code in there. I don't remember what it was, but I think that's what Olivia means. Here, I think I still have it on my phone. Let me play it." Ashley began tapping on her phone.

"Great," said Min. She took a sip from her water. "I have to compliment your choice of glassware."

Ashley looked up and laughed. "Yeah, Olivia got those. She thought it was cool to drink out of lab equipment. She liked things that were conversation starters. I felt it was novel, and I've grown attached to them. Plus, they're great to measure how much you're consuming."

"I might try using one at work to see how people react," said Min. "Then again, knowing who I work with, they wouldn't even bat an eyelash."

That got a chuckle from Ashley. "Here we are, 'How the Wow! Signal Works,' released June 9, 2015." She hit the position slider to jump past the intro. It began playing at 2:23.

#

Chuck: …fascinating stuff because this is something that even the most hardened skeptic hasn't been able to fully debunk.

Josh: Yea that's, that's a good point.

Chuck: It's pretty neat that they're, they're upset probably.

Josh: So we should say that we keep saying the Wow! signal, and Chuck's talking about skeptics and everything. There is evidence of a potential transmission from an alien civilization…

Chuck: Mm hm.

Josh: …here on earth, and it's been here on earth, printed out, sitting in the Ohio State University archives, since the 1970s.

Chuck: Yea. And "potential" is the key word there. I think that's where most skeptics' heads will pop off.

Josh: Right but again…

Chuck: You gotta say potential. You…

Josh: And I did. I don't want anybody's head to pop off, you know. Um, the thing is, like you said Chuck, no skeptic has been able to say, "here's your explanation, dumb dumb", and they've tried. There have been plenty of explanations but every single one has been systematically addressed and reduced to rubble, basically.

Chuck: Yeah.

#

Min interrupted, "When do they actually say what it is?"

Ashley said, "If I remember correctly, they don't describe it until further in. They do this a lot. It's their way of building suspense."

She hit another spot on the position slider, and it jumped to 5:11.

#

Chuck: So SETI, the search for extraterrestrial intelligence, it's not a single organization, although there is the SETI Institute now since the early 1980s. But SETI is a bunch of different groups that are not tinfoil hat-wearing crackpots who are bound and determined to find if there's life out there, but they're open-minded folks that say if there is life out there let's get ahead of the game here and listen out for 'em and see if they're trying to say something to us.

Josh: Right. They're basically people who say there's just too many stars out there that have planets and that are potentially habitable to life, for us to just, it boggles their mind to think that we are the only living beings.

Chuck: They're scientists.

Josh: Right, and to these scientists the much more logical conclusion is that we're one of many civilizations out there and so they have dedicated their astronomical talents to searching for that.

Chuck: Yeah and this all started happening in the early 1970s in earnest and…

Josh: I think it actually started in the '60s in earnest but with the Big Ear it was in the '70s, with their SETI program.

Chuck: That's right 1973, The Ohio State University Radio Observatory.

Josh: Ha ha.

Chuck: I love that you laugh at that every time. Ha ha. They have something called the Big Ear, or had something called the Big Ear.

Josh: Yeah.

Chuck: They needed a golf course though, so they got rid of the Big Ear.

Josh: Even worse than that, the Big Ear radio telescope at Ohio State was demolished, not to build a golf course, but to expand an existing golf course.

Chuck: Um, we need another nine holes.

Josh: Right, we need another clubhouse.

Chuck: Well I think the Big Ear had seen its best days by that point, so don't feel bad for the Big Ear.

Josh: I still feel bad for the Big Ear.

Chuck: So 1973, the Big Ear starts scanning, listening for stuff out in outer space.

Josh: Hence the name.

Chuck: Hence the name. And what would happen is, because it was 1973, it would print stuff out on a dot matrix printer, and a student assistant would take that printout of what it was listening to and take it to another volunteer — teachers, professors — and they would just basically look at all these numbers page by page by page.

Josh: Yeah, if you've ever seen the Wow! signal it's just numbers, 1's, 2's, maybe a 3 here or there.

Chuck: Yeah, it's the level of background noise in space.

Josh: Exactly. So a 1 is a blip, a radio transmission, that was one times the intensity of the normal background noise in space on a particular frequency, right?

Chuck: Yeah.

Josh: A 1 is nothing, like there's 1's all over the place all the time.

Chuck: 1's, 2's and 3's.

Josh: All very common stuff. So these, these poor astronomers who are donating their time to the Big Ear telescope were basically analyzing this stuff with their eyes.

Chuck: Yeah. There wasn't like a computer program to spit it into.

Josh: …they would look at a whole night's scan of deep space from a radio telescope, again, with their eyes, going over the sheets and sheets of computer paper, dot matrix printer paper. And that's what this guy named Jerry Ayman, who is an astronomer at Ohio State, was doing on August 18, 1977. He was looking over some stuff from three days before.

Chuck: Yeah. And so he's scanning all the stuff and there's 1's, 2's, and 3's and he's, you know, he's watching Love American Style on TV and eating his TV dinner and he's bored out of his mind.

Josh: I used to love that show.

Chuck. Ha ha. Love American Style?

Josh: Mm hm.

Chuck: And he's bored out of his skull and then, um, well here's another important thing to point out because it was also 1977 at this point. They didn't have double-digit printouts, it just went 1 through 9 and then started with the letters A, B, C, as 10, 11, 12, and so on.

Josh: Right, exactly.

Chuck: So he's reading this stuff and he sees 6-E-Q-U-J-5 which means the transmission at its peak of U peaked at thirty times louder than anything they've ever seen before…

Josh: Than the normal background noise.

Chuck: And he circled it, and put 'wow exclamation point' on the paper, and that's why it's the Wow! signal.

Josh: Exactly. And this is a big deal. I mean, like in this huge ream of dot matrix paper filled with 1's and 2's and maybe a 3 here or there, there's a U standing in the middle of this string, this transmission…

Chuck: It started at 6, which was high.

Josh: Yeah. I mean 6 alone would be like this is kind of significant. This thing went up to U! And, uh, like you said, he circled it and wrote 'wow' next it and it became the Wow! signal and, almost immediately, they started investigating this thing.

Chuck: Sure.

```
Josh: And there are a lot of details to the
Wow! signal that, uh, make it even more impres-
sive than just the fact that it peaked at U. It
started at 6 and ended at 5 and peaked at U.
There's a lot of different aspects to the Wow!
signal that make people say, "what in the name
of God is this?"
```

#

Min reached over and pressed stop on Ashley's phone. "I see what you mean. The password must be 6EQUJ5."

"Is that long enough?" asked Ashley.

"Six characters should be, for a minimum length."

"Okay, so now what?"

"So now," replied Min, "I play detective, find the hidden system, and break into it. Give me some time. I'll get to the bottom of this."

"Okay, please let me know what you find out."

"I will. Thank you for your time and the water."

"No problem. Speaking of time..."

"Yes?"

"Would you like to hang out and watch a movie?"

Now? Min thought. Then she looked at Ashley, who seemed shaken. It was obvious that she could use a friend right now, and Min wasn't going to work on the problem until tomorrow anyway. "Yes, that'd be great," she said.

"Cool!" Ashley gave Min a wide grin. "I'll make some popcorn."

262

CHAPTER 32 - CONFINEMENT

"You can chain me, you can torture me, you can even destroy this body, but you will never imprison my mind." - Mahatma Gandhi

Sa·ma stirred in the darkness and changed positions. The barren floor beneath him was less than ideal for sleeping. A slight vibration through the ground indicated the approach of a visitor. Light flooded the room as a large door was pried open from the outside.

The cell was triangular at the base and tapered to a point. It was the hollow interior of the Council building. The room had no windows and only a single large door which now stood open. Long ago, this room had been a shelter against attacking Zalisk, at a time when the Colony was much smaller than today. In Sa·ma's lifetime, it had only been used for storage and had all but been forgotten. Until now. It had been repurposed as the Polyan's first prison.

The room was completely empty, save for a shallow hexagonal pit in the center. The light faded as the door was closed, replaced by the dim glow of a small yellow shard. Ga·zo walked over to the pit, tossed it in, and sat. Sa·ma crawled over to the edge of the pit, across from Ga·zo.

"I was sent to confirm you're still alive," said Ga·zo. "I

could care less really. If it weren't for Fa·ro's wishes, I would end you right here and now."

"Ugh," grunted Sa·ma.

"That all you've got to say?"

"I have a lot to say," hissed Sa·ma, "you just don't want to hear it."

"I must remain here a little while. If you talk, I've got no choice."

"It doesn't matter. You have a closed mind, and those like you are the reason our Colony will perish."

"Ha! The Colony is stronger than ever. The Leaders are the problem. They are weak, and only now, with Fa·ro engaged, are decisions being made. We used to flounder, paralyzed by indecision. Now the Council defers to him to end the gridlock. He is a god among us. We've entered a new era, and the Colony is unstoppable."

"Nothing is unstoppable. Even the largest Troaten will grow too large to sustain its own girth; it'll shrivel and die." Sa·ma regretted not being able to refer to the story of the Rift. "That belief is delusional."

Ga·zo poked at the shard with one of his legs, flipping it over.

"You're wrong," he said. "Your caste can't understand. All you understand is how to build. You don't understand strength, don't understand power, don't understand how to kill. We Soldiers live and feel death, and it sustains the Colony. We're more organized now and can hunt better than ever. The Leaders are useless. Fa·ro tells us when to go out, and the Council just bends to his will. And soon there will be two of them, and the Leaders will be that much more unnecessary."

"What do you mean 'two of them'?'"

Ga·zo beamed. "There is a violet bubble rising toward the Source. Soon we'll enter a breeding season. Fa·ro has demanded that the Council make another seven-legged Polyan, another god. With two, the irrelevance of the Council is assured, and the Leaders don't even realize it."

Sa·ma pondered this. Ga·zo seemed to enjoy having made him uncomfortable. The two opponents sat in silence, mesmerized by the glittering yellow shard.

"You need to stop this," Sa·ma finally said.

"Stop this!" scoffed Ga·zo, leaning back on three of his five legs. "I can't wait for it to be done."

"Listen," pleaded Sa·ma. "I know the Council members have trouble agreeing on decisions, but that's okay. Only the important ones are actually needed, and those are the ones they agree on. The real danger is having one Polyan making the decisions. There will be no balance, no counter opinion. Everything will be in service to Fa·ro's personal agenda."

"Correction. Fa·ro's and the new god's. It can't be selfish with two of them. Together they can fulfill the purpose that the Council has floundered at."

"So what of the Council then? What role does it play in all this?"

"I'm not sure. I'm not involved in those discussions. But I would guess the Leaders will debate and provide options, and the gods will then decide on courses of action."

"I find it hard to believe Fa·ro will care about anyone's opinion. Something doesn't add up. Why would he want another god to compete with him?"

"Gods don't think the way we do. They are divine, after all. They don't get caught up in the paralysis that prevents the Council from making decisions. Fa·ro calls it the 'duality,' two gods are stronger than one."

"Fa·ro was created by the Council. He may have seven legs, but he is no god. We both have seen his rage, his temper tantrums, his loss of control. That's not the behavior of a god. That's the behavior of a child with too much power and no constraints. Our blind devotion to him merely because he appears to be god has weakened the Colony. It's divided us, pitting Polyan against Polyan. Look at me in this cage. It was never like this before. We always worked as a cohesive unit, a single mind functioning together for the good of all."

"He is no god?" mused Ga·zo. His vision sensors focused, and he stared at Sa·ma. "You will pay for your blasphemy. Once Fa·ro hears your words, even he won't be willing to keep you alive any longer." Ga·zo grabbed the yellow shard and stood in one quick motion. The door opened, again bathing the room in light. Then with a crash, the room returned to darkness.

Sa·ma sat in the stillness. His fate was with the gods now.

CHAPTER 33 - COFFEE BREAK

"I like coffee because it gives me the illusion that I might be awake." -
Lewis Black

The lighting in the office was reduced to a scattering of incandescent lamps on desktops. Min was the only one still there. The others had all gone home, having worked most of the night. Tomorrow was a big day. Graham was arriving early for an update on their progress, and they wanted to have reliable results. Their continued funding depended on it.

Min needed to finish a critical set of calculations for a report. She'd gotten used to working late, becoming a night owl, so she didn't mind it in the least. She kept working, even after the cleaning crew came and went, shutting off the main lights when they left.

She rubbed her eyes beneath her glasses. They felt gritty, as if she was developing rheum while awake. She blinked a few times and the lines on her monitor blurred.

"Blasted numbers!" she exclaimed out loud. She looked around embarrassed but realized nobody was around to hear her. So she shouted, "BLASTED... NUMBERS!" It felt good.

She stood up and, grabbing her over-sized mug, walked to the kitchenette. The Keurig blinked its yellow LEDs like a puppy asking for attention or to get a treat. Min complied, feeding a Dark Embers k-cup into the machine. Soon her mug was filling up with the glorious liquid fuel. Since one wasn't enough, she put in another cartridge and filled her cup to the rim. After taking a sip, her vision seemed to instantly clear.

"Ah," she sighed. "That's better. Good boy," she said, patting the coffee machine.

Upon returning to her cubicle, she noticed her screen had changed. It was all blue with large white letters. It said, "System Failure, reboot required," along with a bunch of meaningless numbers.

"What the…"

She pressed enter but nothing happened.

"Goddamn, son of a bitch!"

The computer wouldn't respond.

She pressed ctrl-alt-delete. Nothing.

She moved the mouse. There was no visible cursor.

After a moment of frustration, she turned off the power. The screen went black. She took another sip of coffee, noticing the similarity of the fluid to the monitor before her. After about 20 seconds, she turned the computer back on. It booted up to the login screen, and she entered her credentials. Once the desktop appeared, she clicked the icon for the "Spheria Development Environment." Her screen changed again to the words "System Failure, reboot required."

"Huh?" she muttered, now puzzled.

It must be the server, she thought.

She drummed the desk with her fingers, trying to decide

what to do. She knew the key code to the server room, but she'd never been in there alone. And she'd never logged into that terminal before. But nobody was at work, and she wanted to get a lot more done. She stood up, threw on her sweatshirt because it was cold in the server room, and grabbed her mug.

Walking over to the server door, she entered 6174 into the keypad. It beeped and turned green. She opened the door, and a brilliant pink light washed over her. It took a few moments for her eyes to adjust to the brightness as she stepped into the room. The door closed behind her with a satisfying click and beep. She wasn't sure, but it seemed that there were more red Qubes than usual. She shrugged and moved to the desk on the far wall. Sitting, she placed her mug in front of the keyboard. Then, thinking better of it, she moved it to the empty stool next to her.

She wiggled the mouse, and the screen lit up, blue with white letters: "System Failure, reboot required." Yep, this confirmed it. Something unusual was happening.

The server room consisted of the panels of Qubes, four tall server cabinets, and a work surface. Two of the server racks contained nothing but hard drives to store the massive amount of data being produced. The third rack held actual servers. The fourth rack was for future expansion, so it was currently being used as a storage closet.

Under the desk, on the floor, was a Lenovo System x3500, which was used to generate the human-simulation interface or HSI. It served two roles: to provide image data so the humans could see what the world looked like in their visors, and to allow them to interact with the world. This was the machine that their own personal workstations were connected to.

The architecture of the project was distributed, meaning the various pieces performed their roles in relative isolation. A rack of Stratus ftServer 6800 machines, designed specifically never to crash, managed the state of the world. They tracked the location of every virtual object in Spheria. The Qubes were utilized when Polyans made choices. And the HSI was used to bridge the human and simulated worlds.

Because of the relative isolation of each subsystem, Min knew she could reboot the HSI without affecting the simulation. She hoped this was the issue since she didn't dare to touch the servers. She slid back, got onto her knees, and crawled under the desk. The mini-fridge sized box sat on the floor, black and silent, with only one LED on the front, pulsing red.

"That can't be good," Min said to herself.

She fumbled around the back looking for a power switch, but after not finding one, decided to press the red light.

The computer made a loud "pop" which startled her. She jumped, hitting her head on the top of the desk. "Ow! Dammit!" she exclaimed rubbing her head. The computer was now dark, no lights at all. She pressed the front again, and a loud whine started as the fans turned on. Then the light turned blue; a good sign.

She slid out from under the desk and collided with the stool. It tipped over, and she heard a smash. Before she saw it, she knew what'd happened. Her mug lay shattered, and coffee was spreading across the floor panels.

"Shit!" *Max is gonna kill me.*

Without hesitation, she took off her sweatshirt and threw it onto the spill. It soaked up much of the coffee. *A stain is worth not getting fired.*

Then she realized that she was sitting on raised panels. They're used in server rooms to allow wires to run beneath the floor: cabling, power... electricity. *Damn!* She had to get down there.

She opened the rack used for storage. There was a roll of paper towels hanging from a dispenser inside the door. Right above it was a bumper sticker that said "Screw Minecraft."

Ha. But she felt too much urgency to chuckle.

She pulled a bunch of towels off the roll and shoved them under her sweater lying on the floor. Then she rummaged through the contents of the cabinet: a broom, a plastic bin of screws, a flashlight (*that would've been helpful*), a set of raingear (*what's that for?*), and on the top shelf, the item she was looking for. She reached up and grabbed the "double cup floor puller." The device looked like a bar with a large suction cup on each end. It was clever actually. You placed it on one of the floor panels, turned a lever, and you instantly get a handle to lift off the panel.

She did this to the panel next to her spill, and removed it, setting it aside. She grabbed the entire roll of paper towels and peered under the floor. It was too dark to see anything.

She retrieved the flashlight and tried again. The floor was littered with wires crossing in every direction. Some were data, but others were larger, and probably power. Those were the ones she was worried about. She reached under the spilled-on panel and began wiping the underside. She felt this would be better than lifting it since she wanted to prevent more coffee from dripping through.

Feeling satisfied with the panel, she next tackled the underfloor. She climbed down into the space, which was about two feet high, and began dabbing between the cables. Luckily, there wasn't too much fluid down there. She had reacted fast enough, the risk was averted, and nobody would know the difference.

She turned the flashlight off and placed it on the floor above. As she started to exit, something unexpected caught her eye in the subfloor darkness. She squinted again to confirm. Indeed, her eyes were not playing tricks on her.

CHAPTER 34 - PUTSCH

"The so-called lessons of history are for the most part the rationalizations of the victors. History is written by the survivors." - Max Lerner

The Leaders stood outside the columned Chamber, atop the Council structure. They watched the violet bubble grow closer to the Source as it rose on its ascending trajectory. Inside the columns, Fa·ro paced about, apparently nervous about meeting another of his kind.

It was a tough sell, but Ga·zo had convinced the Leaders that having another god would be a wise decision. There would be backup for Fa·ro, and they could take turns breaking ties. They could both travel with Sa·ma to learn the ways of the Lumenaries. That is if Sa·ma ever returned from wherever he was off to.

The Council members were divided, once again, about this option. But Fa·ro broke the tie, choosing to have another of his kind. The Leaders were pleased by his decision since he would now share their attention with another. This was as close to an act of selflessness as could be made. The Leaders' respect for him had grown that day.

Fa·ro checked to make sure that everything was in place. An empty seven-sided core crystal was sitting in the center of the room. Seven orange elongated crystals had been set near each facet of the core. Nothing was left to chance, and the Council had experience and practice to build on. It should go smoother this time.

The eight Leaders entered, and seven took a place near each leg crystal. Ki·sa was the odd Polyan out this time, and he stood next to Fa·ro. They'd both watch the action and assist if something went astray.

The color of the Source shifted, and it cast a violet hue across the world. The Polyans didn't have to look at it to know this – they could all feel it, the strong urge to replicate themselves. Even Fa·ro felt it, although he didn't know what to make of the desire. He fidgeted as the surging energy made him uncomfortable.

The Leaders in their positions began to gyrate in slow circles, first clockwise and then counterclockwise. Even Ki·sa made these motions next to Fa·ro. Fa·ro tried to copy them but was less graceful. Regardless, their cores began to glow with building energy, illuminating the inside of the Chamber.

Each of the positioned seven Leaders, at the same time, touched the base of their body core onto the point of the leg below them. Their life force flowed out, filling each leg with their surplus energy. But these legs were larger than normal, so each Council member became nearly depleted. This outcome was expected, and they rolled onto their backs exhausted.

Fa·ro and Ki·sa then moved around the empty core in the middle, attaching each of the legs one by one. As they did so, the energy from each leg flowed into the new core, turning it violet. But, like when Fa·ro was made, it wasn't enough to animate the new Polyan; the core wasn't yet opaque, and the new god did not move.

"This happened last time," said Ki·sa. "It took all eight

of us to provide enough energy. I will add mine now."

With that, he climbed onto the core, pressed his body against the point, and allowed his energy to drain out. As he approached depletion, he gave Fa·ro a wave of success before falling off onto his back and lying still.

For a moment, nothing happened. Then the legs of the new god began to twitch. Fa·ro sprang into action. He jumped on the nearest leg and pried it from the core, severing the link between them. Then he systematically repeated this for the remaining six, until they all lay dormant beside the legless body.

Having come full circle, Fa·ro again faced Ki·sa's prone form. He straddled it and pressed the point of his core down, draining his remaining energy. Ki·sa's legs fell lifeless to his side.

Fa·ro repeated this process on Me·sa, then Wu·sa, then Co·sa. He drained them one by one until their life force was completely gone. By this time, Fa·ro was full to capacity, so he dumped some of his energy into one of the large detached leg crystals. When it became full, Fa·ro felt hungry once again. He proceeded to eliminate the remaining helpless Leaders: Yo·sa, Ju·sa, Pi·sa, and Vu·sa. The room was a mass of intertwined limbs and clear Polyan cores. For good measure, Fa·ro circled again and smashed each former Leader's core to pieces.

Hearing crashing noises, the three Soldiers guarding the chamber entered. They couldn't believe their eye sensors. In the center of the room lay the large seven-faceted core, gleaming with an abundance of violet energy. Around it, a mishmash of body parts lay strewn like a giant wreath. The Soldiers looked at Fa·ro in astonishment, expecting some kind of explanation.

"Friends!" began Fa·ro. "The Council has failed. The

Leaders are no more. I am now taking their place as ruler of this Colony. Call your brothers! The feast in this room is a prize for the Soldiers."

The three guards paused, trying to make sense of what they were seeing and hearing. Ga·zo, remembering Sa·ma's words, had a brief sinking feeling.

"Are you with me?" asked Fa·ro.

Ga·zo looked around at the shattered remains of their previous government. Then he looked at Fa·ro standing bold and majestic, glowing like the god that he was. Turning to the other two Soldiers, he commanded, "Follow me." He left, and the others rushed after him.

A few moments later, Ga·zo returned. A line of Soldiers, depleted from their own procreation rituals, entered behind him. One by one they mounted the central core, each taking a drink of refreshing energy. Eventually, the core and the additional leg were empty. All the Soldiers rested in the Council Chamber.

Fa·ro climbed onto the inert god's core, towering above the milling audience. "The tragedy today is what legends are made of," he said. "The Council has failed to create another god, and it has cost the Leaders their lives. This proves that there can only be one of me and that my rightful place is leading you all. I promise not to take this responsibility lightly. In this role, I will make this Colony more prosperous than it has ever been before. Alone, I will rapidly make decisions without bias. The paralysis of the Council, which has crippled our ability to react and adapt, is no more. Bow before me. Bow before your god!"

Puzzled looks were seen among the Soldiers. Then one bowed, then another, then all of them bowed before the glory that was Fa·ro.

#

Later, Fa·ro stood alone in the Council Chamber. It was his chamber now. *Fa·ro's Chamber.* He had each Soldier carry a piece of debris when they left, so the room was clean and empty now. He lay upon the central dais and called forth, "Pi·ro, I've completed your test. Come take me to the Source."

Pi·ro appeared before him.

Fa·ro felt a rush of excitement; the time was here. He was finally a god.

Then Pi·ro spoke. "Fa·ro, you are an impressive speci-men, more than worthy of joining our ranks. You have indeed passed the test. Well done. Now you may join us in the Source."

"I am ready. Take me."

"I'm afraid it's not that easy. I cannot take you there."

"What do you mean, you can't take me there?"

"Like each of us before you, you have to find your way. Then you may take your place beside us."

Fa·ro squinted at the god before him. Betrayed and furious, he hungered to strike him more than anything he ever wanted to do. But he wasn't stupid, so he held back.

Pi·ro continued, "You have this entire Colony at your disposal. With this many Polyans, you should be able to move mountains and bring the Source to you." Then with a big smirk, "I will tell the others to await your arrival." With that, he vanished.

Fa·ro looked up at the Source. It appeared to be far above them... but not that far. He dropped down, rushed out-side between the pillars, and nearly collided with the guarding figure of Ga·zo.

"Ga·zo! Go, bring me Sa·ma. Quickly!"

CHAPTER 35 - THE SHADOW ROOM

"Evil is a source of moral intelligence in the sense that we need to learn from our shadow, from our dark side, in order to be good." - John Bradshaw

"What the hell," Min uttered to herself. Yes, it was definitely there. Through the darkness under the floor, toward the back of the room, a faint red glow illuminated that area.

She retrieved the flashlight and focused it on the light. It looked like some kind of hatch leading through the cement floor. To make matters even stranger, an assortment of red cables converged in a bundle and descended through the same hole, propping the lid open a crack. This allowed the red light she saw to spill out.

Next to it, a red pipe descended from the base of the Qube incinerator and seemed to continue through the subfloor to somewhere below.

Not what I expected, she thought.

She crawled under the floor toward the light, in her excitement not realizing that she could've removed a panel closer to it, if not right above it. Anyway, she was small and nimble, so it only took a few seconds to reach the porthole. It looked like something from a submarine, like a manhole cover with a locking wheel on it. Actually, that's what it was. She didn't know if it was typical or not to have something like that connecting floors. But she did suspect that the cables coming through it were definitely not normal. Her first thought was, *Someone is stealing our data.* Her heart raced, and her face turned red with anger.

She lifted the cover. It squeaked, but moved smoothly. It was heavier than it looked and fell backward with a loud clang that echoed down the open shaft. She listened. No sounds emanated from below, but the red light was definitely coming from down there and was brighter now.

She peered down onto the top of the drop ceiling of the floor below. Alternating, like squares on a chess board, were white ceiling panels and black fluorescent light fixtures. Through a cutout in one of the panels descended the bundle of wires. And through this rose the bright red glow. What surprised her more, however, was seeing the red incinerator pipe emerging through the cement floor and continuing down through the ceiling tiles.

"This can't be good," she whispered to herself. Then she caught herself, listening to see if anyone below might've heard her. Only electronic white noise could be heard.

Min reached down to where the wires passed through a ceiling tile, grabbed it, and flipped it over. Directly below, propped against the wall, stood a folding ladder, as if beckoning her to descend. Curiosity getting the better of her, she rotated her body and slid through the hole feet first. Supporting her weight with her arms, she touched the ceiling tiles with her feet, found the opening, and then made contact with the ladder. Testing it to see if it would support her weight, she ducked down and descended the rungs.

What she saw in the room below astounded her. It was an exact replica of the server room above. It had a secured door, eight panels of Qubes, four server racks, and a table with a monitor in the exact same location. The big difference, however, was that every single Qube was glowing bright red!

"What…. the… hell!"

She hung there, halfway down the ladder, in puzzled shock. *Why? How?* Those were the words running through her head, finishing with *Who?*

She stepped off the ladder. Then she noticed one other difference. Instead of having an incinerator, the red pipe descending from the ceiling came to rest on the table top. Spilling from a hole in the side were a handful of inactive Qubes.

"No way!" Min exclaimed, too loudly. She startled herself.

It didn't take her long to put the pieces together. Only one explanation made sense. The incinerator above was fake, and the Qubes they put in to be destroyed instead fell through the floor emerging here. Since they were all bad Qubes, they got plugged into the panels here, which is why they were all red. She remembered Max saying the Qubes were useless to the Spheria Project. But they could be used for nefarious purposes. So they needed to be destroyed to keep them out of the wrong hands. That apparently wasn't happening.

Min felt anxious like she had to get out of there quickly. She had to tell Max. No, she had to tell Dana. No, her mind was paralyzed. *What if one of them was behind this? What if it relates somehow to Olivia's death?* She didn't know who to trust.

Her eyes drifted to the monitor. That was the answer. She needed to break in and find out what was going on.

CHAPTER 36 - ENSLAVED

"If you must break the law, do it to seize power: in all other cases observe it." - Julius Caesar

Ga·zo and Za·zo entered Fa·ro's chamber, dragging the limp form of Sa·ma between them. Fa·ro perched on the empty core crystal, as if he were on a throne, his seven legs dangling over the sides. He casually glanced down upon them. They threw Sa·ma on the ground before him.

"Rise," commanded Fa·ro.

Sa·ma looked up, got his shaking legs under him, and stood.

"Look at your ruler, the sole leader of this Colony. I command the Soldiers, the Workers, and the Drones."

"What of the Council?" asked Sa·ma, looking around.

Fa·ro laughed. "The Council is no more. Its era has passed. The Leaders' lethargy won't hold us back any longer."

"Where are the Leaders?"

"They've outlived their time in this Colony. Their complacency and inaction have resulted in their elimination. I am now all that remains at the top."

"What makes you think any of us will follow you?"

Fa·ro climbed down and approached Sa·ma, who expected to be knocked over or struck. But instead, Fa·ro propped him up with a leg and led him to the edge of the structure. Ga·zo and Za·zo followed, taking positions on either side of them. The four stood gazing down upon the expanse of the Colony. The many hives were quiet, occupied by their exhausted inhabitants.

"Fellow Polyans!" Fa·ro called out, projecting loudly. "Come out and hear me."

The Soldiers, who weren't as tired after their bonus meal, were the first to emerge from their dwellings.

Ga·zo motioned to them to enter the hives and bring the others out. This they did, and soon the ground was packed. Everyone in the Colony – Soldiers, Workers, and Drones – stood looking at the top of the tallest building.

"Everyone. I have sad news," mocked Fa·ro. "The Council's intent to create another god has failed. Tragically, the attempt cost them their lives." The crowd shot concerned glances at each other. "Shortly after this terrible disaster, I was visited by another of my kind, the god Pi·ro. He came to lift me up to the Source to join with my brethren. But I declined his offer for the benefit of the Colony. The failure of the Council made it all clear. It is my purpose, my divine destiny, to lead you into a new era of prosperity. Look at the Mountains enclosing us from the edges of the Rift. Now look at the other valleys over and around us. These lands are unconquered and contain resources waiting for us to take. Together, fellow Polyans, we will tame all Spheria! Together we will have everything we ever need in infinite abundance. When this has been completed, I will bring down the blessings of the gods. You will never want for anything again!"

Some cheers erupted from the attentive listeners.

"Bow before me, my subjects."

Many of the Polyans glanced at each other, unsure. But the Soldiers assisted them all into squatting. The entire community bowed before its new ruler.

Fa·ro whispered to Sa·ma, "See, they're having no problem listening." Then louder, "Go! Return to your hives and your new family members. Celebrate the giving of life that happened tonight. Tomorrow, we begin the glorious journey to greatness."

As the Polyans began to stand, Fa·ro turned and led Sa·ma back into his chamber.

"Phase two of my plan is a special project for the Workers. You're going to guide them as you used to, and in exchange, I'm sparing your life."

"What kind of project?" inquired Sa·ma, not wanting to cooperate.

"Remember your vision in the cave?" Sa·ma nodded. "You said you saw 'how to make larger and stronger structures than anything we've ever built before.' It didn't interest me at the time, but now it's *exactly* what I need."

286

CHAPTER 37 - SPLIT DECISION

"For years I'd thought my color was black: deep, dark, thoughtful, mysterious. Black, you can hide behind. But now I know it is red." - Jami Attenberg

Min's eyes had grown accustomed to the red light in the replica of the server room. She sat at the terminal and hit the keyboard. The screen awoke and a login prompt appeared. It had a single field with a blinking cursor: Passcode.

She typed "12345" and hit enter. The computer beeped and a message, "Invalid passcode. You have one more tries before lockout," flashed in red letters. *Nice grammar*, she thought. Her mind drifted to Olivia, her deleted file, and the conversation with Ashley. Min typed in 6EQUJ5, the values of the Wow! Signal. The words "Login correct" flashed on the screen and a desktop appeared.

"That was too easy," she muttered. The knowledge that Olivia somehow made this possible gave her chills. *This is wrong, very wrong.*

She searched for the Spheria Development Environment, but it wasn't installed. She looked at the running services. The one consuming most of the CPU was called Gridway. She opened a browser, but got an Internet restriction error. She pulled out her phone and searched on there. Wikipedia claimed it was "an open source meta-scheduling technology that enables large-scale, secure, reliable and efficient sharing of computing resources." In other words, something that spreads calculations across many different processors. *Interesting.*

She opened the task manager and flipped to the network traffic tab. A bunch of data was being sent out. This was mysterious, considering there was no open Internet connection. She drilled into the sending application, and it was listed as Tor. This one she had heard of. She'd played with it many times out of curiosity.

Tor was developed in the mid-90s by the Navy as a secure and untraceable means to communicate over the Internet. Tor soon fell into the wrong hands. It was adopted by black market weapons and drug dealers to sell illegal goods online. The most famous site was Silk Road, run by someone calling himself "Dread Pirate Roberts," a reference to the movie The Princess Bride. The FBI arrested the owner in 2013 on charges of hiring a hit man, and the site was shut down. Shortly after that it was reopened by another "Dread Pirate Roberts," further playing homage to the reference.

Tor... Gridway... no direct Internet. Min began to connect the dots. The Gridway program was using the banks of red Qubes to process some kind of calculation. It was sending the results somewhere over Tor in an untraceable manner, possibly on a dedicated line. Figuring out where it was sending was going to be impossible.

Instead, she dug in to find out *what* data was being sent. It didn't take long. She found a folder on the root drive called Project Disintegration. Inside was a wealth of information. Financial transactions in Bitcoins funding offshore accounts. Spreadsheets of feeder data. Business rule files containing algorithms to process. And, best of all, blueprints.

Min opened them one by one and was shocked. They represented some kind of large weapon, like a cannon. Yes, definitely a cannon. The next image showed it mounted to the deck of a ship. A close-up showed the connection to the deck, and a room below with wires wrapped around cylinders. A second set of wires led from the cylinders to the ship's power generator, a nuclear reactor.

It took a while to digest all the information. Min learned that the weapon was called an "Advanced Field Augmented Electromagnetic Linear Accelerator." It was the latest iteration of a type of weapon called a coilgun or railgun. This design could accelerate a simple projectile to nine times the speed of sound. The stored kinetic energy would produce a destructive force greater than any conventionally delivered explosive. It would eliminate any single target, airborne or ground based. Calculations suggested it could even destroy enemy satellites in orbit.

This technology, unlike versions built so far, required a much faster energy delivery mechanism. It needed a type of capacitor that could be charged to 800 kilowatts and then discharged almost instantaneously. The problem was, such a capacitor did not exist. In fact, there was no known substance that could perform this way. That was the problem being worked on. This entire bank of Qubes, more powerful than any super computer ever built, was crunching the numbers. It was performing chemical simulations to find the perfect composite material for the super-capacitor.

Digging further, Min found more disturbing designs. The theory was, once this new substance was found, it could charge portable cartridges, like energy bullets. They'd hold enough power in a handheld laser weapon to kill a human with a single pulse. There would be no delay between pulling the trigger and instant death. And the evidence would be untraceable.

Min's focus was broken when the keypad buttons outside the room's door began to beep. She froze. Someone was entering an access code to enter the room. She instinctively looked at the clock on the monitor - 8:50 a.m. She'd been reading all night! Her heart pounded, and she turned to meet whoever was about to enter, fearing for her life.

#

The door indicator showed red, then turned off. The keypad beeped again, and once again the indicator turned red. A third time, keys were used and this time the indicator turned green. The latch clicked and the door swung open. Max entered the room.

He squinted in the brightness and, seeing that the room was empty, closed the door behind him. He stood motionless for a minute, taking in the scene before him, allowing his eyes to adjust. Noticing the open ceiling tile, he walked over to the ladder and peered up. He frowned at the sight of it open.

Min could see him through the slits in the server rack door. Like the room above, this one had an empty rack used for storage. She'd stowed away in there, saved by the luck of Max entering the wrong combination twice. Now she watched in disbelief, discovering that Max was behind this weapons research. Knowing that he violated the trust placed in him by Graham. Knowing that he lied about not wanting Qubes to fall into the wrong hands, at the same time they were his hands.

As if reading her mind, Max scooped up some Qubes from the incinerator pipe opening. He rotated them with his fingers, examining them. Then he walked over to the nearest panel and plugged one in. Like the others, it began glowing bright red. He plugged in another and then another, and stood watching, mesmerized.

Finally, he looked at the computer monitor. He seemed

less concerned with it being on and logged into than he was about seeing the opening in the ceiling. He sat down and began examining the blueprints Min had been looking at. He flipped through the designs, pausing longest on the handheld weapon.

Something was tickling Min's nose. *Oh no.* This room wasn't as clean as the one above; there was a buildup of dust in the cabinet. She pinched her nose, and her eyes watered. Her body convulsed with a suppressed sneeze. Max cocked his head to listen. Another came, and this time Min couldn't suppress the slight constricted sound from her throat.

Max looked at the cabinet. He'd definitely heard her. She watched him stand and walk toward it, staring and listening. He drew closer and placed his hand on the rack's door handle.

/ PART THREE /

EFFLUENCE

CHAPTER 38 - THE PLAN

"Sometimes we let life guide us, and other times we take life by the horns. But one thing is for sure: no matter how organized we are, or how well we plan, we can always expect the unexpected." - Brandon Jenner

"Which way do we go?" asked Hi·ma.

"Straight, off the trail. We walk straight until we come to two mounds with a tree on each. We go through and then turn right. Then we head toward the highest mountain peak," answered Pu·ma.

"Are you sure we leave this trail?"

"Yes. Sa·ma was specific about that. That's how the meeting place has remained hidden. He takes a different path every time so that no trail ever forms."

"Makes sense." Hi·ma looked up at the darkening Source. Their travels would become difficult if they didn't arrive before darkness. "Did Sa·ma say why we're meeting like this? I mean, in the dark?"

"Yes. He said it was essential that we keep this a complete secret from the Soldiers. It's so we're not seen, let alone followed."

"This is unusual. It must be important then," said Hi·ma.

"I believe so," agreed Pu·ma. "He only gave the instructions to six of us and told each to bring another. That way the twelve lead Workers would arrive while minimizing exposure."

Hi·ma walked in silence, following close to Pu·ma. He was curious about what Sa·ma had in mind. He wondered if it had anything to do with the incident today. "Is this related to the drop?"

"That's a logical conclusion, but the arrangement was made before the incident." Pu·ma recalled the earlier visit from Fa·ro. She'd been working on unbinding a stack of beams in preparation of lifting more to the top of the tower. Then it happened, and at the worst possible time.

#

Sa·ma and Fa·ro walked side by side around the perimeter of the new structure.

"This is quite impressive," complimented Fa·ro. "You've exceeded my expectations already with height. Yet it's much thinner at the base than I was expecting."

"I understand why you think that. The structures we've built in the past, the buildings in town, are all based on stacking rocks. Since they rely on just a push downward for their strength, they have to be wide at the base and taper off at the top. Otherwise, they'd collapse over time. But in my vision, I saw a better way to build things. By using longer rocks and attaching them at the ends with joint pods and making a pattern of alternating left and right angles, we can make a structure that's hollow, but stable."

Fa·ro looked up. Rising over them, perfectly straight, was the tower. It didn't look pyramid-shaped like his Chamber building. Instead, it looked like something completely alien. It was four columns rising up in straight lines, forming a square footprint. They were connected to each other by beams – some leaning to the left, some leaning to the right, in an alternating pattern. From the Colony, it looked like one giant hollow cylinder. Up close, the emptiness was more apparent and made it look brittle.

Workers were climbing up and down the outer beams, using them as a ladder. Some were carrying new beams to the top, others were returning to get more. Fa·ro marveled at the efficiency of the operation, something he'd never admit to Sa·ma. He backed up to get a better look, and stumbled over a pile of beams on the ground. Pu·ma, who was working on getting them arranged, helped him up.

"How dare you touch me! Why's this hazard in my path?"

"Uh-um," stammered Pu·ma. "Sorry, your Majesty." Fa·ro raised a leg to swing at her, but paused at the word 'majesty.' With Fa·ro's rage mitigated, Pu·ma answered his question. "These are new beams being prepared to carry to the top."

Fa·ro looked at the beams then returned his leg to the ground. He watched as a Worker took one from the pile and began carrying it up the side of the tower. His eye sensors followed the activity to the top where two Workers were placing a new piece of the column in place. They seemed to be struggling with the vertical alignment. They both grabbed it at one end and attempted to hoist it up. As it got to about forty-five degrees, they lost their grip and it plummeted down off the tower.

Fa·ro jumped back, knocking over Sa·ma, who in turn barely had time to roll away. The beam crashed to the ground, making a large crater and spreading fragments all over them.

Pu·ma ducked the other way, getting as far out of sight as possible.

"What the Rift!" exclaimed Fa·ro. He glared down at Sa·ma, rage filling his being. He grabbed Sa·ma, dragged him to the crater, and threw him in. He climbed over him and glared down. "If you fail me, with your exotic design, I'll make good on my threat to have your legs removed one by one and hurl your body into the Rift where you can spend the rest of eternity falling."

#

"So why did they drop it?" asked Hi·ma.

"They didn't drop it; it broke as they were raising it. The push from the Source is getting stronger and stronger the higher we go. It's nearly impossible to attach any new beams to the top now. The last level took us five times longer than normal. If our progress slows too much, Fa·ro is bound to notice."

"Is that what the meeting is about?"

"Probably. I sure hope Sa·ma has a plan. If we can't reach the Source, we're all doomed to a fate like the one threatened upon him. This way."

Pu·ma squeezed through a crevice. Hi·ma saw this was the space between the two mounds with trees; kind of hard to miss. He squeezed through, turned right, and followed Pu·ma toward the tallest mountain.

The rest of the journey was made in silence. Although neither spoke, they both knew what the other was thinking. As members of the working caste under the rule of a tyrannical dictator, their value to the Colony was diminished. A light ahead indicated the squat opening to the cave. They ducked through and entered.

The inside looked unusual. The walls and ceiling were naturally formed, and as such were somewhat jagged; nothing like the smooth inside surface of their dwellings. In the center of the cave, a large yellow crystal emitted a reassuring glow. It lit the other Polyans who formed a circle around it. A quick count indicated they were the last to arrive.

"Sit," beckoned Sa·ma.

Pu·ma and Hi·ma did as told, completing the circle of Workers. In addition to the twelve of them plus Sa·ma, there was one additional four-legged Polyan. They had never seen him before.

"Fellows," continued Sa·ma, "let me introduce you to my master, Lumen Elder Go·ma." Go·ma stood and bowed.

"How is this Polyan not of our Colony?" asked Pu·ma.

Before Sa·ma could answer, Go·ma did. "I *am* from your Colony, but from a time before you can remember. Being a Lumen Master will drain your life core faster than normal, so to speak, so we grow tired of the role. I know you all believe that a Learner is elevated to Master when the previous Master dies. That can happen, but if the Master lives a long life, as I have, we elect to go into exile, passing the title to our apprentice Learner. Thus I'm a Lumen Elder, a retired Lumen Master. I've been watching the Colony from afar for some time. Nothing like Fa·ro's rise and the murder of the Council has ever happened in our oral history. It's a dark time indeed. I offer you my home here in this cave to have this meeting, where the fate of you all will be decided." Go·ma glanced at Sa·ma, giving him permission to take over.

Sa·ma stood as Go·ma sat. "Thank you all for making the trek out here this evening. We need to be brief and then complete our work before daybreak." He glanced at Le·ma. She nodded encouragement to go on. "We all, as slaves of Fa·ro, have been building his tower to the Source so he may join the other gods in their home. We all know this to be an impossibility, as the push of the Source is becoming too great to continue. This isn't unexpected. I knew this would happen, and we'd reach this point where we couldn't go on."

"If you knew that, then you've doomed us all and sealed our fate," shouted Pu·ma.

"Quite the contrary, my fellows. I've sealed our freedom from the tyranny of Fa·ro forever!"

His plan was shared, in detail, with the others. They all agreed to participate, not that there was any other option. Still, they were amazed at the resourcefulness of their Lumen Master.

"Elder Go·ma," said Hi·ma, "will you come with us?"

"I'm afraid I'm too old to attempt such a journey. I'll remain here and keep an eye on the Colony in case I can ever be of assistance again."

"Thank you, Elder," said Le·ma.

"Thank you, Elder," the others said in unison.

CHAPTER 39 - MALA SANCTIS

"If you die in an elevator, be sure to push the Up button." - Sam Levenson

Min knew she was screwed. Max was much stronger than her, and she was essentially trapped in this room with him.

Her adrenalin kicked in. She braced her back against the inside of the cabinet and her feet flat against the door. As Max turned the handle, she kicked it open with all her might. It smashed hard into his face, crushing his nose and knocking him backward. He tumbled into the ladder, which fell on top of him. He began flailing, not knowing what had just happened.

Min took the opportunity to dart toward the door. She didn't get far. As she exited the cabinet and took a step, Max was able to stick out a leg and trip her. She fell forward into the center of the room. Furious, Max threw the ladder toward her. But his aim was wrong, and it crashed into the panels on the right side of the room. It knocked loose several hundred Qubes, and they spilled across the floor toward the door, turning dark. The ladder clanked down next to Min.

Min pushed herself up onto her hands and knees and tried to move ahead. As she pulled her foot forward to crawl, something held it back. She lost her balance and fell sideways onto her hip, now able to look back toward Max. He had rotated around, still on his back, and was grasping her ankle with one hand. She kicked at it with her free foot.

His grasp was firm, and her feeble attempts to get him to release her were futile. He pulled her along the floor toward him and tried to grab her other foot with his free hand. He missed, and she pounded her shin into his face. He released her ankle and covered his eyes with his hands.

"Ahhh!" he shouted.

She didn't wait to have a conversation, and spun again toward the door. She moved too quickly and fell immediately over the prone ladder. She tucked and rolled into a ball, feeling jabs in her back from the pointy corners of the spilled Qubes. She had too much at stake to let pain slow her down, and she quickly stood again right next to the door. She hit the unlock button.

The door beeped, and the lock disengaged.

"Stop!" yelled Max as Min grabbed the handle. He was there before she could open it and placed both hands on the door to hold it shut.

"Let me out!" she yelled.

"What the hell are you doing in here?" he demanded.

"I'd ask you the same thing!" Her heart pounded. She didn't want to be talking, fearing for her life.

He took one hand off the door and reached for her neck. This was her opportunity. She pressed down on the handle and yanked the door open. For some reason, Max wasn't prepared for this, and it forced him to take a step back. His foot landed awkwardly on a single Qube and slid sideways. He tried to steady himself with his hand on Min, but his grip closed around the thin strap of her gris-gris, which snapped under his weight. Max fell backward and hit his head, with a dull thud, right on the side of the ladder.

A part of Min wanted to run over to him, to put a cold compress on his head, to soothe his pain. But she fought the instinct and darted through the door. It led into a small dark room filled with filing cabinets and storage boxes. There was one other door that said "Exit" above it. She pulled that open and it led into the main hallway. As she left, she glanced back as the inside door was closing. She saw Max lying on the floor, rubbing the top of his head. He was conscious.

#

Max tried to rise. A sharp pain shot through his brain, and he literally saw stars. He sat for a second, trying to regain his orientation. He quickly recovered and realized he had to stop Min. Finding her in the room was the last thing he expected, and it was imperative that he prevent her escape.

The urgency compelled him to push through the pain and stand up. He crawled to the door, worked through the locking mechanism and exited the computer room. In the storage room he called out "Min!" No answer, not that he expected any. She might be hiding in here, but he doubted it. He ran to the other door and exited.

Just as he stepped into the sixth-floor hallway, he heard a ding. Turning toward the elevators, he saw Min enter one of the two.

"Wait!" he shouted and began to run toward her. Each step was met with a jolt of pain in his forehead.

Hearing his voice, she turned and saw him charging toward her. Her previous look of panic was replaced with calm deliberation. She pressed an elevator call button, then stepped in the one that was open. It closed just as Max reached it.

Damn, he thought.

He watched the numbers over the elevator change from six to five and pressed the down call button. The up button was already lit.

Double damn. She'd pressed up. It would cause a delay, but only one floor since the building had seven floors.

He watched the second elevator rise through the numbers, stopping for what seemed a little longer on five. Finally, it opened, and he jumped in. He pressed button one, and that was when he noticed the problem.

"God dammit!" he shouted, and kicked at the number panel.

#

Moments earlier, Min watched Max charging at her. She knew what had to be done. She pressed the up button. It would call the second elevator, which usually parked on floor one. That would give her enough time.

She got in and pressed five, then one. The doors closed. She heard Max's footsteps outside as the elevator began to descend. *Ding.* The doors opened on five. Min opened the utility door inside the elevator and pulled the stop lever. The elevator locked in place. This was a seldom known feature of elevators, but one she used before loading dorm items, not wanting it to take off without her. She jumped out into the hallway and pressed the up button, just in time, too. The second elevator door opened.

She ran in, holding the doors open with one hand, and pressed every button on the panel. *That should help,* she told herself. Returning to her elevator, she disengaged the stop, and the elevator began descending once again. Max would take a ride to seven, then on the way back down he'd have to stop on every floor except for six. That should give her a couple of minutes of lead time to get to Dana.

CHAPTER 40 - THE MACHINE

"Imagination and invention go hand in hand… Shift a few pieces of furniture around the living room, and you have yourself a fort." - Alexandra Adornetto

In the dim, hazy light, Fa·ro rested in the chamber at the apex of the largest structure in the Colony. It was spacious when empty. Looking around, he recalled the carnage that filled this room when the Council was eliminated. It was his Chamber now. As the sole ruler of the Colony, sitting on his throne, he was truly the greatest Polyan in the world.

He heard footsteps approaching from outside. He stretched his legs long, intending to intimidate any who entered. He awaited an arrival.

Ga·zo appeared and approached the throne. The leader of the Soldiers never wavered from his loyalty to Fa·ro. As such, he was one of the few allowed to approach without permission. Still, it was early, and Fa·ro wasn't fond of being awakened. Ga·zo stopped in front of the throne, bowed, then looked up at Fa·ro.

"Your honor," said Ga·zo, "we have a problem!"

Fa·ro eyed him wearily. He grumbled, "A problem?"

"Yes, the Workers... the Workers are gone. All of them!"

"What do you mean?" inquired Fa·ro, not comprehending.

"Gone. There are none in the Colony. They seem to have vanished during the night."

Fa·ro, only caring about a possible delay to his project, jumped off his throne. He ran through the columns to where he had a perfect view of the tower and the mountains beyond. The tower stood majestic in the dim light of the morning Source, a silhouette against the world beyond. It rose halfway to the Source, the tallest erection that ever existed. Taller even than the mountains.

He activated his artifact and scanned the horizon. The outline of the tower appeared yellow in his vision, as this was the thing he'd tuned it to observe. However, he could also sense, even through obstructions, every living creature, outlined in violet.

Not far beyond the tower, he could thus see a milling herd of Zalisk. *Very dangerous*, he thought, *even to a god*. Then he noticed them, a large mass of Workers huddled around the base of the tower. They were moving about, forming lines of some kind. Something was happening, something he hadn't approved.

#

Hi·ma stood at the base of the tower, facing the Rift, which was nearby. The next bubble, green, was just rising over the edge. She followed its trajectory with her eyes to the Source. It was still dim from the previous night. Soon the bubble would hit the Source, and the world would be filled with green light causing the plants to grow. Her gaze shifted to the tower. It was so tall, even half finished, that the top seemed to vanish at a single point. It would never be completed.

Several more Workers arrived from the foliage. They made their way through the crowd to Le·ma, who stood beneath the tower.

"It's done," said Pu·ma, "The perimeter is secured."

"Good," said Le·ma. "That'll buy us the necessary time. Is anyone else there?"

"No," answered Pu·ma. "I walked the length and it's complete. I was the last one out."

"Then things are going smoothly." Le·ma had a bad feeling but didn't want to show it. Sa·ma should have been there by now. They definitely didn't have unlimited time to execute their plan.

As if reading her mind, Hi·ma asked, "Where's Sa·ma?"

"He's completing the last piece of the plan and will be here shortly." Trying to distract her questioners from his obvious tardiness, she changed the subject. She stepped on a pile of beams to speak over the crowd and said, "It's now or never. Whether this plan succeeds or fails, we'll never be accepted back into the Colony. Any caught by Fa·ro will certainly be killed. If any of you are having second thoughts, now is your chance to return to the Colony."

"There is no return," said Pu·ma.

Le·ma realized she was right and the error of her words. Before she could form a response, Hi·ma did. "Nobody wants to return; we're in this to the end. One way or another, Fa·ro will oppress us no longer."

"For the Colony!" they all said in unison. Le·ma didn't miss the irony.

As if on cue, the foliage on the far side of the tower

began to flutter. Sa·ma emerged, pulling some sort of contraption. The gathered Workers stood motionless, not comprehending what they were seeing. It wasn't a structure like a building, but an interconnected series of various colored stones, similar to a sculpture. It resembled a cylinder, lying horizontally, but wasn't completely solid. The shape was formed by six long segments. Each was a sandwich of colored rock: brown on the outside, then red and blue toward the inside of the cylinder. Between the blue surfaces was a hollow tube-shaped space.

Sa·ma dragged this jumble of parts toward the tower. Others, overcoming their surprise, rushed to help him.

"Grab the base," he said. The structure was supported by a brown rectangular platform, which behaved like a sled. Those who could fit pushed it along. Sa·ma guided it up to one of the legs of the tower. He shifted it so that it formed a line with both the closest leg and the one beyond it.

"All, gather over there and take hold of the rope trailing behind it," directed Sa·ma. Those who'd been pushing it moved behind as told. Indeed, a line was dragging on the ground. It fed through the cylinder and emerged from the front as well. The length inside floated in the air, repulsed by the surrounding blue rock. Sa·ma took a beam from the construction pile. He attached the front end of the rope to it and held it near the sculpture.

"Pull," he said, "and don't let go."

The Workers began to pull on the rope, and it easily slid backward. The beam touched the front, and a massive amount of tension developed on the line. The blue crystals were pushing the beam away. But since there was a space between them, the beam slid inside, suspended in the center, as had the rope.

"Pull!" commanded Sa·ma again.

They pulled harder. Slowly, the beam moved deeper into

the cylinder. It wobbled and spun a bit, as the conflicting forces of the blue rock competed to eject it. The rope creaked with the strain, and pulling became harder.

Sa·ma joined the others and grabbed the remaining length of rope. They all strained together. The beam moved further into the cylinder and was nearly to the back.

"On the count of four, release it," directed Sa·ma. "One… two… three… four!"

The rope was released. The beam was ejected out of the front of the cylinder with incredible speed and force. It slammed into the first leg of the tower, completely obliterating it, and continued into the second leg, knocking it to the side.

#

Fa·ro watched as the Workers lined up around an object. They seemed to be forming a line and moving slowly away from the tower, stopping, then moving a little more. They all fell backward at the same time.

Something caught his eye. The tower appeared to shudder. He focused on it, and something wasn't right. The tower wasn't pointing exactly at the Source but leaned slightly to one side. It began to tilt, slowly at first, but then faster. In a blur, it collapsed sideways. His dream of reaching the Source had been thwarted by the same Workers he'd enslaved to create it.

If Fa·ro's core could've turned red, it would have. "Ga·zo! Gather your Soldiers. I want all of them, every last one, destroyed."

CHAPTER 41 - BUTTON MASHUP

"One thing I'm not going to do is chase staying alive. You spend so much time chasing staying alive, you won't live." - Patrick Swayze

The elevator arrived on the first floor, and Min exited. Sunlight rained down through the skylight, illuminating the potted trees and benches. It was blinding to her red, puffy eyes. *What time is it?* she wondered. She looked down the hallway in the direction of campus security but headed in the opposite direction instead.

\#

Dana was preparing for the board meeting. In one hour, she was to present their grant awards to Graham in the Experience Room. Appropriate, as this was their gateway to another world – a world with different rules that made sense, in a weird way. It was completely opposite of the grant process on earth. She wondered how anything ever got done given that some of these government agencies were still functioning in the Dark Ages. She saved her presentation to a flash drive just as Min stormed into her office.

Min was out of breath.

"Can I help you?" Dana scowled at her.

"... Max... wrong.... weapon..." she stammered, barely able to get the words out.

"Weapon?" Dana was intrigued. She stood and assisted Min to a chair. "Relax. What's gotten you so flustered?"

"It's Max... I found a room... a duplicate of the server room... but all red... he's working on a super weapon... working for the military."

Dana stared at her blankly, trying to process what she'd heard. Min knew what she said didn't make much sense. But she also knew she was in danger. She needed Dana to know about the room in case something happened to her.

"Olivia... It all makes sense now," said Min. "She didn't commit suicide. She was onto this, and something bad happened to her. I want you to know before it happens to me."

Dana rose, went to her office door and locked it from the inside. Then she pulled a bottle of water out of her mini fridge and handed it to Min.

"Please, calm down," she said. "We're safe here. Let me know what this is all about."

Min twisted open the bottle cap and began to chug it down. She realized she'd not drunk anything all night and was parched from the dry air in the server room. She drained the bottle.

"Well, I sense you've had an exciting night."

"Very," Min replied.

"How so?"

"I was in the server room, our server room..."

"Our server room," Dana repeated. "What other server

room is there?”

“I'm getting to that. I was up in the server room and spilled my coffee.”

“You know drinks aren't allowed in there!” Dana scolded.

“I know, sorry. But I was cleaning it up, and it got under the floor tiles. That's when I found a duplicate server room directly below ours, and it was full of only red Qubes. There was a terminal there, and I hacked in. The Qubes were being used to calculate a power source for a new military super weapon.”

“Is this some kind of joke?” Dana asked, incredulous.

“No… No… I wish it were. I'm serious. Max found me in the room, and he tried to kill me. He was furious.”

“Max,” Dana said with a look of shock. She walked back to her desk and squatted underneath to get her purse. “We need to find him.”

“No. Why? He's after me!”

“We need to question him.”

“No, we don't. We need to get out of here.”

“Maybe you're right. Let's go to my house. We can talk there without him around.”

Dana unlocked the door and exited the office. “Follow me,” she commanded.

Min trailed behind her.

#

Chelsea tried to stay awake as Dr. Reynolds lectured from the podium in Massey Auditorium. Behind him was a large projection of a fractured bone. He zoomed in on a clump of blood cells in the gap between the break.

"After the bone is set, these hematoma cells will gradually be replaced with hyaline cartilage," he said. "It will then be calcified into new material, fusing the bones together. Your assignment over the weekend is to research how this process works – a process we call 'endochondral ossification.' Please turn in a two-page paper on Monday describing it. And if you copy it from Wikipedia, I will know. Have a great weekend."

He turned off the projector and began packing up his laptop.

The students began to mill around. Some talked in small groups. Others gathered to privately ask the professor questions, having been too shy to do so in front of the class. The rest began to shuffle into the hallway.

Chelsea loaded the thick textbook into her backpack and hoisted it onto her back. She followed the crowd out of the lecture hall. For the most part, the students all headed toward the academic lobby, which led to the building exit. A few stragglers went to the library, or in the opposite direction to another class or a laboratory.

Two women abruptly rushed into the same hallway from one of the management wings. They seemed to be in a big hurry, and Chelsea watched them curiously as they merged into the flow of students.

Suddenly a tall man appeared on the opposite side of the crowd, seemed to recognize the women, and began to push through the crowd. Beneath unsightly fresh bruises, his face was red with anger. The gaggle of people moving towards him impeded his progress.

The older woman noticed him, grabbed the other's arm, and pulled her in the opposite direction. "Let's get out of here fast!" she said. "Stay close."

They broke from the crowd and rushed down the corridor, entering an inconspicuous door on the side of the hallway. The man pushed his way through the students, shoving many aside.

Chelsea heard rumors of other experiments going on in the research building, but now she decided she didn't want to know. She continued on her way, wondering about bone ossification.

#

The door led into a stairwell. "We can get to the parking lot this way," said Dana to Min. She dashed downward. Min pumped her legs to keep up.

As they reached the bottom, they heard the door above open and someone start down, skipping stairs.

"This way," whispered Dana. Instead of ducking out the exit door, they entered the basement and sprinted down a long hallway. Min knew Max had heard them since he was just one floor above. He'd assume they went outside, so Dana was trying to throw him off their trail. They got about 30 yards down the corridor when the stairwell door opened, and Max nearly fell through. Min and Dana both glanced back and locked eyes with their pursuer.

"Shit!" said Dana. "C'mon." She made an abrupt right turn and headed deeper into the basement. This area was a maze of storage rooms, partitioned from floor to ceiling with rusted chain link fencing. The lighting was dimmer, and it looked like something one would see in a Grade B horror flick. Min was confused but assumed Dana knew the area and could find a place to hide. Or maybe a shortcut out the other side and they'd lose Max in the twisting passages. Min didn't have much time to think about it as keeping up with Dana took all of her focus.

Max crashed into the fencing behind them. He was closer now. They turned again and again. It seemed like they were slowing, and Max was catching up. It was possible to see through the walls and across the stored debris – tables, chairs, medical equipment, a ping pong table. It didn't provide enough concealment; their escape was failing!

They dashed into a caged room. It was empty save for a large iron boiler-like apparatus. It was a dead end.

"Shit," Min whispered to Dana.

They turned around. Max stood in the doorway, blocking their egress.

CHAPTER 42 - STORM WIND

"Don't ever take a fence down until you know why it was put up." - Robert Frost

The mass of Soldiers was too many to keep to the trail, so they fanned out, pushing through the foliage. Somewhere ahead, the remains of the tower would lie, surrounded by the disloyal Workers.

Or at least Ga·zo hoped they were still there. But he doubted it. Whatever motive led them to this organized betrayal must've also made them scatter and hide. It would've been easy to predict the reaction of the Colony.

"I expect the Workers have fled," said Ga·zo to Za·zo, who followed close behind. "When we get to the tower base, we'll need to spread out and find them. Each of us should be able to kill a couple of them, and if we find them one-on-one, we'll wipe them out in short order."

"Agreed," responded Za·zo. He was too enraged to have a conversation. Ga·zo sensed this so he fell silent. When they reached the tower ruins, he'd gather them up and give additional instructions. The pursuit of the Workers into the foliage was his plan. But since it was unexplored territory, he figured they'd take it slow, lest they fall into a river.

Bam!

Za·zo was knocked onto his back by Ga·zo's body, which spontaneously reversed direction. Dazed, they both picked themselves off the ground. Regaining their senses, they observed a blue glow before them. A long channel had been cleared through the foliage, perpendicular to their heading. In the center of the track, forming a wall, was a continuous line of vertical blue rock. It stretched in both directions as far as they could see.

"What the Rift?" said Za·zo.

"Indeed," mused Ga·zo. "The Workers are more cunning than expected." He looked up and down the clearing as the remainder of the Soldiers emerged from the foliage. They came to a halt, looking puzzled and discouraged.

"Find the edge," shouted Ga·zo to the Soldiers on his immediate left and right. They, in turn, communicated the instructions to their nearest neighbor, and so on, until the message traveled to the furthest Polyan at each end. These charged away, seeking to locate a way around the fence.

Ga·zo held up a leg, and the Soldiers gathered around him. "Fellow Polyans. What's been committed today is nothing short of an attack on the heart of the Colony. Our beloved leader, Fa·ro, sought only to take his natural place next to the other gods. And he'd look down upon us with respect and admiration.

"He would've rewarded us with a continuous and endless yellow Source. This would've halted our need to replenish energy. We Soldiers would no longer have had to hunt for violet energy cores. And the Drones would no longer have had to forage for green power crystals. By destroying the tower, the Workers have dashed our hope for a simpler life. Their act has been a betrayal of Fa·ro, the Colony, and each of us as individuals."

The Soldiers listened intently to their chief. They stood motionless, and an eerie silence spread through the dim morning light. Ga·zo continued.

"Never before has Polyan opposed Polyan at this level of intensity. After the purge of the Leaders, Fa·ro thought their evil guidance had come to an end. But now we see their destructive ways have corrupted the honor of the Workers. It's clouded their judgment and desire to serve the collective. By wrecking the tower, they wounded us all.

"Brothers, we must now do the unthinkable. We must slaughter our own kind. We must redeem the wrong done to our society – the wrong done to the very fabric of our culture. We must end every life that participated in this disgrace! The Workers' act was an attack on us all, and we must respond in equal measure."

Cheers erupted among the Soldiers. They danced around, revved up to complete their mission. Ga·zo raised his whip, holding his leg in the air. He twirled it around and caught the end with another raised leg. Stretching the strap over his sensors, he shouted, "For the Colony!"

"For the Colony!" the others said in unison.

Just then, both scouts returned. They rushed through the crowd to Ga·zo.

"Commander," the first said, "the wall goes all the way to the Rift. There is no way around in that direction."

"It's the same the other way," said the other, "it goes all the way to the river."

"So we're completely blocked," brooded Ga·zo. Then to the entire gathering, "We must find a way through. It's time we learned to work without the Workers. Let's breach the wall!"

The Soldiers huddled and began speaking with each other as they discussed his request. Ideas began to form. Ga·zo watched in anticipation, waiting for someone to come up with a plan.

The first to do so were Te·zo and We·zo, who'd been traveling together. They returned to the foliage and brought forth a large branch that they noticed when they arrived at the wall. They lifted it and attempted to lay it across the wall. But it bounced and bobbed until it was finally thrown back at them. A couple of other Soldiers joined them and attempted to hold the end of the branch to steady it over the wall. It bobbed, but remained pointed at the other side. We·zo began to climb across it. But as he approached the wall, his weight lowered the branch, and the blue rock repelled it more forcefully. The branch thrashed violently, throwing We·zo back into those holding it. The branch flew up and landed on the other side of the wall.

Ga·zo watched with disappointment. He glanced at the branch on the other side and wondered if they could somehow do that with a Polyan. Before he could verbalize his thought, a group of five Soldiers began picking up brown rocks. These they hurled at the blue rocks forming the wall. Before colliding with the blue, the rocks were each deflected. Some shot upwards, some backward, and some went over the wall. None made contact with the blue columns.

"Come," said Ga·zo to the group. "Five of you, pick me up, and throw me over."

The five that had been throwing the rocks each took one of Ga·zo's legs. They hoisted him so that he was standing on their backs. They approached the wall as close as they could get. There they knelt, and in unison stood, flinging Ga·zo into the air toward the wall. It wasn't high enough. He was deflected backward and landed on top of a gathering of Soldiers, who sprawled about in a tangle of legs.

Ga·zo looked up from the morass of Polyan bodies. There stood Fa·ro looking down at him.

"I'm disappointed in you Ga·zo," he hissed. "You're unable to solve this simple problem without my help. I bet any Worker would be able to find a way through. This is why they need to be destroyed. They're a danger to us all for as long as they live."

Ga·zo and the others watched. Fa·ro had a bunch of red rocks stuck to his back. He used a brown rock to detach one of them and held it like a handle. He flung it at the obstruction. Unlike the brown rocks alone, the red rock struck the wall with sudden force, knocking one of the blue columns aside. Fa·ro repeated this four more times, hitting away four more blue segments of the wall. Finally, there was an opening big enough for them to pass through single file.

A cheer rose from the crowd, and more than one statement of "Long live Fa·ro," and a couple of "For the Colony."

Then they began to storm through the breach, heading toward the fallen tower.

#

No one was in the real server room. Had they been, they'd have seen several entire panels of blue Qubes begin to shift to red.

CHAPTER 43 - THE INCINERATOR

"When you're cornered, there are two things you can do: move or fight." -
Josh Fox

Max stood motionless, looking at both Min and Dana, who faced him like cornered animals. The rage was gone from his eyes, but a tension existed like a wall of frost.

Dana took two steps away from Min. She shifted her eyes from Max to Min and asked, "Can someone tell me what the hell is going on here?"

Min thought, *thanks for throwing me under the bus.*

Max's eyes followed the voice and he stared at Dana, realizing who he'd been chasing. A look of confusion washed over his face, then paralysis, as he wondered what to do next.

Anger returned, and his face turned red. He spoke to Dana, slowly and deliberately. "I would like *you* to tell *me* what's going on here!"

"Sure," Dana replied, her body language relaxed as if it was no big deal. "Min came to find me because she thinks you're trying to kill her."

His eyes snapped back to Min.

"Kill her?"

"Yes," said Dana.

"Min, why would I be trying to kill you?"

Min was shaking. Her shoulders slumped in a posture of defeat. She mumbled, "Because you found me in your secret server room."

"Min," he said, "nice try bluffing your way out of this. That was the first time I was *ever* in that room. You're obviously the one running it. I want to know right now what it is. What were you doing in there and why does it even exist?"

Min glanced at Dana and back to Max.

"Max, how do you even have the nerve to pin this on me? I hacked into the computer in the room. I know what you've got to hide – the weapons. How could you do this? How could you compromise our values for money? And murder!"

Max looked shocked.

"Yes," continued Min. "I know Olivia was murdered. She discovered the same thing I did, and it cost her her life. I hacked her journal and knew she was onto you."

"No, no, no," stammered Max, confused. "Something isn't right here."

He stepped forward and grabbed the sides of Min's shoulders. She'd given up and didn't resist. She noticed his grasp was lighter than expected.

Max continued. "I swear. I was at your desk and saw your computer had crashed. I rebooted it and logged in to see what might have happened, which is when I found Olivia's journal. I read the whole thing, and something jumped out at me. There was a message embedded there. Every first letter of each entry spelled a message, 'F-L-O-O-R-6-C-O-D-E-2-4-6-5.' Floor 6? I knew we had a storage closet down there for paper files. And I remembered seeing a keypad in there but never thought much about it. Until now. I grabbed the key, let myself into the storage room, and Olivia's combination worked – at least once my eyes adjusted enough to enter it correctly. The room that lay beyond, the red server room... that's the first time I saw it. I was trying to make sense of it all when you attacked me."

Min was processing what he said. "I wish I could believe you, Max. But that's a huge coincidence."

"It's the truth. And I agree it's a big coincidence. Why were you in the room?"

"I was in the real server room above and spilled my coffee. I was cleaning it up when I found a conduit under the raised floor..."

"Enough!" shouted Dana.

They both looked at her. She stood blocking the exit from the cage. A silver and black pistol in her hand pointed in their direction.

Max looked at the gun and said, "It all makes sense to me now."

"Of course it does," spat Dana. "You two brainiacs make a cute couple. But that's enough. This little secret must remain a secret. Believe me, I'm fond of you both, and I hate to kill you. It's going to slow the Spheria project. And your disappearance will be harder to explain than Olivia's. But I don't intend to leave evidence this time."

Min asked, "Why are you doing this?"

"What do you think I am? Some kind of super villain about to explain my motives before killing you? Not going to happen. I'm sorry, but I've got no choice in this matter. It's your lives or mine. Now turn around and climb through that door."

They both turned to look in the direction where she was pointing the gun. There was no other exit. Then they realized that the door she was referring to was part of the substantial boiler-like apparatus taking up the bulk of the room. It was a walk-in medical incinerator. It was massive, large enough to wheel gurneys into before dumping the bodies for disintegration to ash. The roof of the chamber was high enough that Min could stand upright.

"Otherwise," Max clarified, "you will... shoot us?"

"I'll shoot you and drag you in there. So, either way, you're going in. But if you won't go in yourself I will first make it painful."

"Burning to death isn't exactly painless."

"True, but the burn is quick." She was right. After a brief pilot lighting period, the incinerator would heat to 2,000 degrees Celsius in about 15 seconds. Death would come in about 4 seconds. Not even enough time to realize the flames had begun to blast from the injection ports.

"Now in!" Dana ordered.

Max took a step toward Dana. Without hesitation, she fired a shot into his foot. She had good aim, and he fell sideways into Min, who caught him with her body. Both tumbled to the ground.

"Owww. Fuck!" Max yelled.

Tears began to run down Min's face. Her eyes shot

daggers toward Dana. "Please don't do this," she pleaded.

Dana said, "Get into the incinerator *now* and I'll give you the explanation you desire. Consider it your dying wish. Don't get in and I'm going to start shooting body parts until you can't fight me. Either way, you're going to die. One way you'll know why, one way you won't."

Min started sobbing but grabbed Max around the torso from the back. She began dragging him into the doorway. He helped push with his functioning leg, wincing in pain when his other foot jostled over the threshold. A trickle of blood left a line on the floor like a crimson arrow.

Satisfied that they'd complied, Dana kept her word. "I'm truly sorry to have to do this, and sorry about Olivia also. I was convinced that it'd look like a suicide, but Captain Brennan wasn't so sure. He investigated her death and almost discovered the truth. This time, I can't have any bodies."

"But why?" Max asked through gritted teeth.

"Isn't it obvious? You know we're having funding issues. DARPA had its eye on your pet project since the Solvay Conference. But Graham's contract preventing military investment was an issue for their administration. So they approached me, and we worked out a deal. Not only did we get enough funding to keep this going, but I also will receive a beautiful piece of land in Costa Rica for my retirement. I've worked for Graham a long time, and I'm not getting rich doing it. I'm sorry you got caught in the crossfire, Max. But I promise you, I'll keep your project going as long as I can. Good stuff will come of this. I wish you luck in the afterlife."

"I doubt we will meet there," Max spat.

"You sound ungrateful. I could just shut your project down." As she said this, she walked up to the large iron door and slammed it shut. She locked it with a large metal latch.

Min and Max were in pitch darkness – at least until a small pilot light in the corner flared on, casting a blue hue in the chamber.

CHAPTER 44 - THE GREAT DIVIDE

"Hope is being able to see that there is light despite all of the darkness." -
Desmond Tutu

Hi·ma entered the open end of the tower. It now lay horizontal instead of standing vertical. In this position, the four sides of the structure created a tunnel. Its zig-zagging girders formed enough of a surface to stand on. Hi·ma moved ahead, and the ground disappeared, revealing the chasm of the Rift below for as far as she could see. She paused, then continued more slowly since there were plenty of significant gaps. For a second she got dizzy and lost her footing, but caught herself before falling in. Looking straight through the tunnel steadied her, and she resumed moving again. Others began entering behind her. So much had changed, it was hard to accept this was actually happening.

Mere moments ago, she was pulling the rope protruding from Sa·ma's strange contraption. On his command, she let go, as did the others. Somehow, as if by magic, a beam shot out of the device. It violently removed two of the four support columns of the tower, the two closest to the Rift. The tower seemed to emit a pitiful groan followed by a series of creaking sounds. Then the unimaginable happened.

She gazed up the length of the tower, which pointed at

the Source above. As she looked at the top, it began to drift from its position. The separation between the tower and the Source began to speed up as the structure began to lean.

Sa·ma yelled, "Back to the woods! Now!"

There was a lot of commotion as they ran from the base into the surrounding foliage. Hi·ma turned back and saw the massive tower leaning at a 45-degree angle, falling toward the Rift. It was gaining speed, and the remaining distance was closed in seconds. But instead of falling into the chasm, the top of the tower touched the other side of the Rift! The middle sagged under the strain, so much so that she was sure it was going to snap in half. But then it sprang back and bounced up at both ends, shifting, then coming to rest. They'd done it! They had actually built a framework long enough, and strong enough, to span the Rift.

#

Crossing the bridge took longer than expected. Since the Polyans had to place each leg on a girder one by one, they couldn't rush. When about a third of them had gotten onto the bridge, the Soldiers arrived.

They emerged from the foliage into the clearing and formed a line along the edge. The remaining Workers spread out inside the clearing, having no choice but to confront the Soldiers. Then Fa·ro emerged. A sense of impending doom spread among them.

"Sinners!" yelled Fa·ro. "You disobey the will of a god! You have no right to exist in this world any longer! Don't expect the Qubessence to be kind to you either. Soldiers, now!"

The Soldiers rushed ahead. The Workers stood their ground. They met in the middle of the clearing.

The Workers pushed and batted at the Soldiers, trying

to knock them off balance or drive them back. But lacking combat experience, they were no match. The Soldiers began snagging the legs of the Workers with their whips. They pulled in opposite directions, snapping them off, leaving a trail of dismembered violet cores in their wake. They would return later and drain them of their energy, rendering them lifeless.

Fa·ro joined the battle, his lust for revenge more than he could resist. Having an even larger stature than the Soldiers, he proved a natural at combat. Pinning a Worker with one large leg, he used four others, in sets of two, to snap off its legs. When it lay helpless, he pierced the Worker's core with his point, drinking in its life-giving energy. This he repeated, and took delight in all his victims, one by one.

At the entrance to the bridge, Sa·ma and Le·ma stood, shocked. The blue wall had failed. Their carefully laid plans were crumbling. The freedom of their people had given way to death. The situation was grim. In short order, the Soldiers will have gotten them all.

Then something clicked in Sa·ma's brain. It was like a switch lighting up a transistor, opening a new pathway of creativity. He replayed the image in his mind. *It could work.* "Le·ma," he said, "I saw something when I was making the cannon. I need your help, but at high risk to you."

He told her his plan.

"Let's do it!" she exclaimed.

#

Back in the server room, over half of the Qubes had now turned pure red. And many of the blue ones had begun blinking.

CHAPTER 45 - ASHES TO ASHES

"What progress we are making. In the Middle Ages they would have burned me. Now they are content with burning my books." - Sigmund Freud

Their oxygen was depleting fast, and it smelled horrible.

Min stood to take a fresh breath.

Max pulled his phone from his pocket and began to dial. "Damn!" he said, "No signal."

Min saw a reflection at the back of the chamber and walked toward it, holding her hands out to feel it. Instead of hard metal, her hand contacted something squishy. She pulled out her phone, turned on the light, and shrieked. On a shiny metal gurney lay a corpse, sewn up in several places after apparently being used in an anatomy class. She now recognized the scent of embalming fluid mixed with propane.

"It's all right," Max reassured her.

"All right!" Min screamed. "We're about to die a fiery death with Frankenstein next to us!"

"Hey, that's no way to treat the dead," he said. "I have an idea. Look at the ceiling."

Somehow his calm voice helped her regain her mental clarity. She shined her light upwards. At the top of the domed roof was a human-sized opening – the exhaust vent.

"Stand up the gurney," Max requested. "We can use it as a ladder."

"Ladder? To go up there? Why?"

"That opening should lead to the chimney. Most chimneys have a clean-out door. Maybe we can open it."

Min didn't have much hope for his plan. But she knew the air would be better up there, and breathing was becoming difficult. She dumped the body and stood the gurney on end. The folding mechanism on the underside created a makeshift ladder. She scaled it and, with Max feebly attempting to hold it steady, stood in the opening.

"It curves downward," she said.

"Yes, it should. Slide down it."

She disappeared. There was a thud followed by, "Ugh!"

"You alright?" Max shouted.

Faintly, he heard her say, "I think so."

#

Min shined her phone's light around, trying to figure out where she was. Indeed, she was in a circular chamber made of bricks, about 8 feet wide. It rose into the darkness. Metal rungs protruded from one section. The other side had a small iron door.

She ran toward the door and tripped on something. It was a shovel, completely soot covered, as was everything, including her. It must be stored here for cleaning out the chimney.

"It's getting hot over here," she heard Max's voice echo down the vent shaft.

Heat was coming through the passage, but it wasn't more than what the pilot light produced. Soon, even here, she'd be burned alive, or maybe suffocated.

She picked up the shovel and tried to pry at the clean-out door. It was futile. Thirty years ago, they made things to last. She looked up. Nothing. Not even a view of the sky.

Not knowing what else to do, she began climbing the rungs. *Maybe,* she thought, *I could climb to the top of the chimney and hang over the side to avoid the poison gas or heat.* After about 15 feet, she hit her head on a ceiling. It was metal, but soft. She turned her light toward it. It was an aluminum sheet, newer than the original structure.

Then it hit her: *a scrubber.* That explained the lack of light. At some point, to prevent toxic waste from being released into the atmosphere, the U.S. government had the foresight to require that medical incinerators have a scrubber installed. They used activated carbon and cooling chambers to prevent solids from exiting with the rising vapors. In the middle was a fan, spinning slowly, but deliberately. The opening was large enough for her, but the fan would chop her to pieces.

She heard a rumbling. The fuel injector was pressurizing. They had seconds to live!

"Min, I love you," was barely audible above the loudening din.

No, it can't end like this. I won't let it.

She jumped down. It was farther than she expected and she almost twisted an ankle. She groped in the dark and found the shovel again.

A series of rapid clicks began as the intake valves opened. Max started screaming in agony.

CHAPTER 46 - INTO BATTLE

"Ideas can be life-changing. Sometimes all you need to open the door is just one more good idea." - Jim Rohn

Le·ma stopped a Worker who was about to enter the bridge. "Pu·ma, I need to go with Sa·ma. Can you help others get on the bridge?"

Pu·ma looked at the ensuing battle. A third of the Workers lay destroyed. The Soldiers were advancing through their ranks as if they were making an inspection: slow, but unchecked. She glanced at the bridge; another third were crossing or had made it across. That was the group she wanted to be with. But she looked at Le·ma, who had a pleading expression, and agreed, "Yes."

Le·ma took off after Sa·ma. He'd pulled the cannon away from the fallen tower and into the open.

"You six!" he called toward a huddled group of Workers. "Help us!"

They came immediately. Sa·ma was tying the rope onto Le·ma. The other end he passed through the inside of the cannon. "Like last time, grab and pull. Pull as hard as you can!"

They formed two rows of three and grabbed the cable. They pulled it backward, just like they'd done earlier when they fired at the tower. Le·ma positioned herself near the opening and folded her legs.

"Harder!" shouted Sa·ma.

The six pulled more, straining against the resistance. Le·ma began to slide into the barrel of the cannon. The crushing force of the blue rock pinned her legs to her sides, fiercely squeezing her.

"Harder!" yelled Sa·ma again.

The six fought the resistance and hauled the rope back bit by bit. Le·ma sank deeper into the barrel. Sa·ma rotated the cannon, then, using his back, lifted up the front and pointed it into the air. When he was satisfied with the angle, he blurted, "One...two...three...now!"

The six let go. Le·ma shot out like a rocket, flying through the air, making a gentle arc. The Soldiers, focused on their violence, didn't notice. More importantly, Fa·ro, who was feasting on another kill, hadn't noticed either. Bam! Le·ma slammed into him. Sa·ma's aim was perfect!

Fa·ro tumbled over and over, coming to rest on his back, his seven mighty legs flailing in the air. He looked up at the Source, confused, and the world seemed to be spinning. He tapped his legs together a couple times, not comprehending where the ground had gone. Then he felt it. *Snap!* His artifact was removed.

In an instant, Fa·ro's seven legs shot out. Pushing with three of them, he flipped himself over. He stumbled sideways, then stood. He couldn't believe what he saw. The diminutive body of Le·ma, kneeling on the ground, sat with the artifact attached to her head. He roared in fury. He raised his front two legs to smash her. But before bringing them down, he paused.

She just sat there, not moving, not trying to flee. She bowed before him with the artifact.

CHAPTER 47 - CLEAN-OUT

"I would imagine that if you could understand Morse code, a tap dancer would drive you crazy." - Mitch Hedberg

Walter pushed the canvas laundry cart full of dirty linens off the service elevator. It always frustrated him how much laundry the facility generated. Someone once told him that the hospital operated the busiest laundromat in the city, and he believed it. He wheeled the basket down the long basement hallway heading toward the washer room. As a candy striper, he performed a variety of tasks. Transporting laundry was one of the least inspiring. Getting people to their appointments was the one he preferred the most because he liked conversation.

As Walter passed the storage cages, he heard a faint banging sound. He couldn't make it out and looked at the pipes running along the ceiling. *Maybe air bubbles in there*, he thought.

He continued pushing his load, and when he came to the next side passage, he heard the banging even louder. He cocked his head left, then right, trying to get a sense of the direction of the sound. Yes, it was definitely coming from the side hallway. He abandoned his basket and ventured down to find out where it was coming from.

As he emerged into the maze of cages, the banging

stopped. He shrugged and turned back toward his basket. Then he heard it again.

Bang, Bang, Bang... Bang... Bang... Bang... Bang, Bang, Bang.

He listened.

Bang, Bang, Bang... Bang... Bang... Bang... Bang, Bang, Bang.

It was some kind of pattern. He'd no idea what it was but figured that bubbles wouldn't do that. So he turned again and followed it. After a few twists and turns through the dim clutter, he came to the incinerator chimney. The sound was coming from behind the clean-out door. It was locked shut.

Bang, Bang, Bang... Bang... Bang... Bang... Bang, Bang, Bang.

Louder this time. The hair on the back of his neck stood up.

Ghosts, he thought. But he never believed in that supernatural stuff, so he decided to open the door.

He fumbled through the key-chain the janitor had given him. He found the old iron key, the only one of its kind. He put it into the lock and jiggled it around. It made little scraping sounds.

Bang. And then nothing.

Whatever was making the noise had stopped. Walter guessed he was making the noise now. Maybe it was rats. No, that was impossible. It'd have to be a giant rat. He imagined such things existed and had second thoughts about opening the door.

Then he heard a faint "help" from the other side. Rats don't speak, no matter how large they are.

Walter finished fiddling with the lock, and it clicked open. He lifted the thick bar and began to swing open the door. As he did so, it was flung open from the inside. A short Asian woman, almost black with soot, darted past him. "Thanks," she said as she disappeared around the corner of the cage.

"Wait," he said, chasing after her.

She led him to the main incinerator door. It was completely dark. She tried to lift the bar but it was too heavy, or stuck. He walked over and pushed it with her, and together they swung the bar up and pulled the door open. A man crawled out, gasping for air. His shirt was wrapped around his foot.

The woman squatted down and hugged him. "Thank God you're alive!" she said.

"Thank God for us both," he said.

"Um," said Walter. "Why are you guys in the incinerator? That's only for bodies, you know."

The woman looked at Walter and said, "Thanks for letting us out. You saved our lives. I'm Min, and this is Max." Min looked at Max's foot, then back at Walter. "He needs help. Can you get us a wheelchair please?"

"Of course," Walter said, and he shuffled off to find the cage where they stored them.

Max smiled a sooty grin and asked, "So, care to tell me how we're still alive?"

"Dumb luck I suppose. I got through the vent, but the clean-out door was locked from the outside. So it was hopeless.

I tried to climb the chimney, but it was blocked by a scrubber of some kind. I was blocked from every direction, so we were both about to die. That's when it hit me. They wouldn't install a scrubber like that without putting in some kind of fail-safe mechanism. After all, what's the point of having it if it could fail and release hazardous materials into the air? So I grabbed a shovel I'd found and wedged it into the fan. It nearly pulled me up and took my arm off, but it stuck, and the fan stopped. The system shut off and, judging from the cooling airflow, the pilot lights went off also. It worked! We were saved. Or at least I was. I tried calling you, but you never responded. I was sure you were dead."

"I thought so too," said Max. "I said something to you because I heard things starting up and knew the blast was about to fire up. The last thing I remember, and I don't even know why, I stuck my finger into the hole in my foot to see if there was a bullet there. My finger passed right through, and it hurt like hell. I started screaming, and I think I passed out from the pain. I don't know for how long. But when I awoke I heard you banging. I tried to call out, but it was too noisy for you to hear. My foot was still bleeding, I've no idea how much blood I lost, so I took off my shirt and wrapped it around my wound. I think I stopped the bleeding, although it hurts like a son of a bitch."

Walter reappeared with not only a wheelchair but also a teal patient robe.

"Thank you!" said Min and Max in unison.

"Glad to help," said Walter, as he assisted Max into the chair.

"Now where can I take you?"

"The seventh floor," said Max.

"No," said Min. "I know what I need to do. You go to

security and bring them to the board meeting. I'll join you there."

CHAPTER 48 - LIBERATION

"Liberation is not deliverance." - Victor Hugo

As Fa·ro paused, the ground began trembling beneath him. Then a sound like thunder rose in the distance, getting rapidly louder. The foliage around the clearing shook violently.

A herd of Zalisk burst forth, flooding onto the battlefield! They immediately impaled the five nearest Soldiers, shattering their cores and flinging their limp carcasses into the others. More Soldiers went flying. Others were trampled. Some began to retreat. A handful of the best, led by Ga·zo, managed to flip one of the beasts with their whips. But before they could finish, another bowled into them scattering them like teetering rocks.

It became evident to everyone that for some unexplained reason, the Zalisk were only attacking the Soldiers. The Workers were ignored. Those mixed with the Soldiers were stepped over, unharmed, and were freed by the flailing beasts. The Workers began running for the bridge and resumed entering single file. Fa·ro was the only one with an explanation, and his fury reached an all-time high. He flung his legs down with such force that they dented the ground. But Le·ma was gone.

He glanced toward the bridge; she was running toward

it. While distracted, he'd let her escape. He charged after her, but his path was blocked by a Zalisk, who seemed to take a particular interest in him. It thrust at him, but he dodged it, jumping onto its back. It thrashed around, spinning, trying to dislodge him. He hung on, pulling it onto its side. It dug in three of its six legs and rotated itself on the ground, but Fa·ro stayed behind its back. Grabbing the top three legs for leverage, he managed to snap one off. The beast went wild. It rolled its body over on top of Fa·ro, flattening him. It jabbed its tusks into the ground, pinning four of Fa·ro's legs in place.

Ga·zo arrived with three others, and they snared the beast. They began pulling it off Fa·ro, but it was hooked into the ground. It tried to claw at Fa·ro with its remaining legs, but the whips held them back. Fa·ro looked at Ga·zo, then toward the bridge and commanded, "Get her! Get my artifact!" Ga·zo followed his gaze. At the entrance to the bridge, Le·ma disappeared, followed by Sa·ma. They were the last remaining Workers. The battle was between the Zalisk and Soldiers now.

As commanded, Ga·zo abandoned his master and sprinted toward the bridge. Two Zalisk converged on him, but he managed to leap back, and they collided, knocking each other over. He clambered over them and had an open field before him. With all the speed he could muster, he closed the distance and peered into the tunnel across the Rift.

When he visited the tower in the past, he'd stand under it and admire the view. It seemed to go on forever, the four vertical lines converging into a small distant square. The thought of the height and the Workers up there made him dizzy. Now before him was that same view, and he was about to enter. Halfway across, he could see the Workers moving away. Closer, not yet finding their rhythm, were Le·ma and Sa·ma.

Ga·zo entered. He walked up to the edge of the Rift where the ground stopped, and the immense chasm began. Only the zigzags formed by the girders provided support, and there was much more empty space. He stepped onto a beam. It seemed stable. He brought two other legs there and reached out to the next beam. Then with two and three working together, he began to move across.

He looked up along the hollow passage, and it was empty. The Workers were either too far to see, or on the other side. More puzzling, Le·ma and Sa·ma were missing. *Did they fall?* He doubted it. Then he suspected the answer. He stood on one of the side beams and popped his eye sensors through a gap in the ceiling. There they were, moving along the top surface of the bridge, faster than the others. They were buoyed by the knowledge that if they fell, they had another layer to grab onto.

Ga·zo climbed onto the top as well. He proceeded slowly at first because the gaps were at a different angle than before and he had to relearn where to place his legs. But having five helped, and he soon found a rhythm that he used to get some momentum. Indeed, he was moving quite a bit faster than the two Workers he was chasing. They looked back, saw him approaching, and attempted to speed up. But that just made Le·ma lose her footing, and Sa·ma had to help her back up. Their pursuer was closing in on them.

"Keep going!" shouted Sa·ma.

Le·ma glanced back to see Sa·ma turning to face Ga·zo.

"No!" she said.

Without looking at her, he repeated, "Go! I'll handle Ga·zo."

She hated to leave her master but knew the artifact must not fall into Ga·zo's possession. She sped up as best she could.

Ga·zo arrived and stopped before Sa·ma. "Let me pass!" he said.

"Never, Ga·zo. Your false god has corrupted you and your kind. Return to him and figure out how to survive without Workers."

"You speak blasphemy! For that, you won't be forgiven, even by the gods!" He struck Sa·ma with a leg, but Sa·ma parried with one of his own. Ga·zo swung at him from the other direction with another leg, and again, Sa·ma blocked it. With Sa·ma teetering on just two legs, Ga·zo leaned forward and threw him off the bridge.

Sa·ma flew a good distance, then stopped abruptly. Ga·zo was yanked to the side and barely managed to grab a girder. Sa·ma had managed, just as he was getting thrown, to grab the loose end of Ga·zo's whip. He fell, swinging beneath the bridge, and came up on the other side. Ga·zo and Sa·ma both hung from the top of the bridge by two legs, facing each other.

Ga·zo didn't hesitate. He kicked through the bridge at Sa·ma's core, but Sa·ma released a leg and swayed to one side. Ga·zo slid over and kicked again at where Sa·ma was, but he did it in the other direction. Ga·zo noticed Le·ma making progress to the other side of the bridge. *The artifact.* He glared at Sa·ma hanging there, disregarded him, and began moving quickly along the top of the bridge. He had the advantage now, and would reach Le·ma before she made it to the end.

She looked back to check on them and saw Ga·zo gaining on her. But even worse, a line of Soldiers began entering the bridge. The Zalisks must've given up attacking when she lost the focus to control them any longer.

She turned and tripped, nearly falling through the bridge. She recovered and sped forward. But it wasn't fast enough. Ga·zo was within striking distance and raised his whip to snag her. As he flung his leg toward her, it stopped in mid-air. He yanked again and again it stopped. Turning, he saw that Sa·ma had reached him, and had attached the loose end of his whip to one of the girders.

"Enough with you!" fumed Ga·zo, and he swung into the bridge, coming up underneath Sa·ma, kicking him into the air. Sa·ma tumbled and fell through a gap on top of the bridge. He extended his legs just in time to stop from falling past the bottom level. Before he could react, Ga·zo dropped down on top of him, hitting him dead center with all of his weight. Sa·ma's legs folded, and he slid through the gap. He plunged down into the black void of the Rift below.

Le·ma screamed, "Noooooo!"

Ga·zo saw her standing inside the bridge, but on the other side of the Rift. It wasn't too far away, and he began closing the distance, skipping every other girder now. She grabbed the end of the bridge and started pushing. "Help me," she called. Other Workers joined her, pushing sideways. The bridge began to shift, the end moving toward the edge of the Rift.

"Push!" the Workers shouted in unison, and the end lost contact with solid ground. They heaved it into the chasm with Ga·zo and the Soldiers still inside it. Le·ma gripped it a little too long and lost her footing, falling to the edge of the Rift, hanging by two legs. Two Workers grabbed her to prevent her from slipping, and began pulling her up. But she seemed heavier than she should have. They peered over; Ga·zo was hanging from her other two dangling legs. He reached up, ripped off the artifact, and attached it to his own core. The world spun, and she would've fallen had the Workers not been holding her legs. Ga·zo paused for only a second, then began climbing up over her.

As he reached the rim, the two Workers holding her backed away. He stood on her two legs, locking her in place.

"Push him!" she screamed at them.

They hesitated, not wanting to risk her by shoving him so close by. Ga·zo, reacting to their delay, reached down and lifted her up, holding her in front of him.

"Back off, all of you!" he said, "or I toss her into the Rift."

The crowd of Workers cleared a space around them. Ga·zo crept sideways along the Rift, dragging Le·ma with him. A forest of dense foliage began mere steps away. He was about to escape into it, possessing the artifact.

Le·ma understood the implications. Although he would be the only Soldier on this side, he would hold the artifact. This would put their new freedom at risk. It would jeopardize all they had fought for. Would they be able to establish a new homogeneous Colony with his interference?

With her last bit of strength, she pushed the ground away, and both she and Ga·zo tumbled backward into the Rift.

CHAPTER 49 - PROJECTION

"We talk a lot about hope, helping, and teamwork. Our whole message is that we are more powerful together." - Victoria Osteen

Dana entered the Experience Room looking disheveled. The rest of the team, minus Min and Max, was already seated around the table, ready to begin. The panoramic screens each showed the simple spinning logo for the Spheria Project.

Graham stood near a beverage cart that had been brought in for the meeting. "Tough night?" he asked.

"You could say that," Dana replied. "Last minute preparations, etc. The typical stuff. We all were working extra hard."

"Glad to hear that. I love the dedication. Here, have some coffee."

Graham poured Dana a cup from the dispenser. "How do you take it?"

"Cream and one sugar, please." This was odd, a billionaire serving her coffee.

"Sure thing." Graham began dumping the requested additives into her cup. "Where's Max?" he asked as he stirred.

"I'm not sure," replied Dana. "I got a strange message from him this morning saying that he had some things to take care of. He told me to start without him."

Graham frowned. "That's unexpected. I hope he's okay. The future of this project depends on him." He handed the cup to Dana.

"Yeah, I hope so too," she said, taking the cup. She sipped the coffee and then cleared her throat. "But I'm sure we could keep it going without him. The team has its act together. It's a great crew."

"Even still. Sometimes a great team goes nowhere without a visionary leader. Look at Apple. Brilliant engineers couldn't save them. It took one guy to lead them from the brink of irrelevance. That's rare to find. Just look at me." He smiled a sheepish grin, having just compared himself to Steve Jobs.

Dana nodded.

Graham took a seat at the table with the other staff. As he did this, Dana walked over to the wall panel and plugged in her flash drive. Three of the screens in the room showed her first slide: "Quarterly Report." This was a convenient arrangement so that anyone sitting at the round table could see the materials.

A computer voice announced from the speakers: "Incoming event." Frankie hit a button on the remote.

"What was that?" Graham asked.

"Oh," said Frankie, "the computer is always monitoring Spheria. If something is happening that it detects would be of interest to observe, it'll automatically play it on the screens here. That way we don't miss anything. But it gets recorded anyway so we can check it out later."

"Good to know," said Graham. "I'd like to check out the recordings after this meeting."

"We can definitely give you access," said Dana. "But even if you just watch the most interesting ones, you'll be watching for days. You're free to have at it if you wish."

"I'm in no rush," he said, countering Dana's attempt to discourage him. He watched for a reaction.

Dana smoothed her blouse with her hands. Graham noticed her fingers were dirty, and this left a dark smudge on her shirt. Before he could comment, she began.

"This has been a record quarter for the Spheria Project. The team has made some valuable and insightful observations. Plus, Max and I have found several new sources of funding."

"I like to hear that," commented Graham.

Dana nodded to Frankie.

Frankie clicked the remote and the slide changed to "Agenda." It listed the following items:

1) Quarterly Goals (Max Moreau)
2) Cultural Progress (Jean Evens)
3) Flora and Fauna (Abina Andam)
4) Subterranean Passages (Frankie Pompeo)
5) Financial Analysis (Dana Carter)

Dana continued. "These are the five topics we will cover in this meeting. I will talk more about the funding at the end. Max was supposed to discuss the first item. But since he's not here yet, Jean, can you go first? We'll circle back when he arrives."

"Uh, sure," Jean said. As Dana sat, Jean rose and walked over to one of the screens showing the slides. "Flip to slide 8, please."

Frankie fumbled with the remote, skipping past a bunch of charts. He stopped when the screen showed "Cultural Progress."

"So, for this quarter, our primary focus has been on the power shift of the Colony. The godhead, specifically."

"The what?" asked Graham.

"The godhead. It means 'the essence of being a god,' and that's what this Polyan is."

The slide changed to show a close-up image of Fa·ro. He stood on the dais in the center of the Colony, striking a statuesque pose.

"So this is Fa·ro," continued Jean, "the first seven-legged Polyan. At the end of the last quarter, just after our report to you, something unusual happened. The Polyans created him of their own volition. Whenever we materialize in their world, we always appear with seven legs. That's because the most the Polyans could ever build was six, and we wanted to appear more powerful in some way. In hindsight, that may have been a mistake. They based their entire social class, as well as their mythology, on the number of legs. But I digress. Other than this, their social structure formed naturally into a well-run insect-like…"

The computer voice once again announced: "Incoming event."

"Again!" blurted Frankie. He clicked the remote to suppress its playback.

"Hmm." Jean frowned. "Should we check it out?"

"No," said Dana. "Not until after this presentation."

"Okay, then," Jean continued. "I was just saying how the Polyan social structure resembled that of an insect colony."

"Until now," added Ravi.

The slide changed to show the eight Leaders in a circle in their chamber atop the tallest building.

Jean continued. "This was the Council. The members ran the Colony using a simple but equitable system of rule. They voted on actions, and the majority prevailed. At some point, they decided too many tie votes were happening. For an unknown reason, rather than making another six-legged member like themselves, they made one with seven."

"Interesting. But how could we not know why?" asked Graham. "Isn't that the point of this project, to learn these things?"

"Yes, it is," answered Jean. "We're still reviewing the logs and recordings to find out why. We will figure it out, but I suspect they wanted to see if they could do it, to see if they could touch divinity."

"Makes sense."

"So, anyway, the Leaders found a way to make a seven-legged Polyan. They did something we never expected. They used an additional contributor during the breeding ritual. This provided the excess energy required to jump-start seven legs. But that's not the most significant thing that happened. In a relatively short period of time, this occurred."

A video of the eight Leaders, being slaughtered one by one by Fa·ro, played in its entirety.

"What the hell just happened?" asked Graham.

"Exactly what you think," said Ravi. "Fa·ro eliminated

the Council and took ultimate control of the colony. He elevated himself to godhead and instantly changed their society into a dictatorship. He won over the Soldiers and used them to his advantage. With their larger numbers, he was unstoppable. The remainder of the Colony had no choice but to accept his rule."

"Well, this isn't unlike coups we've seen involving humans, right?" asked Graham. "Take Cuba for example."

"It's exactly the same, which is what makes this so interesting," said Jean. "History repeats, even inside our little virtual world. It shows the realism that un-deterministic destiny can lead to and that societies go through inevitable stages of formation. It validates a few of our theories about human nature."

"Impressive," said Graham. But he wanted to gauge the weight of this discovery by the reaction of the project's creator. "Where the hell is Max?" He pulled out his phone and checked it for texts. "Dana, do you have a message from him?"

She took out her phone and pretended to look through her emails and text messages. "None, sorry."

"This isn't like him. There's nothing he cares about more than this project."

"Yeah, he's never been late for a quarterly meeting," said Frankie.

"I hate to proceed further without him," said Graham. "But I guess we should. Jean, is there more?"

"I could go on and on, but that's all I have in the report. If there is time at the end, I'd like to discuss what they're building."

"I'm intrigued," said Graham.

"Next up," announced Dana, "is Abina, who'll cover flora and fauna."

Abina took the remote from Frankie and stood. With her thick accent she began. "So the world is full of various plant-like and animal-like creatures now. It is starting to become a vibrant place. Even so, we created six new species this quarter, which averages two a month, a record for us."

She clicked the remote, and the slide changed to a graph showing the number of new species created every month. It was a sharp upward trajectory, starting slowly and then taking off like a hockey stick.

"I think we are in our groove modeling and coding these now. I mean, we are performing as a team."

She clicked the remote again, and the slide changed to a topographical map of Spheria. It was broken up into triangles, some connected to others, each showing a piece of landscape. "This is a modified Dymaxion map. It shows the entire inside surface of Spheria, preserving, for the most part, the relative sizes of each land area."

She clicked the remote again and regions of color over-laid the triangles. "These areas show where we have placed the new species. The center is the location of the Colony."

"Wait," said Graham. "Can you go back a slide?"

"Sure." She clicked the remote, and it returned to just the topological view.

Graham stood and walked over to study it up close. He pulled a pen from his pocket that had a laser pointer on the end. He attempted to shine it on a couple of triangles, but the red dot wouldn't show up against the brightness of the screen. He frowned, looked around, then walked over to the rack behind the door and took one of the pool cues. Returning to the screen, he used the stick to point at the edge of a triangle that wasn't connected. "What should be here?" he asked.

Abina said, "Look carefully. There is a faint blue arrow that connects that side to the side of another triangle."

Graham squinted. "Oh. I see it." He traced the line with the tip of the pool cue, actually making it darker from the chalk. It was apparent that the topology at the two edges matched. "I get it now. It's as if it's unfolded into triangles. Go on."

The slide advanced to the colored regions again. "To not make things too unstable, we have placed several of the new creatures a safe distance from the Colony. The yellow areas show where. They are far enough so that the Polyans will have to venture further before they encounter the new species. We have also placed several on the other side of the Rift, where the red areas are. The current set of Polyans will never encounter those. This will allow us to compare their evolution under the influence of intelligent beings to those without such influence."

"So you put some of the same types of creatures on each side?" asked Graham. "And you'll see how they mature with and without encounters with the Polyans?" He touched the referenced regions with the stick as he spoke.

"Exactly. So you could say this is the first time we're adding an observation of the 'culture of non-sentient life forms' as I like to call it. I'll give an update of my findings next quarter."

"Looking forward to it," said Graham.

Abina continued, "Instead of talking about the new creatures I wanted to show a video of them. Some are the craziest and most creative we have ever made. I thought a visual representation would have more of an impact than descriptions."

She advanced the slide. A video began playing on the screens. It was not, however, a video of the creatures.

CHAPTER 50 - INTERRUPTIONS

"I don't believe in the no-win scenario… I like to think there always are possibilities." - James T. Kirk

The screens in the Experience Room began playing a video. It wasn't the video Abina had intended to play. Instead, Dana's face filled the screen, and she started speaking.

"I'm truly sorry to have to do this, and sorry about Olivia also. I was convinced that it'd look like a suicide, but Captain Brennan wasn't so sure. He investigated her death and almost discovered the truth. This time, I can't have any bodies."

"But why?" Max's voice said from off camera.

"Isn't it obvious?" said Dana on the screen. "You know we're having funding issues. DARPA had its eye on your pet project since the Solvay Conference. But Graham's contract preventing military investment was an issue for their administration. So they approached me, and we worked out a deal. Not only did we get enough funding to keep this going, but I also will receive a beautiful piece of land in Costa Rica for my retirement. I've worked for Graham a long time, and I'm not getting rich doing it. I'm sorry you got caught in the crossfire, Max. But I promise you, I'll keep your project going as long as I can. Good stuff will come of this. I wish you luck in the afterlife."

"I doubt we will meet there," said Max, again from off camera.

"You sound ungrateful. I could just shut your project down." The screen went black as a large iron door closed in front of the camera.

Every eye in the room was now staring at the real Dana.

"What in God's name have you done?" demanded Graham.

"N-n-nothing," Dana stammered.

"Where the hell is Max?" demanded Graham again, even louder.

The door to the room flew open, and the head of campus security entered. Captain Brennan scanned the room, and upon seeing Dana, stated in a calm voice, "Miss Carter, please come with me."

Dana stood abruptly, pulled her hand out of her purse, and raised her pistol. She aimed it toward Brennan. He simultaneously drew a Taser and aimed it at her.

"Back off!" screamed Dana. "I'm leaving now, and nobody needs to get hurt."

"People have already been hurt," said Brennan. "Drop your weapon and nobody *else* needs to get hurt."

"No. Nooo! I will shoot if you don't get out of the way." Her gun was small, the perfect size for her hand. Her index finger was wrapped solidly around the trigger. It twitched in time with her heartbeat as she wrestled with her adrenalin.

Brennan was trained for situations like this and would've already discharged his Taser. Except the jolt would make Dana clench her hand, thus firing her pistol. He couldn't risk a shot going off around people if he could help it.

Then she saw them. Through the open door, Min stood, holding onto a wheelchair in which sat Max, his foot tightly bandaged. Their expressions turned from curiosity to fear as they saw her looking at them.

"Damn you, Min!" she shouted and, changing aim from Brennan to Min's head, squeezed the trigger.

Nothing happened.

She squeezed it again, but her index finger was pushed away. Poked deftly between the gun's trigger and the grip was the tip of a pool stick. Before Dana could comprehend what she was seeing, the gun was flicked out of her hand. It flew through the air and crashed into the screen on the opposite side of the room, shattering it.

"What the..." she began to say but was cut off when the 50,000 volts began to surge through her body. She twitched and fell to the side. Graham guided her limp body to the floor with the pool cue he'd used to stop her from firing. Brennan ran over as she lay helpless, bound her hands in cuffs, and flipped her over.

Everyone looked down at her as she regained her senses. Max sat there with Min by his side. A single word was uttered from Dana's lips, "How?"

Min tapped her glasses. "Spy gear. My glasses have a camera in them. I recorded your whole spiel before you tried to kill us. Sucks for you that Max talked you into spilling the beans."

"Well done, Min," said Graham.

Dana responded, "I'd have gotten away with it if it wasn't for you meddling interns."

"Get her out of here please," said Max.

"My pleasure," said Captain Brennan. He dragged her to her feet and led her out of the room.

"Sorry we were late for the meeting," Max teased, "but our ears were burning." Min giggled.

Graham frowned. "You know, Max, I love this project as much as you. But nothing is worth murder. Poor Olivia was a victim of some sinister plot to exploit your technology. That's exactly what I was trying to prevent from happening. What started as an engaging quarterly report has turned into a disaster. I don't need to give this any more thought. I'm pulling the plug on this project. There will be no more funding, and I want all of its assets to be liquidated for market value."

Max stiffened, his jaw opened, and his eyes widened. "Please... sir."

"No," said Graham. "This isn't negotiable. I know this isn't your fault, but it happened. There is too much risk involved here. Dana was a trusted friend, and she betrayed me, betrayed all of us. How can I trust anyone to run this project now, given the stakes? The military is out to get this technology, and they can be very persuasive."

"You can trust *me*," pleaded Max.

"I wish I could. I really do. But the only person I could ever trust is myself. All of you, please make preparations to shut everything down. I'll remain here another two weeks to make sure it is done."

"Mr. Neilson," said Min. "Is there any way to change your mind? This project means everything to this team. You told us how important this is for human knowledge."

"Sorry kid, this may set the world back a bit, but the knowledge will come in time through other means."

The room speakers startled them as they once again announced: "Incoming event."

Graham looked at the ceiling, and then at Abina, who still held the remote. "Play it," he said.

She clicked a button on the remote and all the intact screens in the room lit up. Each of the eleven monitors showed a close-up of a different Worker. This created the impression that the observers were surrounded.

In unison, the Polyans began to chant:

Oh mighty gods, hear our words.
Please return Sa·ma from the Rift.
For we are lost without him.
We pray to you.
Our lives are yours.
Take us instead.
For freedom... For freedom.

CHAPTER 51 - HAND OF GOD

"Liberty must at all hazards be supported. We have a right to it, derived from our Maker. But if we had not, our fathers have earned and bought it for us, at the expense of their ease, their estates, their pleasure, and their blood." - John Adams

"Abina, pause the playback," commanded Max.

The circle of Polyans froze in place.

"What's going on here?" asked Graham.

"I'm not sure," said Max.

Jean answered, "They're... praying. This is the first time we've ever seen such behavior." She lied.

"This is groundbreaking!" exclaimed Ravi.

"Why did this happen?" snapped Graham.

"Abina, replay the last two recordings," said Max.

Abina hit some buttons on the remote. The screens went black, and then in green numbers, a timestamp flashed. It was from about thirty minutes ago. A view of Spheria faded in as the letters faded out. Nobody in the room could believe what they saw. The enormous tower that the Polyans had constructed fell sideways. The top hit the land on the other side of the Rift, forming a span. A group of Workers huddled in the nearby field began to cross toward the other side.

"What?" asked Graham. "I thought you said it'd be impossible for them to get to the other side."

"Um," said Jean, buying time. "Uh. That was what I said. And, I believed it was true."

"Their resourcefulness is quite astonishing," said Ravi.

"Just like humans," muttered Graham.

The screens went black again, and the green numbers showed a time about 20 minutes ago.

The same field was now cluttered with a huge mass of Polyans, moving every which way. The Soldiers were slaughtering the Workers, ripping their legs off and abandoning their carcasses. Fa·ro stood prominently in their midst, doing most of the damage. At one point a smaller Polyan flew through the air and landed on Fa·ro, knocking him over. The Polyan took something from him and froze. Then a herd of Zalisk charged into the battle, decimating the Soldiers.

The small Polyan, who was now recognizable as Le·ma, ran. Ga·zo pursued her and Sa·ma onto the bridge. What ensued was a fantastic set of acrobatics resulting in Sa·ma, the bridge full of Soldiers, Le·ma, and Ga·zo falling into the Rift.

The screen went black. The team stood dumbfounded.

Min was the first to break the silence. "Genocide."

"A diamond with a flaw is worth more than a pebble without imperfections," said Graham. "Ingenuity. Fighting for freedom. Deference to a higher being. These creatures are indeed sentient. How could I shut them down? How could I punish them for our transgressions, crimes in a world beyond which they could possibly conceive? That would be akin to God snuffing out our universe because His angels fought. We can't let their prayers go unanswered. Max, can we rescue Sa·ma?"

Max replied, "He's in the Rift. If we get creative, we could probably come up with some way to save him."

"No, wait," said Graham, briefly recollecting his life experiences. "We're the gods here. Let's act like gods. Let's only partially answer their prayer and give them a sign at the same time."

"What do you mean?"

"Rescue the little one instead."

#

The circle of twelve Workers continued to chant. Every other Polyan joined in, forming circles around circles. No one noticed the bubble rising from the Rift. Inside its semi-translucency was an opaque geometrical form. Even more unusual, instead of floating straight up toward the Source, it floated over the congregation.

It came to hover above the center of the circle. As it cast its yellow hue upon the crowd, someone spoke out, "It's a miracle."

The mass looked up. At that moment, the bubble burst and Le·ma fell into their midst.

"Praise the gods!" said one.

"They've chosen our new leader," said another.

"Hail Le·ma, our Lumen Master," said a third.

They all bowed to her. And together spoke, "Lumen

Master, lead us to salvation."

EPILOGUE

Sa·ma watched the walls of the Rift rushing by as he plummeted sensors first into the dark depths. He flailed his legs and found he could control his orientation. He righted himself, leaned, and gradually approached one wall of the vast chasm. He tapped it with a leg, which caused him to flip out of control. He could see the brightness from above, narrowing into a mere slit, alternating light, dark, light, dark. He slowed his spin again using his legs and realized that he had drifted to the opposite side. He continued falling there waiting to meet his end.

Then he saw something below him. Something, for lack of a better description, shiny. It was on the wall and growing larger as he approached it. He began to drag a leg against the side, this time not tapping, so that he didn't get flung away. This seemed to slow his descent. He added another leg to the wall and slowed even more. The shiny thing was much larger now and appeared to be some kind of irregularity in the side of the chasm. It was directly below him and getting bigger. Then he was upon it. Somehow, a gash was cut into the side of the Rift, and it converged into a small ledge.

As he passed the ledge, the two legs he was dragging caught and stopped. The rapid deceleration slammed his body into the face below the ledge, but he managed to hold on. He hung there, perplexed, before pulling himself up onto the outcropping. It was triangular in shape, with one point leading into the Rift wall like a shallow cave. He went in but found that it went nowhere.

A loud scraping sound caused him to turn around. He looked up to see the remains of the tower falling toward him. It rotated horizontally in the center of the Rift and made a lazy spin clockwise. When its ends scraped the sides of the Rift, it made the loud grating sound again. Then both ends caught firm, the whole thing came to an abrupt stop, and the center sagged down. A couple of beams in the middle snapped, weakening it, but it hung there forming a giant V-shape. Several Soldiers lost their balance from the sudden stop and fell off. They went careening past Sa·ma into the abyss below.

Sa·ma felt the walls around him, and they were somewhat rough. He began to contemplate a way to climb up to the tower. Maybe it could provide some means to scale out of the tomb. *If only I had some red stone*, he thought.

From nowhere, the falling body of Ga·zo, who was spinning out of control, slammed into the center of the tower. The remaining beams snapped, and the tower folded completely in half. The two sides fell, bouncing against the walls, with Ga·zo hanging between them. As the wreckage passed Sa·ma's perch, Ga·zo noticed him and glared at him. His look of terror was replaced with one of fury. Then he was gone, a mere speck in the darkness below.

Sa·ma sat for a moment, pondering his fate. He returned to the inside of the cave and rubbed the walls. They were smooth. He tapped on the walls and swore that part of it made a different sound, almost like it was hollow. He banged on that section harder, but nothing happened. He slammed his body into it. Still, nothing happened. He noticed some small rocks littering the surface of the ledge. He picked one up and pounded it into the wall but failed to even make a dent.

To pass the time he began playing with the rocks. He stacked them different ways over and over, making various sculptures. He finally left them as a depiction of Fa·ro, as if signaling a warning of what lay above.

He spent days sitting on that ledge. This he knew because he could count the bubbles rising past. He watched their iridescent colors and faint glow, and witnessed the dimming of his own core. His life force was running out; he wouldn't last much longer. He escaped the fate below, but would die here anyway, sitting on this ledge.

Maybe he had lost his mind, or maybe he was morbidly curious, or maybe he couldn't bear the solitude any longer. Regardless of the reason, he walked to the edge, looked down, and leaped off.

AUTHORS NOTE

Dear reader. I hope you enjoyed this novel as much as I enjoyed writing it. My objective was to create the story I have always wanted to read, and I think I achieved that. Specifically, I wanted to make a fun narrative based on thought provoking concepts. As Socrates declared on the eve of his death, "seek truth and wisdom… question everything". Thus it was my intent not to provide answers, but to encourage questions. If you liked it, **please consider leaving me a review** where you bought it and **recommend it to your friends**. This is the only way an independent author can be found above the sea of noise out there.

Oh, one last thing, I have some great ideas for some sequels. The more successful this one becomes, the more likely there will be for continued adventures of the Polyans. In fact, if you sign up for my mailing list, I will send you a **free** related story called "Spheria: Olivia's Log." Sign up here:

http://www.codyleet.com/spheria-signup

Thank you,
Cody Leet
2016

P.S. I would sincerely enjoy hearing your thoughts, good or bad. You can contact me at any of the methods below.

Website: http://www.codyleet.com

Email: me@codyleet.com

Facebook: http://www.facebook.com/cody.leet.writer

Twitter: http://twitter.com/Cody_Leet

CODY LEET

SPHERIA

ΛPPENDIX - POLYΛN LΛNGUΛGE

When I first embarked on writing Spheria, it was my goal to make the Polyans seem more "computerized." In an attempt to show this, I set out to invent a new primitive written language that you might expect a computer AI to process easily. This I called "Polyan" as in "Polyans speak Polyan."

After making the language, I wrote the first several chapters using this for all Polyan dialog. It soon became apparent that I could not effectively express emotion through this language, so could not develop characters through dialog, so abandoned this technique. It also created a learning curve for the readers, which would have become a barrier for entry, which I did not want to require. So I abandoned this idea. So if you feel, after reading this novel, that the Polyans are a little too human, it's to allow good storytelling, at the expense of realism. Touch choices, but I feel it's a more approachable novel as a result.

In case you're curious what it would have looked like, the following is an excerpt from a talk that was going to be given by Ravi, the Sociologist on the project. This talk was describing how the team implemented the language.

#

There were several things we just didn't want to wait to see develop naturally, language was one of them. We wanted to give the Polyans a basic means of communication so we could focus on seeing how their culture evolved without their needing to invent that.

Our goal was to keep things very simple but expressive, and at the same time allow their speech to be human readable. So we crafted a basic structured grammar using a vocabulary based on a reduced set of English words. The results came out sounding like 'caveman', which was not an entirely unbelievable outcome.

In transcripts, you will always see their language expressed in Pascal case, where every word is capitalized, but without spaces. Distinct thoughts, or sentences, appear on separate lines. The structure of each sentence follows the pattern:

<Actor><Verb><Target>

Some examples would be:

GrogJumpRock
ZuggClimbTree

A name followed by a colon at the beginning of a sentence will indicate the Polyan who is speaking. An example would be:

Grog: MeGoHunt

For those speaking to others, the recipient is named after the speaker, separated by an angle bracket, followed by a colon and the sentence.

Grog > Zugg : ThongGoNorth

If the recipient is the actor, as in the case of commands, the actor need not be mentioned again:

Zugg > Grog: GoNorth

Compare this to the following, which is a description of where Grog went:

Zugg: GrogGoNorth

One thing to note above is that tense is implied. The language is always in the "present" tense. If something happened in the past or future, a modifier is used to express the time frame:

    (past)
    Zugg: GrogGoWhereBefore
    Grog: MeGoNorthYesterday

    (present)
    Zugg > Grog: GoNorth
    Grog: MeGoNorth

    (future)
    Zugg > Grog: GoNorthLater
    Grog: MeGoSouthTomorrow

Any statement can be converted to a question by either replacing the target with a question word or appending one after the target. The question words are: where, when, how, why, what, and ask. "Ask" is a special case that makes a sentence that looks like a statement into a question, analogous to a question mark.

    Grog: ThongGoWhere
    Zugg: GrogWantThongWhy
    Grog: ZuggShareMeatAsk

Lastly, modifiers can be used after the sentence to behave essentially as adjectives, to provide emphasis on the target, or otherwise affect the meaning. Some Examples:

    Zugg: GrogThrowRockFar
    Grog: ZuggEatMeatCold

Instead of having variations of modifiers to show degrees, such as "cool", "cold", or "freezing", we borrowed a concept from George Orwell's Newspeak and added the "Plus" and "Minus" modifiers to express more or less of something:

    (cold) Zugg: WaterIsCold

(cool) Zugg: WaterIsColdMinus
(very cold) Grog: WaterIsColdPlus
(freezing) Grog: WaterIsColdPlusPlus

The last modifier "not" is used to reverse the meaning of the
sentence. Used as so:

Zugg > Grog: NotGoNorth
Grog: NotGoNorthWhy
Zugg: NorthIsColdPlusPlus

Putting it all together we can get rather complex conversations,
like so:

Zugg: MeHuntBearLater
Grog > Zugg: NotGoNorth
Zugg: NotMeGoNorthWhy
Grog: NorthIsColdPlusPlus
Zugg > Grog: GoSouth
Zugg: BearIsSouth
Grog: MeKillBear
Grog: MeCookBear
Zugg > Grog: ShareMeatAsk
Grog > Zugg: MeGiveMeat